C000261024

It Takes a Girl

Atima Srivastava

Cover by
Dean Stockton

Published by Bite-Sized Books Ltd 2023

Bite-Sized Books Limited

8th Floor, 20 St. Andrews Street, London EC4A 3AY, UK

Registered in the UK. Company Registration

No: 9395379

ISBN: 9781739152444

The moral right of Atima Srivastava to be identified as the author of this work has been asserted by her in accordance with the Copyright, Designs and Patents Act 1988

In memory of, and with gratitude to,
Kirti Choudhary, Onkar Nath Srivastava
and Ajit Kumar, my mum, dad and uncle who were
my greatest influences.

Chapter 1

I knew exactly where I was going and why. You see I just had to go there. Where? To Pumping Iron. It's a gym in North Finchley near Argos. It has boxing and weights, no annual membership fee and it's open 24/7 so obviously it's full of men. Mostly illegals and part time workers who can't afford Virgin, and like a lot of gyms there's as much business going on there as exercise. I've heard you can get all sorts in there: poppers, passports, prostitutes you name it. You can't imagine such places exist alongside the trembling cherry blossoms and tranquil avenues of our neighbourhood, but they do. Dad, believe me I wasn't exactly happy about going there but it's where he goes to train, so that's where I had to go.

Lino on the floor, no soda machine and the harsh smell of bleach had you in an arm lock as soon as you walked in. A big clock on the wall said 10.45am. The receptionist, a frothy blonde with diamante pink nails and resting bitchface told me to wait, so I sat down on the plastic bench, palms sweating. I caught a glimpse of myself in the mirror behind her. Although I'm a proud 5' 4 with strong arms and legs and excellent core body strength I looked insignificant in my little pony tail and sweat pants. My glo white Adidas sneakers looked like they belonged to Mickey Mouse. I wasn't projecting the image I wanted. Instead of exerting authority beyond my 19 years I looked what I was, a frightened teenage girl out of her depth. So I adjusted myself and sat up straight.

A man weighed down with the worries of the world, maybe he was an Afghan or a Syrian, shuffled into reception and sat down too close to me. Oh dad he looked so *broken* in his crumpled suit and bloodshot eyes. I wondered who he was waiting for? He stank of unwashed armpit and I desperately wanted to move away but I didn't want to be rude. It's important to be compassionate, as you've taught us to be. It's what proves we're human. That poor man was just the type that Max exploits.

Max!

He took his time coming out to see me. Mid thirties, slicked back hair, tight white shirt, walking like a baboon, fingers perpetually brushing his crotch. He wasn't much taller than me and skinny rake. He had a sharp face with sharp features like a rat. I'd only ever seen him at a distance two months ago, and that too through a blurred pub window but he wasn't the muscly he-man you might imagine.

"You asked for me?" he said in a low voice. "What's it about?" His face was blank.

The receptionist was intensely playing Candy Crush. The world could have come to an end and she wouldn't know.

I didn't say anything

He motioned for me to follow him. I followed. He was wearing a fake Rolex. Was I scared? Not at all. I kept thinking 'you're a short ass, you're a pimp, you're scum, you don't intimidate me.' We went into the 'juice bar' a room with Formica tables and plastic chairs. He pulled out a chair for me and I just automatically sat down which was stupid because then he was standing and I was sitting.

He asked me if I wanted a drink and I said no thanks and he sat down opposite me.

"So what do you need?"

"I need you to stop seeing my mum," I said looking him in the eyes.

He blinked. "So you're the daughter?"

I felt sick.

"Yes"

"Mum know you're here?" he said with a frown.

"If you don't stop seeing her I'll tell my dad. He won't be happy about it."

"Isn't he a pensioner or something?"

How rude! What kind of ignoramus thinks 55 is retirement age? Maybe in his scumbag criminal profession, not in a real profession like teaching.

"Never mind. I just want you to stop it."

He kept staring at me like I was some kind of freak in the circus.

"It's not right what you're doing," I said at last.

"It's not *right*?" He smiled creepily. "What are you the daughter or the mother?"

"I know what you do. If you don't stop seeing my mum, I'll report you to the police."

His face drained of all emotion.

"I understand your concern. Don't worry. You won't see me again."

I left the gym feeling foolish. I knew I'd just made things a whole lot worse. I knew he'd be on the phone to mum the very next minute. It was 5pm by the time I finally put my key in the door hoping she wasn't back from work yet, knowing I'd handled it all wrong. Ash met me in the hallway with a finger on his lips and a winning grin. He's taller than me now. He was barefoot in his usual manky dressing gown thrown over the t-shirt and boxers he sleeps in with the stale smell of beer hovering on his breath. Mum never tells him off because a) he's an Indian boy and therefore automatically The Jewel in the Crown and b) he's bound for Oxford or Princeton.

"Don't you ever get up before tea time Ashi?"

Genius or not, he was getting to be a slob lately. He was bored with the humdrum summer holidays and too lazy to get a job and anyway he was supposed to be studying. He wasn't the kind of autistic nerd you imagine brainboxes to be, just annoying in the way all 15 year old boys are, because they think the world revolves around them.

"Watch this it's hilarious," he whispered and beckoned me.

I sighed and stood behind him patiently compliant. The door to the kitchen was ajar. Sunshine pooled in from the window making a perfect square on the parquet squares. Mum took out a glass from the tall cabinet and walked across to the sink, her glossy black hair swaying gracefully, her toned upper arms golden brown. She was in her work clothes, which were smarter than most womens' going out clothes: White sleeveless silk blouse, neatly ironed pencil skirt, doe eyes makeup, high heels.

"Wait." Ash held up his hand as if I was oncoming traffic.

Mum turned on the tap and the jet of water sprang back ferociously from the sink and drenched her. She shrieked, stepped back and turned it off.

"That's the second time this week!" she wailed.

"I know!" said Ash giggling and walked into the kitchen. I followed behind him.

"It's not funny Ashi. Just my luck. I wanted to wear this top tomorrow but it's dry clean only. It's ruined! I've got this unlucky star over my head that follows me around. I just can't get a break! Just my luck."

"It's got nothing to do with luck mum," said Ash handing her a tea towel. "The fault is not in the stars."

"Shaani!" said mum glaring at me, water dripping off her face. "There you are."

"It might be the washer. I'll take a look at it," I said in a feeble voice.

"Look here's the culprit. Reason, not luck," said Ash fishing a teaspoon out of the sink and waving it in the air. "The water came out of the tap and bounced off the side of the bowl of the spoon, which created a trajectory that then ricocheted on to you. The velocity *thus* increased. See? Shouldn't have left a dirty sink you dirty gremlin."

"Wow," said mum. "I *was* in a hurry this morning. That'll teach me."

"It's not wow, it's just science," he said with a yawn. "What's for dinner?"

"Your hair looks nice Ashi. I like it like that," smiled mum looking at him with pride.

His hair had got long and it fell over his eyes and he pushed it back with the back of his hand in a gesture of impatience.

"Did you put that spoon there?" I hissed as he walked past and was immediately sorry because he looked wounded and gormless like a dazed chick. I felt bad because I knew I was projecting my guilt on to him. I had to take responsibility for my actions. I'd done something inappropriate and now I had to fess up and it was so *embarrassing*.

Mum said shut the door and we both listened to him going upstairs. He'd be in the shower for ages. God knows what he does in there, she said. But we both knew what he probably did in there. He was a normal 15 year old boy. Well, not quite normal because Oxford and Princeton had

6

both offered him a scholarship to study for a Physics degree at age 16. He could recite the alphabet backwards and forwards at age 3 and he'd self published a paper on the Net when he was 12 which had been picked up by Professor Mitch Rosenthal, Head of Physics at Leicester university. Mitch had become his champion, mentor and our family friend.

Of course Ash wasn't the youngest knowitall brainbox that ever lived. Some in our generous-supportive-not-at-all-envious Indian community had been quick to point out that there had been prodigies who had challenged Einstein's theories and gone to university at the age of 9, which was the *accurate* age for a child to be *actually* called a prodigy. Well, Ash might not have had Stephen Hawking quaking in his wheelchair just *yet*, but he was *our* knowitall brainbox and we were very proud of him.

Chapter 2

"Put your hood down Shaani, you're inside the house. Where have you been all day?" mum said.

"Window shopping for my chair?"

She lowered her voice. "I know you went to see Max."

I didn't say anything.

"What have you got to say for yourself?"

"You're having an affair," I said looking up.

"Keep your voice down! How dare you talk to me like that?"

"Deny it then."

She crossed her arms. She smelled heavenly of Pomegranate Noir which was £60 a pop but she wore it all the time. She said it was her 'signature scent.'

"I don't have to deny it, I'm not up in court."

"You've been weird ever since Dad went away."

"No I haven't," she said crossly.

"No you've been weird ever since we moved to *London*. You haven't been right for the last four years mum, what's wrong with you?"

"What's wrong with me? Well my mum died four years ago Shaani if you remember? Excuse me for grieving. Maybe you'll find out what it feels like one day and then you won't be so quick to judge."

Harsh!

Mum's always had a sharp tongue but I was honestly shocked. Where had all this come from?

"We all miss Naani, but that was four years ago and I thought the anti depressants...."

She put her hands on her hips. I could tell she was getting herself all worked up to fishwife timbre.

"You think grief has a sell by date? You're nineteen years old and you think you know everything. You walk around in your entitlement! You haven't suffered a day in your life. Do you have any idea of the things that people have had to go through, no?"

"Well—"

"And your dad, since you bring it up -- he's been gone for seven months now. Seven months, four letters, no Skype, no email. It's very hard for me being without him. Who abandons their family for seven months?"

"He hasn't abandoned us!"

She suddenly tapped the side of her head as if to shake the conversation out.

"Sorry, sorry my darling I didn't mean to say any of that. Of course he hasn't. It's not in him to hurt a fly let alone his loved ones. He'd cut off his arms for us. We're all he has left.

It's really important what dad's doing. I support him all the way, you know that. We agreed on it."

"He's always been there for us," I said.

"Yes of course he has. He's the sweetest most darling man in the whole world. He's one of the best ones you know Shaani? Everyone knows that! And I should know given the men in my family. God strike me down, I just got discombobulated when Max phoned me. But Shaani you can't just go and *speak* to people like that. Max is a friend. Aren't I allowed to have male friends? What do you think he thought of you?"

"What do I care what he thought of *me*? And what could you possibly have in common with him?"

"Well, what do I have in common with your dad? I didn't grow up in a big fat house in India with doting parents listening to classical music. His name was on the door of their house, can you imagine that? His name, then his mum's name and then his dads name. That's unheard of! We moved fifteen times when I was a kid, from one rented deathtrap to another. Why d'you think I know London like the back of my hand? My dad was a drunk and when the rent didn't get paid the landlord threw our stuff on the pavement! I can't sit in a room and read a book all day like he can but we've been married for 20 years sweetheart. You relate to people for all different reasons."

"Ok but where did you meet that creep?"

"Just in a pub."

"What pub?"

"Which pub," she said trying to make me laugh. "I went to a porsche grammar school you know? Had to queue in the line of shame for free dinners but I *was* taught syntax. And how to speak properly. I've forgotten it all now."

It was a simple statement of truth but her voice had a terrible catch in it. I looked at the abandoned empty glass on the counter, water dripping down its side. It could have been a tear running down my cheek. Mum was like mercury, she went from dark to light in seconds and back again. She had an altogether different kind of power over me than dad did. Something in her pulled at me. She had survived hardship and even though I was the daughter not the mother, I had always wanted to keep her safe. To make up for it maybe? I took my lead from you dad, because you've taken care of mum forever and treated her like a goddess.

She was right that I hadn't suffered a single day in my gilded cage life. She had hated everyone knowing her mum was on benefits when she was at school. "No one respects you when you're poor Shaani, don't let them tell you it makes you real. The truth is the shame strips you like battery acid and makes you numb." I've never forgotten her saying that to me at Naani's funeral when all the hypocrites in the Indian community were lining up to praise Naani when they had shunned her in the street when she was alive. I've never forgotten how guilty and responsible it made me feel.

I know I should have talked to her, dad. I shouldn't have gone steaming in to confront Max the way I did. It was disrespectful to mum. When you love people you have to give them your respect. It's the unwritten contract of being human. They don't have to earn it, you have to give it. Employers and MP's and teachers have to earn it, but the people you're connected to have inalienable rights over you. Your mum and dad are your pillars of strength, the foundations of your esteem, the shoulders on which you stand. It doesn't matter if you don't like them, you still love them. They're the only ones you'll ever get. You told me that dad.

So why can't I ever talk to mum? About anything.

Because I don't trust her judgement that's why. I can't help it. I've never asked her advice on anything. She just shoots her mouth off, she doesn't think deeply enough about things. She's never had to because you've always steered the ship. She even jokes about it, *"that's why I don't have any wrinkles because my husband deals with the stress of my life,"* when it's the Botox injections. Yes she has them dad! You don't notice! I went mad at her when she first had them. She doesn't even need them! Why would you put that gunk into your body, it can kill you! And she said, "I just want to look pretty sweetheart," like that was her religion I was knocking.

"Which pub," I said miserably.

"Why does that matter?"

"Because."

"Alright. It was the Green Dragon in St. Albans. Manish took us there for lunch, about two months ago. It was his 30th. We couldn't believe it, you know how tight he is?" She grinned and looked at me but I was looking at the floor. "He made a toast to his dad Old Mr. Popat and I was the only one who remembered him from when I was a little girl and the practice was pure NHS. All the clients were Asians back then and he used to make you hold the sluicer yourself, no dental nurses! Only I remembered. Nicolau and Gosia and all the other dentists, they're all new and it's a big practice now. Anyway blah blah, then they all went off and I had the afternoon free and he'd left a tab running and…"

"So you stayed in the pub drinking on your own."

"It's not against the law Shaani! Just because you're tee total, don't judge everyone by your standards. Yes I sat and drank and had many thoughts. So what? When I was growing up and we didn't know where my dad was half the time, or my brothers come to that, the one constant in our lives was Old Mr. Popat. He was my mum's dentist. She was terrified of the drill but she also had terrible teeth. He gave me a lollipop every time we went and said I was a very pretty and good girl for holding my mum's hand. My brothers never went with her and she was always terrified and I always went with her. All the Asians in North London went to him. They snubbed us but Old Mr. Popat treated us with kindness and respect. It was like all those lost years started swirling around me. And now my boss is his son who's 11 years younger than me. And I'm working the reception desk, a teenagers job.

And feeling sorry for yourself 24/7, I felt like saying but I kept quiet.

She picked up the large gold embossed card on the kitchen counter and turned it over:

You are Cordially Invited to Henna and Sangeeth for the Auspicious Wedding of Pushpa Kumari, beloved daughter of Krishna Sharma and Anuradha Dev-Sharma of Sparkbrook, Birmingham, grand daughter of Lata Kumari Parmeswari Dev. In handwriting, Anuradha aunty had written *Please (underlined) come and do it, we must have you Dolly, you are the star in our galaxy, love Anu.*

"You have to go to that Mum, you know how traditional dad's family is."

"Nah," she said and tossed it.

"But you're the star in--"

"You know how two faced Indians are, they don't mean it."

"Mum? What happened? You can tell me. We're connected to each other."

She smiled at me then, that vivid dazzling smile that I remember from when I was a baby and she'd sing me these awesome Hindi lullabies and my eyes would get as big as dinner plates. We were her world. She's 41 but she could be 31, she looks amazing for her age, for any age. I know she had a horrible childhood but why can't she see the talents she has? Her smile lights a room. Her voice is like a nightingale.

"I felt this blackness Shaani. Just drowning in it. This really strong feeling that I was just dirty water disappearing down a plughole. I shouldn't have gone off those anti depressants I know, but they were so strong. Mind you these Nightsleeps knock you for six, God knows what's in them, liquid cosh

14

they call them. But they don't help with anxiety. I felt so anxious. How many pills am I supposed to take? I don't want to be rattling into my old age Shaani."

"Mum but you're young."

"And then this stranger on the other side of the pub, he sees me having this meltdown and he comes and says hello I'm Max, are you ok? I mean, it was kindness you know? And I thought he sees me. He *sees* me!"

"Ok I don't even know what that *means*, but you can't see *him* anymore. You just can't."

"Ok," she said and started emptying the dishwasher.

It was the same way Max had shut me up.

"I saw you in that pub," I said bitterly. "I came to pick you up as a surprise. I saw you and him in the window. I drove off. I didn't know what to do. It…freaked me out."

"And you've kept it under your hat for two months," said Mum crossly. "Why'd you have to go and see him now?"

"I didn't know how to talk to you —"

"It was just a drunken kiss you saw. Nothing more."

I knew she was lying.

"So you've never had sex with him?"

"Of course not. What is this, an interrogation?"

My heart suddenly started beating hard.

Max had taken advantage of my mum's vulnerable state. He'd spied her and then he'd slithered across the pub and then he'd swooped in with the flattery. He was that sort of man. Maybe he'd taken her to a hotel and bought her more wine.

"He's a proper low life. He's into all kinds of things mum."

"Can't you just forget about it Shaani?"

"What if dad knew? He'd be devastated."

"What's it got to do with him? He's not here. What's it got to do with you? It's just something of my own. It isn't what you think. It isn't an affair. I didn't have sex with him. I wouldn't! Why did you have to go there? It's nothing, it's nothing! Why won't you accept it?"

"Ok I accept it," I said.

"Thank you."

She left the kitchen and went upstairs to talk to Ash about something, probably to make sure he was cleaning his room. I sat at the breakfast bar immobile. The kitchen cabinets, the ticking clock all seemed to waver as though they were made of paper. The sun disappeared and the kitchen was cold and dark . I got up quickly, the scrape of the stool setting my teeth on edge. Putting up my hood I took the stairs two at a time and went into my room. We don't lock doors in our house so I made sure it was closed tightly and then I sat down at my desk and took out my airmail letter.

Chapter 3

Rain started coming down, a soft rain folded in with the soft wind. The light from the lamppost lay a wobbly square on the thin sheet of blue airmail paper on my desk. I couldn't think of fun stuff to write you. I couldn't say seven months are an eternity. I miss you dad, I wish you were here to take the reins, maybe she would never have met Max if you were here. I tried to imagine you 7120km away, or 4424.16289 in the old money as you call it.

I saw you sitting in your dilapidated guest house in rural Chayaa waiting for our letters. Going to court every day in something called "the three wheeler," but "Indian courts move slower than a tortoise on Valium," to quote your last letter. Forget Skype and email, they don't even have electricity 24/7 in Chayaa because the generators keep going down. Which is ironic because Chayaa means shade!

There was a poem we were given in English Lit written by that guy who makes exceedingly good cakes. The teacher read it out with gusto and we all just sat there giggling. I'd forgotten it but it was quite good, there was a nice rhythm to it dad.

> If I were drowned in the deepest sea,
>
> *Mother o' mine, O mother o' mine!*
>
> I know whose tears would come down to me,
>
> *Mother o' mine, O mother o' mine!*

If I were damned of body and soul,

I know whose prayers would make me whole,

Mother o' mine, O mother o' mine!

I started thinking about how you must have sat waiting for your mum's airmails when you were studying in London, renting a 'bedsit' in Willesden Green with a gas cooker in the room! You lived on hard boiled eggs that you shoved in your overcoat pockets to keep your hands warm, and then ate for lunch. When London was still 'black and white' as you call it.

You didn't consider yourself poor, London was exotic and exciting to you, transgressive even. Those eggs were a delicacy to you because you'd been brought up a strict Brahmin and never mind meat, chicken and fish, you weren't even allowed to eat eggs. But in the Yoookay you had to or you'd have starved. You couldn't find Indian vegetables or supermarkets then. You were my age when you left India for the Yoookay as you still call it.

Thirty six years later you can still only cook boiled eggs!

The guest house in Chayaa gives you three home cooked meals a day, remembered dishes of your childhood that 'fill my senses,' dishes that you had to forget about when you were trudging up Willesden Hill with your warm delicacies in your pockets. See, I read and re read your letters just as you do ours. I wonder if you miss our cheese sarnies.

I never met your mum but I know about her from you: She came in a covered rickshaw from a tiny village called Chayaa to a small town called Lucknow to marry your dad and live in a big house with electricity and a flushing toilet. She had a BA in Hindi that she had passed through correspondence course because there was no university in Chayaa and she kept that diploma scroll in her suitcase rolled up with her marriage shawls and mothballs. Her dream was to be a teacher but there was no possibility in those days and so she devoted herself to you, her only child. She carried on living there after your father died and when she died the house was sold to developers and razed to the ground.

Now there's nothing left of you in India. Except for a small piece of land that belonged to your mum's people in Chayaa. You used to visit it when as a kid your mum took you to stay with her family in the summers. It was just a stretch of dormant land with a fence around it and your mum would point to it proudly and say it was yours. You hadn't thought of it for years until that official letter landed on our doormat at Christmas, informing you of the new rules.

It's been mired in legal limbo for 40 years and if you don't fight for it now, the Indian government will steal it. Some people here think you're on a strange and sentimental mission on your sabbatical. Most academics just write a book. I can't imagine what it must feel like to have no parents, no siblings and no childhood home, but I do understand why that piece of land means so much to you. I have this conviction that if you don't claim it, you'll be lonely all your life.

So what if we never build a house there, or live there? It's our heritage and our history. It'll connect me and Ash to India and to you, and to our paternal grandmother, and her people before that who planted the spreading peepul trees and dense mango groves you played in during your childhood summers. Also, it might be worth a few bob one day because India is on the world stage now!

But seven months are an eternity.

I know there's nothing you can do to make the wheels turn faster on a comatose reptile, but people have started to wonder how many times Air India will let you change the return date, and aunty Anuradha said I hope it doesn't go on like "Jaundice and Jaundice" (she's been watching the BBC serials). I know you can't abandon the project because to you it's Home, which is the same as Love.

I know you love the UK and you've got a British passport, but your heart will always belong to India, to Lucknow, to Chayaa, to the earth where you were born and where I know you want to die (but not until I'm an old lady!). I was born in Chesham General but neither the County of Aylesbury nor the Chiltern District mean a thing to me. I prefer living in London, in the Borough of Barnet and it doesn't feel like I've only been here four years, it feels like I've always lived here. They say the idea of Home is complicated, yet to me it feels smooth like those Russian dolls, homes within homes, layers within layers. I feel like I'm from Chayaa too even though I've never been there.

I like the way I've arranged the furniture in my bedroom. I like my desk underneath the window so if I want, I can stand up and look directly in front of the house. I prefer this house to the one we had in Chesham, even though it's smaller. We all fell for it when we saw it. Ash said it was ours because it was on a road which had his name in it and I said it's not all about *you* Ash, typical Indian boy, but we all agreed it was a sign.

Just as we all belonged to each other, this house had been waiting for us to claim it. Our garden, our corner and where our road Ashley Gardens intersects with Lansdowne Road, and even that tumbledown path called Lovers Lane. And the fence that goes from it all along the golf course the length of Ashley Gardens. I like being at the front of the house above the front room.

A sparkle bounced on the window frame.

Something, a noise outside stopped my pen in mid air. I knew then that it had been absolutely the right thing to take a gap year. I was needed at home. I stood up. A flare in the dark. In Lovers Lane. A lighter? What was that? I rubbed the condensation on the window but the blurriness was all on the outside as it had started to rain pretty hard. There it was again. A definite flame. Who was lighting a bonfire in the rain? My throat went dry. I bombed downstairs and ran smack into Ash.

He was standing at the foot of the stairs, his jacket on, torch in hand.

"What are you up to?"

"Relax."

I lowered my voice. "You going out?"

He looked upstairs and back at me but said nothing. Mum was coming out of her room. Ash walked into the lounge and turned on the TV. Mum came downstairs.

"Excuse me, mind the gap," she trilled as though we were in a crowded tube station.

She was all dressed up in skinny jeans, red lipstick and re-blow dried hair. She reached for her raincoat on the coat stand.

"Mum! Are you going out now?"

"Yes, I'm going out now."

She looked stunning, eyes shining. Alive, utterly alive.

"It's 9.30pm mum," I whispered. "Are you going out to see him? Is that him outside?"

Her eyes flashed with fury and she put her perfectly manicured hand on my shoulder, lightly but full of animosity.

"I'm going out and I'll be back. That's all you need to know. Go in the front room and watch TV with your brother, there's a good girl. I'll be back soon."

As she went to open the front door something went *whoosh* in my head. *Max* was outside. He was just outside! What if he came to the door? What if she bought him in? No, he was staying that side of the door. And she wasn't going anywhere. I grabbed her arm. She's puny and I'm strong but

I'd never manhandled her before. I was shocked at my own strength.

"Ow," she winced.

"You're not leaving the house," I said tightening my grip.

"Get off..."

"I won't let you," I said pulling her arm.

She looked at me then with an expression I had never seen before. Like she hated me.

"Let me go," she cried pulling with all her might but I had my other hand on her shoulder and I'm much stronger than her. We were in a tussle. It was surreal. But something in me just couldn't let her go. If she went out there, in the rain, anything might happen.

Ash came out of the front room, the TV still blaring behind him. I let her go immediately and stepped back. He was carrying a bottle of beer and he wiped his mouth on the back of his hand. He had taken off his jacket and clearly settled in for the night.

"What's the commotion?"

"Your sister won't let me go out," she shouted.

She sounded deranged. My heart was beating hard. The rain was pelting against the roof. Something so strange was happening.

"Well, it's raining," said Ash unmoved by the drama, but that's Ash. Nothing ever freaks him out.

"Mum."

"Don't you come near me Shaani," said mum.

She was scared of me. I'd frightened my own mother. I felt sick. She stood with her back to the door, her colour high, breathing rapidly.

"I'm going out ok?" she said looking at Ash, her favourite, thinking he being the man of the house would give her permission. Or something. I was reeling.

"Ok" said Ash. "You taking the car?"

"No. I'm just. I'm just going out to meet someone."

"Who?" Ash put his hands in his pockets and stared at her.

It was as though she was hypnotised. She stood there pleading with him silently.

"Who are you going out to meet at this hour?" Ash sounded so stern and yet he didn't raise his voice or move towards her.

Mum began to cry. It was awful, awful.

"Mum.." I tried to extend my hand to her but she swiped it away.

"Leave me alone."

"Go back to bed mum," said Ash.

Obediently she took off her raincoat, hung it up and climbed the stairs slowly, head bowed. Ash and I stared at each other until we heard her bedroom door close. He must know, I thought. Poor Ash. It must be devastating for a boy to know his mum is having an affair. It was devastating enough for me.

"Mum's not herself these days," I said carefully.

"Off her head on meds," he said and walked back into the front room.

"What?" I followed him. "She's not on the anti depressants any more. Anyway they don't-- She not off her head."

He settled himself back in front of the TV and picked up his bottle of beer. Ash gets bored with conversations that aren't about him.

I spoke to the back of his head. "Were *you* going out just now?"

"I saw a guy prowling about."

I gasped. "And you thought mum was going out to meet him?"

Ash turned from the screen and looked at me like I was a moron.

"Why would mum be going out to meet a burglar?"

"A what?"

He sighed. "Don't you *ever* watch the news? Romanian gypsies camped out in Barnet Fields? Council can't shift them because of EU human rights, even though their emmos well known. A group drive out at night and park in a side street. One prowls out, cases all the houses on foot, informs the others by text. Lights, alarms, fences, back doors all the easy entry indicators. The driver stays put while the others fan out and do five houses in each street, bam bam bam, run back with the loot, and they're gone! To do it again in a different street, same night."

"Brazen!"

"Yeah, old school. They're always falling out of windows and jumping off roofs but they just bounce back. Robbing's a game to them. They don't care if people are sleeping in their beds, they just rob around them. There's no precision, it's just pig headed greed. It's a part of their culture in fact. They're nomads, they don't believe in jobs, they thieve therefore they are. I'm pretty sure I saw one of them in Lovers Lane about a half hour ago."

"We should call the police!"

"He'll be long gone by then. I'll give him a bit more time to stew and then I'll run out and flash the torch in his face. Hah! Watch him run! They're good runners."

"Ashi don't. What if he's got gun, or a knife?"

"No knives are weapon of choice for 13 year olds crossing postcodes. These gypsies are just scavengers, the lowest in the food chain. They use fists and feet. They don't frighten me."

He took another swig from the beer bottle and wiped his mouth on the back of his hand again.

"Don't drink anymore."

He nodded and stared at the screen. I suppose he was preoccupied with how he was going to protect us, his jacket and his torch on the table. I suppose he was revving himself up. For all his annoying-ness, Ash is the most responsible 15year old you can meet. He's a serious boy.

"I'll switch on some more lights so they'll know we're home. Then they won't target us. If it is them. Him. Whatever."

"I've seen him before. Nasty little runt."

My heart leapt. Had Max been to the house before? Had he met mum in Lovers Lane before? What was mum doing now? Was she texting him? Was he going to come to the house? He knew we were alone. He could literally ring the bell and say he was a friend of mum's and how could we stop him coming in?

"Ash listen, don't let mum go out tonight."

"Don't worry sis. I'm on it like a bonnet. I'm a staying down here. I won't let the nutter out."

"And you won't go out either?"

"Ok yeah I'll stay here. The standing guard. Or in my case the sitting guard." He opened another bottle of beer.

"Don't drink so much."

I knew he would stay where he was. I knew he wouldn't fall asleep. I knew even if it wasn't quite for the same reason, he felt he had to protect Dolly same as I did. I trusted him totally. We had an unbreakable bond.

"Don't worry sis. Go to bed."

"Ok, yeah I will. Good night."

I went to the front door and put the chain on. Then I double locked it and hung the key back on it's hook. I stared at the door and thought of Max kicking it in and then I turned around and quickly went upstairs. I could hear mum padding about in her room. I assumed she was tidying. She had done a lot of tidying when Naani died and then when dad left to go to India.

How quickly she had obeyed Ash's order.

I felt awful, just awful, didn't want to think about how I'd tried to restrain her. I sat down and took up my pen. The rain had eased. The TV was blaring reassuringly downstairs, not too loud, not loud enough to make out the dialogue, but loud enough to know Ash was there. I must write my letter to dad. I started to think about the "characters" in the neighbourhood and got drowsy at my desk.

'A dour Vietnamese couple had taken over the Spar, and their son kept talking non stop and English people being polite just smiled and took a sneaky look at their watch but he kept talking. After you paid he always said "keep in touch" and I thought he was trying to compensate for the parents' glum faces. How exhausting for him!

Barry who had driven a black cab for 35 years and hated Dollis Cars and Uber, told me he would have liked to be an artist but his parents thought only poufs did that and his wife said footstools cant do anything Barry.

Mr. Patel in the Pharmacy said he could never figure out Dr Hollings signature on the prescriptions back in the day. He said your dad might remember him, a very good doctor but couldn't write to save his life, and I said no we've only been in the area for four years and he said oh yes, and yet I feel as if I've known your family for the longest time. That was a nice thing to…'

The front door closed. Oh my God, she's gone out! I opened my door and raced downstairs.

Ash was standing in his jacket, torch in hand, hair dripping. He had Naani's walking stick with him. He raised a finger to his lips. I followed him into the lounge, furious. He was breathing hard. The TV was on.

"You said you wouldn't go out."

"I found the guy. I bopped him," he said giggling.

"What guy?"

Ash's eyes shone. "I saw him leave Lovers Lane and I followed him down Ashley Gardens, along the wire fence. I didn't know what I was going to do, but I just followed him."

"You've seen him before?"

"Yeah, I told you. Don't you listen? So I followed him halfway down and then when he got to that bit where the fence is broken and there's a ditch, I shone the torch on the back of his head. He twisted around. Wasn't expecting that! He stumbles! I advance! Before he could do a thing I pushed the stick in the back of his knees."

"Ash!"

"Hah, down he went like a sack of potatoes. Element of surprise. His knees gave out. I pushed him with the stick and he rolled into the ditch. Hah! He won't come round here again. Don't look so shocked Shaani. I didn't kill him, I just gave him a scare. That's how you got to be with these people. They need to know they cant mess with Asians. All the Gandhi stuff about turning the other cheek that Dad's always on about is balls. They think we're all meek and mild and we keep gold in our houses and we're no good for anything except running corner shops! They target Asians for that reason! Well I showed him. He or little gang won't be bothering us again, I can assure you of that."

Chapter 4

I woke up and the sun was streaming in. A hot almost clammy light. I jumped out of bed and looked at Lovers Lane. It was beautiful. The leaves were glistening with dew and the bushes were like a crayon sketch; everything looked gorgeous and green. There was a knock.

"Come in"

"Listen darling, I want to talk to you."

She pulled the chair next to the bed and sat down. She was dressed for the day in her black jeans and white jacket.

"Mum I'm so sorry I didn't mean to hurt you--."

"No no my darling. You could never hurt me. You love me. And I love you very much. You're my wing woman!" She stroked my hair and gave me a smile. "I need to tell you something. I hate to lie to you. I did go out for dinner a couple of times with him. I'm sorry. It was wrong. But there was no sexual contact. It was not an affair Shaani. Absolutely not. I promise you. It was just texting, honestly. Just texting. A secret friend. A little message waiting for me. That ding. Elevates the serotonin levels apparently. I know, it's typical of me to do something that teenagers do. Not that my sensible Shaani would ever do anything like her silly mum. I got carried away with the novelty, that's all. I must be in a mid life crisis. Can I have a hug please?"

I hugged her and she kissed my cheek.

"It's finished. I told him last night. I texted him. It *was* him I was going out to meet. I felt I should tell him face to face. He was angry and wanted to know why you'd gone up there shouting the odds. Sorry darling, I'm so so sorry. It was such a stupid mistake. The whole thing. Such a misjudgement. Can you please forgive me?"

"I shouldn't have confronted him. I should have talked to you."

"Sweetheart, can you please forgive me?"

"Have you met him here before mum?"

"Maybe yes."

"In our house?"

"No Shaani, never in the house. Never. I know he's no good Shaani but I don't think he's quite as bad as you made out."

I didn't say anything. I believed her but my brain was racing. So then who had Ash 'fixed'?

"I'm sorry I wasn't in my right mind yesterday, I shouldn't have laid my insecurities on to you. I'm the parent. And the past has passed! And honestly, I like working for Manish, the part time suits me. And you know what, if I never finished college it's because I met a wonderful man and made a choice to get married and have a baby. That was you my lovely."

"I know mum," I smiled.

"You know I love your father very much. He's the kindest nicest man I've ever met in my life. I've never regretted that choice. I might have made some bad choices recently but I've never---"

Mum had tears in her eyes.

"What happened when I wouldn't let you go out?'

"I calmed down and realised you were right and I didn't need to see him face to face at all. His pride was hurt, so what? That's the only reason he wanted to see me. I texted him and said I wouldn't see him and he should go home. He said ok and that was that. I took a couple of NightSleeps and I was dead to the world till this morning. The sunlight hit my face and I realised what a fool I'd been but more importantly that I had to talk to you."

"So it's really over then?"

"Yes of course, but it was nothing. Sweetheart you never have to worry about me falling for anyone. I'm taken. You're my life. You and Ash and dad are my life. Love is the smell of you, the way Ash frowns when he thinks my skirts too short."

We laughed then.

"Are we good?" said mum.

I nodded.

"I'll be home a bit late tonight as I've got Pilaaadees"

She always says it with an American accent as though she's a bit embarrassed about doing it, the same way she says

34

Zumba! with an exclamation mark. It's those moments when suddenly I feel protective of mum. After she left for work I thought: I'm not like that. I can't relate to it. She's spends hours doing her makeup in the morning, she's done that since she was 14. She always had to project a front when she was young because her home life was so chaotic, she had to speak for her parents.

Their chav Asian neighbours would phone to say her dad was drunk and collapsed in the street. Sometimes they'd say they would bring him home and they did, but sans wallet.

The Asians shunned her and she hated them but mum had a love hate thing going on forever with the community. She hates them but she desperately wants them to love her. I think she's always had that insecurity. I didn't think a woman of her age would still feel insecure but maybe people don't really change. Well that just meant she needed more of our love and protection, not less. I went downstairs feeling philosophical and made myself a cup of tea.

Ash's phone rang and I looked at it. Five missed calls from someone keen called G and a text saying LOML. I smiled. Ash has a girlfriend? Who knew? I couldn't stop smiling. The kitchen clock burped. And suddenly from nowhere I stopped smiling. The battery's gone flat I thought, I must put that on the list because it's a little round one. I had the feeling this gap year would change me. But how?

Mum and Dad had spoken about me behind closed doors: Do you think she has a boyfriend? No, said Dad. And good! I don't want her to have a boyfriend till she's at least 35 and they'd laughed. We have to handle Shaani carefully, mum had said. She's got so much inside of her. She'll find the right boy when the time is right and he'll be just right, the love of her life. But then she'll leave us and marry him and go and live with his family, that's not fair, said dad and mum said 'well this is a Brahmin house and she is a good Brahmin girl just like you've raised her to be'.

Where would we be without Shaani to influence us, dad had said. She's the centre of good in our family. I had puzzled about that and wondered what he meant and some time afterwards I heard him talking about a play to a student and he was saying "all the characters are pulled towards the centre of good, it unifies the play"

Mum had shown me how to do the doe eyes soon after that. Was she worried about me never getting a boyfriend? Did she think it was time I had sex? I wasn't worried about it but I did think about it sometimes. I was apprehensive of all it might entail and how falling in love might make me weak and pathetic but I didn't want to have sex with a boy I didn't love. There was this whole problem with love. What it was in terms of a boyfriend, I didn't know.

I knew I was different to my school friends who were man mad, and I definitely didn't dream about being a Princess and meeting my Prince. I thought all that stuff was pink and sappy. I wanted to do something first, have adventures, make a mark on the world. I didn't know what or how but I felt certain that I would. Why not? It was all waiting out there, somewhere. I definitely wasn't going to meet someone in my first week at university and marry them and have a kid because I was scared of going under. I had this crazy conviction that there was nothing to fear in the world, except fear and like that Neville Brothers song you love dad, I was 'fearless, we must be fearless'.

"Ash...!" I shouted. No answer. Dead to the world or gone out.

I looked at the photograph of Ash as a little boy stuck on the fridge with a magnet. He was wearing thick glasses and looked like a nerd. He had become a little celebrity in the Chesham Echo when he was 3. **Brave sister saves genius brother from Chesham Pond** went the headline. The journalist had patted me on the head and called me a brave little girl and I'd pushed his hand off and crossed my arms, stuck my nose in the air and said imperiously. "He's the only brother I've got, what else would I have done?" Apparently I was stroppy even at age 7, and they were far more (rightly!) interested in hearing this toddler recite the alphabet backwards. Was there something magical in the Chesham Pond, they asked? I didn't remember it all exactly but the story had been recited and bragged about so often by mum and dad in company, that it had become part of our family lore and I knew the dialogue off by heart. I smiled at the photograph. The Chinese say when you save a life that life belongs to you and if something belongs to you it's your duty to take care of it.

Ash was hammered last night. How drunk was he? He was stumbling when he came in. He stank of it. Did he really do what he said or was it just some fantasy? The torch was on the hall table. I picked it up and replaced it in the drawer. Ash's words from last night seemed hollow, unreal.... Like a scene from a videogame. Following a burglar along the wire fence.....He didn't do it. What did he do?

I put my hoodie on and went out. No one was about. 11am was the quietest hour in this street. Every single soul was working. There were no housewives here unlike Chesham where they had all been housewives. And there were hardly any cars. It was still wet and murky and I had to be careful. I walked along the ivy covered fence peeking through the gaps at the flat golf course beyond. Tall thick trees lined the fence like railings. I reached the broken bit of fence and looked at the ditch. Nothing. Honestly Ash! I felt relieved, hugely relieved. You're so full of it I thought. I walked on.

Then I saw the body.

It hadn't rolled through the broken bit into the ditch, it was lying there by the good part of the fence. On it's stomach. A mound covered with wet leaves. It was Max. I was almost sure it was Max. I bent down to look. He was in an awkward curled up position as if he was hugging the ground, one arm up like a crab. You could easily walk past. The rain and wind last night had swept a carpet of leaves over him. A dog would find him. He was definitely dead. He looked awful lying there in that position. I felt like I wanted to straighten him up which is ridiculous. I looked around. No one was about. But for how long? And when would Ash come back?

My heart started thundering. I can't wait, I've got to act. The car was a hundred meters away. I looked around and walked briskly to it, looked around again, got in and reversed it back so that it obscured the body from the line of houses to the other side. No one was about. No twitching curtains, no child playing in the No Ball Games area of green. I sat in the car thinking what shall I do? My hands on the wheel looked like strange appendages. Think it out! *Breathe for Gods sake.* Breathe through it like you're doing lengths underwater.

I took my hands off the wheel and shoved them in my pockets. I pulled out a Tesco receipt, on the back of which mum had written the number of AXA Alarm Systems. I screwed it up and put it back in my pocket for safekeeping. I've got to phone them and cancel, that's one of my chores. I've got to move the body. I've got to get it away from the house. If I report it, they'll know it was Ash. He won't be able to go to Oxford or Princeton. But Ash didn't *kill* him. Did he? He didn't know what he was doing. The police won't think so. And it'll come out about him and mum. And dad will find out.

But it's broad Daylight. You can't move a body in plain sight. No one does that. I've never seen it in a movie. But I've got to do it straightaway. I scanned the line of houses. Everyone was at work. *There should be dust balls rolling across Ashley Gardens in the afternoons.* If I get him in the boot…If I can get it in the boot. I got out of the car and went around to look at it.

His eyes were closed. What if they suddenly open? No that doesn't happen in real life. Once the eyes close they're closed forever, the hearing is the last to go. What was the last thing he'd heard…I couldn't connect the swaggering man in Pumping Iron with this inert body, but it was him. He was dead. I can do it physically I thought, he's thin, but can I *do* it? Can I touch a dead body? I bent down and pulled his foot.

I gasped. The body was already stiff. I pulled and pulled until he was out of the ditch. He stank of ditch water. A rat scurried away.

I can't get him in the boot, they always put the body in the boot. I heaved him up pushed him in the back seat and flung the blanket over him. What am I doing? God I'm going to bawl, I just want to sit down and cry. Stop it, it's just fear. Fight or flight? Definitely fight. Energy surged in me. *But there's DNA everywhere.* Ash's and now mine. Too bad. I looked around. Perhaps someone's watching from a window? I don't care let them watch. I got in. You're fine, now drive away from the house. Where to?

The Brook, where else?

Chapter 5

As soon as I started the car, the heavens opened up. Biblical! Lightning and thunder and rain. The rain started coming down in sheets. The wipers couldn't wipe it fast enough. Zero visibility. Drive through the rain, drive through it. Rain is good. Keep your nerve, keep under the limit. I drove down to the roundabout and then left into Dollis Hill until I got to the viaduct. There were a series of modern flats on the right hand side obscured by a range of trees and opposite them was wild countryside and the entrance to the Brook.

The Brook was famous in Barnet. In a way it was a much larger version of Lovers Lane plus running water. A lot of people went to the Brook. But there was no one today. The sky had turned black or darkest grey. The rain was coming down like a thousand running taps drumming on the road. Mud, wet leaves, mud. I backed up the car carefully, *you don't want to slide now,* opened the door peeled off the blanket and pulled him out onto the bank. I stopped and caught my breath.

For an horrific moment I saw his face and I thought I know you, I knew you for a short time. You pulled the chair out for me and you said "so you're the daughter". A deafening crash of thunder broke above me. Lightening smashed the sky open illuminating the rain and then it was dark once more. What sort of day is this, I thought in a panic? How can it be so *dark?* I pushed him hard and he slid easily into the Brook. I stared. The rain was coming so fast now that the Brook was getting full.

What have you done Shaani? He's right here Shaani, you can still go to the police, it's not too late, you can tell them everything. Pull him back, get him back. I kept staring, motionless, hardly hearing my heartbeat. He kept sliding and then stopped. And there he lay in the middle of the Brook. In a few moments it would be too late.

Within seconds the Brook was over flowing and like a paper boat the body began to move away. It looked like a floating black bin liner and then it disappeared under water. I could hardly believe it, as though some divine force had pulled the body in. The rain was coming so hard I couldn't even see where it was. I kept looking, even though the rain was blinding me, I kept wiping my eyes with my sleeve. I had to make sure it was gone. You can't go to the police now.

I stood staring at the bubbling black water, at the urgent cargo of twigs and branches and leaves rushing away. I kept expecting to see the body bob up but it just wasn't there. The water current was too strong. I got back into the car and pulled down my hood. No, get rid of the blanket! I got out of the car and pulled out the blanket, rolled it up and chucked that in the Brook too. Water will wash off the DNA. It was a second hand blanket bought from a charity shop. No one could link it to us. What about the DNA in the car? But we aren't under suspicion. Unless someone saw Ash. Unless someone saw me.

I drove to Barnet Community Leisure Centre and sat in the car park watching the wipers. They were moving manically and still I couldn't see anything ahead. I've done it. So don't think about it. I went inside the Leisure Centre and Troy behind the desk buzzed me in, no need to produce my card because he knew me, and I went into the changing rooms. The reassuring scent of lavender permeated the air. There were just the usual ladies for Aqua and some kids and unemployed people. I put my wet hoody, joggers and underwear under the shower and then in the Rinse n Spin machine and then I had a shower and got changed into the fresh clothes that I kept in my locker for after my daily swim. I took out the spun clothes and shoved them in a plastic bag and then I sat down to compose myself.

What about my footprints? Was the clay or the ground a special one and would it be on my trainers? Had I walked the clay from the Brook into the car and now into the gym? Oh I don't care, I can't think about it now I thought crossly.

"Sixty as usual yeah?" said Troy. "Got your new membership card? The i-ting. Wicked innit?"

"Innit," I said and held up my plastic bag of wet clothes like a trophy.

Anyway they'll have you on CCTV entering the Leisure Centre so they'll know exactly when you arrived and (imp)lying that you've done 60 lengths won't fool anyone. I don't care, I thought crossly. Shall I go back to the loo and put two fingers down my throat? Because I haven't thrown up yet. Why haven't I thrown up yet? A normal person would have heaved at the sight of a dead body. How could I have done it? How did I do it? Shut up keep going. It was drizzling. I got in the car and drove to North Finchley to the American Valet service run by Slovakians and Albanians.

"Full VIP please," I said.

Was it too soon? Was it too rainy, would they do it? Of course. They want the money. And we always have it valeted on Monday every month.

"See you in 30mins, you're lucky you're number 1," said the guy.

"Cheers"

How far was the body now? Had it somehow got obstructed by a rock or a branch? What if a branch had pinned the body against the bank pushing the head out? It would look like a floating dismembered head. What if a little kid found it? It would have blown up like a football. No, I don't want to think about that. It had started to rain again. Hard. Good. Let it rain let it rain. But will he do the service if it's raining? The spores and the fibres would be embedded in the back seat and maybe they'd stop the VIP service half way through and go "hang on a minute, what this?"…No, they'd already started, they wouldn't stop in the middle. They're not forensic officers! But a simple forensic test would reveal everything. And weren't there CCTV cameras on every street? They probably had me from all different angles. Well what can I do about it now?

I went to the café on the high street.

As I finished my coffee I imagined the car going through the super laser rollers getting it's blow dry. We always had the car valeted on a Monday so there was nothing funny about me getting it done today. That was a piece of luck. I'd been for my swim as usual, a bit later than usual but so what? Even if no one saw me actually swimming it didn't matter, I was changed in my fresh clothes and I had followed my routine. And now you have to go home and let the alarm guy in.

No, I cant face it!

You're crazy, you think nothing of shoving a dead body in the Brook and being recorded probably every second on the four hundred and twenty two cameras in London, but you cant face the alarm guy. You think nothing of it Shaani? Go back and undo it, there's still time. Isn't there? Go to the police, tell them what you did, and then...then. I can't. I've done it now, I have to go on.

Mum had written the number on the Tesco receipt which was in the pocket of my hoodie, and now it was probably screwed up from the Rinse n Spin. Why does she bother writing things down when you can just go to the website? I've got 4G.

"Hello AXA alarms"

"Hi I'm calling about 15 Ashley Gardens. Is it too late to cancel the annual service?'

"Because of the weather yeah?"

"Because? Of the. Yeah exactly."

"Yes madam. Our engineers are trained to do the work in all weathers and as you know it's really mostly inside but they do have to check the outside too and."

"Better for him to do it on a nicer day. Unless he's already out on the job?'

"That's kind of you Mrs. Dev. I'll let him know. Phone us back to get another appointment though. You know the insurance isn't valid if there hasn't been the annual service and your contract ran out last week."

I breathed out slowly. I went out and got the car and drove home thinking the AXA receptionist would remember it was me and not mum who cancelled. I shouldn't have pretended I was mum! But I didn't pretend, I just let her assume because it would have been too complicated to--But that's irrelevant. Stick to the relevant points. And who else? There might be a thousand witnesses. The "clean Genie" dangling off the rear view mirror was twirling away like mad.

From this moment you've got to think of every little thing, each minute detail, every microscopic possibility, because you've done it now, you're in it now. Up to your neck. You're in it up to the neck like *him* in the Brook. I shuddered and breathed long and slow. I'm not going to think about it anymore. I'm just going to relax. It's done. Dusted. The sun came out hot and strong and I felt it's welcome healing warmth on my skin. I drove home.

Ash was standing outside the front door.

"I thought the car had been stolen, you nutter!"

"I went to get it cleaned, what's up?"

He looked vague, preoccupied. Hungover.

"Nothing, I just thought. Never mind. Where is it then?"

"What?"

"World Peace, the cure for cancer, what do you think? The car?"

"The car. I just decided to park it outside number 35. The Singhs have gone to India, they said its ok to use their spot."

"I'm starving. Hope you bought eggs. I fancy a desi."

"Come on," I said and nudged him in the ribs out the way.

I went in first and he behind me and shut the door. Suddenly it felt great to be making my little brother a desi Indian breakfast in our warm cosy kitchen.

Chapter 6

"Ash, don't tell mum about last night," I said watching him tuck in.

I'd made it just the way Princey makes it, plenty of green chillies, chopped red onion and a slice of bread to squidge and make it an omelette sandwich. He looked up and grinned, dazed like a new born chick. You are so hung-over I thought. Mum doesn't notice how much Ash drinks. She doesn't notice how much she drinks either. Maybe because I don't drink I notice these things? I suppose it's possible that I'm the weird one, not them. But no, I'm sure I'm the nearest to normal in this house.

"What about last night?"

I thought for a mad minute he had obliterated it from his memory. If only I could. But then he laughed and I knew he remembered, only he had no idea. He assumed the man had come to and run away, because they were good runners and always jumping off of roofs.

"I doubt our house will be targeted again. Saw to that. Let's park in Lansdowne outside the Singhs for the next few weeks though yeah?"

He fixed his stare on me and I nodded. I can see what girls would like in Ash. There's a sort of authority he exudes that's way past his years. He's clever but it's a power he hides because he thinks its rude or showoffy to display it. That's the right kind of clever. I look at Ash sometimes and I know he'll do something amazing in the world, *for* the world, and I feel proud of him. He'll never let anyone or anything get in the way of where he's going. The boozing and the slouching around are just a smokescreen.

"So you know Princey threw her husband out? Apparently he's 'dancing with all the girls' in their neighbourhood and she's had enough." Ash lolled his head to indicate Indian assent.

"I didn't even know she was married!"

"Coz you don't listen!"

When Mitch told him he had a chance for a scholarship to Oxford or Princeton a year early, he said Oxford was better because you can drink in the street in England. He said it in a way that you didn't know if he was joking or serious, just like you can't tell if he's being mean or just honest. Mitch and Ash have a special relationship, they talk for hours but as far as I can make out (because I've walked past and listened) it's never about Physics or Maths or anything like that. They always seem to be talking about nothing, silly little jokes or other stuff that I don't understand. They have a mutual admiration society.

"So did you hear about this thing that happened in Paris?" said Ash. "Hello? Earth to Shaani?"

"No," I said.

"This art thief. Last month he cleans up at the Louvre. He's shoved all the paintings in his van and he's chugging down the Champs Elysees and then he gets slower and slower and finally comes to a stop. The gendarmes steam in. They go, ello elllo ew yew are a very bad robbeur, what append to yew? And he goes I ran out of monet and could not get de gas to make de van go."

People look at Ash and they can't stop looking at him. He's young but underneath his brain is burning bright like a fire. *He's* the centre of good. Every year I tie a thread on his wrist and he gives me a present that mum's bought on his behalf, and wishes me Happy Raxsha Bandhan, which is the promise all Indian boys make to protect their sisters. But ever since he was a baby I've protected him.

"What's wrong?" said Ash from somewhere.

"What?"

"You've been staring out the window for the last ten minutes. Come on, sort yourself out," said Ash and then his phone rang and he walked off leaving his plate of congealing ketchup.

I looked around the kitchen and pushed myself back against the sink. All I could think of was "Don't worry. You won't see me again." That macabre sentence kept playing on a loop in my mind. But what can I do with that? What's the point of thinking about it? The dead don't talk. The dead are dead. That tree is a tree. The grass is green. The dead can't talk. The kitchen door opened.

Ash stood in the archway with a long face.

The police are here, I thought.

"I'm going to Leicester for a couple of days."

"Ok," I said and Ash left.

I washed up the dishes and wiped down the kitchen. Just go about your normal routine. Stop thinking about it. Life goes on. Whatever happens you'll just deal with it. But maybe nothing will happen. Who knows where he'll end up but it'll be far from us won't it? He's missing, that's all. But what if he had a family? A wife. No, he didn't look the type. Didn't hundreds of people go missing every year? Who would miss a man like Max? He sold drugs; there must be another hundred who could fill his place. Mum. Would she try to call him or would she stay true to her word?

I walked down to the local shops and bought milk, a blister pack of batteries of all shapes because it was only £1, and bleach. I put the bottle of bleach in the toilet and replaced the battery in the clock, but it wouldn't work. Cheap Chinese shit, but what's the point of going back, he won't give me my money and anyway it's only a pound. I looked at the blister pack with it's 22 different shaped round batteries that we would never need and put it carefully in the kitchen drawer. Just throw it away, for gods sake just throw it away.

Mum was still out when I went to bed. I need to sleep. I must sleep. The land line rang and I went downstairs to the lounge to answer it. The evening was fading. Princey had put a single rose in a vase last week and it had wilted. Normally I leave the things that are in her domain because she says it's her job but I made a mental note to throw it out. Good old Princey, she was helping us with the economy cuts

51

because we were living on one income these days as well as off the money dad had deposited in an Instant Saver called the Chayaa Fund.

"Hello?"

"Hello, is that Shaani? Hi there, how you doin honey?"

"Hi Mitch!" I smiled. He had a great accent, just like a cowboy and he even wore a Stetson. Born and Raised ma'am, he said when I'd first met him and asked if he was really from the "American South" because I'd thought every white man in the south was a throwback and a racist, not a Harvard educated professor of Physics, but even in academic terms Mitch was a one off. He had been a child prodigy himself, an actual one, by going to university at the age of nine. Now he was in his late fifties and looked like a genial old cowboy, the type that go on forever.

"Honey, I can't get Ash on the phone. Could you call him to the land line for me?"

"I thought he'd gone to see you Mitch? Isn't he answering his phone? He should have got there by now, unless that's some train strike? Southern are usually in talks."

It was 8pm

Mitch sighed.

"What's up?"

"Oh it's nothing honey. It's just a little bit of cancer. He's hightailing it down here because he's pretty upset. And he's not answering the phone because he knows I'll tell him to turn back. I'm an old buzzard, I can take care of myself. I guess I shouldn't have told him flat out like that today but I didn't know what other way to say it really."

"OMG Mitch, I'm so sorry to hear that. Yes he just shot out. Are you ok, stupid question. Is it.."

"Incurable, uh-huh, according to my pessimistic oncologist but I have other ideas. Don't sweat it honey, listen I'll see you soon. I'd better get down to the train station. He'll be waiting for the bus and it don't come more than twice a day now."

"But Mitch. Ok Mitch. You know we love you," I said feebly. "Please let me know if I can do anything."

"Stay out the deep end honey."

Mum walked in still in her Zumba gear.

"Mitch has cancer!" I said.

"I know, it's so sad," said mum bowing her head.

"When did you know?"

"Ash texted me." She looked like someone died. "I'm going to pray for him."

"Is it prostate?"

"Yes," she said and shook her head.

"But they can do a lot for prostate cancer---"

"I don't want to talk about that...that *thing*. Stop saying the word. It's bad luck! Listen Shaani, let's go out tomorrow. A day at the seaside. Just you and me? We can go early. Margate. We can get our palms read and have fish n chips. Well I don't eat chips, but."

"I don't know. I don't like throwing my routine out. It's not catching mum. Cancer is a mutation of---"

"Come *on* darling. You can take a swim there if it's warm enough. Let's go to the sea. It'll be good for us."

"Ok," I said.

Part of me was relieved at getting away. I lay in bed that night thinking "You won't see me again," and why had he said those exact words and then that none of it really meant anything, it was just coincidence. Words couldn't do anything, they were just words. Mum is so superstitious. It's just another word for fear isn't it? Poor Mitch, it was so like him to say "a little cancer", he was more stoic than any Englishman. My brain kept circling everything dad, I couldn't stop thinking. I could hear mum snoring next door. Sometimes when she didn't take the NightSleeps she slept in a funny position and her sinuses blocked up. And I thought about those words she'd used. The sweetest darling man. Nicest man I've ever known. That's the kind of thing you said about your teddy bear.

Maybe it's none of my business and obviously not something I'd care to ponder on but I wondered vaguely if you and mum still had sex. It was a bit gruesome. It's only a fourteen year difference between you but maybe that matters as you got older? You used to be much more lovey dovey, but maybe that changes as you get older too? I could only really think of it as how often you'd shared a bedroom in the last few years and frankly, what with you reading and staying up late and her needing to get up early, the spare bedroom had more or less become your bedroom. It had seemed quite natural and not something I'd thought about before. I lay there that night in a troubled restless sleep and in the morning we went to Margate.

Chapter 7

Mum had her Sophia Lorens on with a jaunty scarf around her neck and she'd made us a picnic of cheese sarnies with the famous coriander chutney. The car smelled fresh and pin needle-y with the little clean Genie Albanian cartoon character dangling off the rear view.

"Yayy," she said as she put her foot down. "We're like Thelma and Louise."

"Don't they drive off the cliff?" I grinned.

One thing I'll say about mum is she is an excellent driver. She handles that thing like a pro. She was driving illegally at age 15 because she had to drive her mum around looking for her dad who was often AWOL. She was their interpreter with English people because my uncles were too uncouth. Back in the day I think mum was quite tough. In photographs of her teenage years she's wearing a leather jacket over her shalwar khameez, but once she got married she looked really traditional in her saris. I don't know when she got into her skin tight jeans and jackets, but the older she gets the thinner and more fragile she seems; she gets worked up and freaked out and sad over the smallest things. The constant in all those pictures was always that mane of glossy black hair, her source of strength perhaps?

She turned on her favourite station Magic which they should call Musak because it's supermarket music.

"Don't sing that!" I said.

"You are the wind beneath my----" She buzzed the windows down and despite my better judgement I sang along with her to that sappy song. Soon we were belting it out anthem style.

"…know that you were my herooo."

"…everything I wanted to beeeeee."

"That film is so corny mum," I started laughing and it felt good.

"It was such a treat when we went to Margate," she said. "We left all the worries behind and mum loved to put her feet in the sea. Even Harish and Ajeet loved it although they were off chasing girls and whatnot. She wouldn't eat the fish and chips without the coriander chutney."

"Really? She was the same when she lived with us wasn't she? Had to have it on *everything*, and the hotter the better! Funny that she still liked it even after she'd gone doolally and demented. She gets her daughter and her grand daughter mixed up, but the coriander chutney she doesn't forget."

"I know it's a terrible disease but in a way I didn't mind that she didn't recognise me sometimes. If it meant that she forgot about dad too. All those times. All those hypocrites whispering about us. She didn't need to remember them. I never forgot. I couldn't."

I squeezed mum's shoulder. Poor mum.

"Remember that time when she put on her slippers and went down the Broadway with her stick? Boy I need coriander, where is coriander, boy? She thought Chesham Broadway was downtown Uganda. She came running home and announced there was a group of Hubshi on the corner and I thought she meant sheep, but she meant Black people. Actual Black people! A group of Black men. OMG! Beyond, beyond! I suppose that's how Indians used to talk about Africans back when she was growing up in Uganda? "

Mum groaned. "I just blamed the Alzheimer's and said she was making words up! Far too complicated and embarrassing to explain Indian racism to the white neighbours. Anyway, the racism was bad enough but those bloody awful slippers. I don't know why you still keep them."

"She's the only grandparent I've ever met. Anyway, they're my size."

"But you don't wear them."

"I know. I just like to have them."

She beamed. "See Shaani, you're not that different from me. You're sentimental. And superstitious."

"I thought Ajeet uncle might want something of hers, but he said we could have it all. I didn't really get that. He came all the way from Australia for the funeral."

"He was in the UK for business that's all. Neither of your uncles could give a damn. They never bothered when she was alive. Harish thinks he did us all a favour by having mum stay with him for the free babysitting but as soon as she showed signs of Alzheimer's, it was oh we can't handle that, we're moving to America, you take her. Your dad insisted we take her and he treated her like a lady, just like she was his own mother even when she didn't know who he was! Both of my brothers married bitches who've made it their business to cut me out. It was different when we were young, we all pulled together."

I sighed. I'd heard it all before, the mixed up sentiment and selective memories, and I didn't want mum to get bitter and upset and start cursing. I was determined to be positive.

"Margate's quite trendy now mum. I'm looking forward to the sea. It's going to be a scorcher today. This was a brilliant idea. We can make new memories. Road Trip!"

We found ourselves in traffic.

"What's this about?" she said craning her neck. "Oh no not an accident!"

"Mum," I said suddenly. The sun was hot on my shoulders and an urgency was stinging my skin. "About…about."

"*Stop it* Shaani. We're not going to go over it again. It was nothing, I told you. It's too stressful."

"Ok," I said and the feeling subsided. We were stuck in traffic, a line building up around us. Windows were down and radios were playing. Nothing was moving.

"We're so close," she said. "I wish we were there. I just wish we were there now."

There was a look of pure anguish on her face.

"Are you ok mum?"

She exhaled. "Hate being stuck in traffic. You've got nothing to do but think."

I looked left at the car next to us. I smiled involuntarily because they were Asians too, or Indian Indians, I can tell the difference. Mum, dad, three kids in the back passing round smelly paratha rolls. They had plastic sport bottles of water called Rajah, an Indian brand and they had lots of reused yoghurt pots and margarine tubs filled with curries. They looked happy and at ease with each other. To white people, brown skinned people were the Other but in a sense this family in the other car were the Other to us. They weren't quite British yet, they were still Indian. And we were a bit Indian still, but more Asian and British. But I guess English people just thought we were all the same.

Home was a complicated idea all right, each car was a little unique home and we were all little unique units made up of funny little people. The Albanian thing twirled madly above me. What is that thing, it looks demented, but it's part of our family now. One time they forgot to give it and mum said hey where's my genie, how do I know my car's been cleaned without it dancing on my head?

"You know Shaani, when I was a young mum, with you and again with Ash, I felt so important. You needed me, you used to crawl all over me; Ash would hold on to my leg like it was a tree trunk, and everyone said don't let them use you as a climbing frame but I loved it, I really loved it. And now, my kids don't need me."

"Well—"

"It's true! You've never discussed the course at Brighton with me."

"Nothing to discuss, I'm doing it in October."

"Yes but. With dad you talk about the ins and outs and you want his opinion and his approval."

"What's wrong with that?'

"Nothing, it's good."

She sighed. She was working herself up again.

"And as for Ash," she snorted.

"What?"

"He just thinks I'm an idiot."

"No he doesn't. *He's* an idiot. He's just about capable of catching a train but he's got no idea about buses. He literally can't read a bus timetable. He'd still be waiting there if Mitch didn't go and fetch him."

"He's a funny little creature isn't he?" she said after a while with such a serious face that I started laughing.

"What?" she said, delighted to have made me laugh. "What did I say?"

"He's a total psychopath!" I said and we both became helpless with laughter.

"There's something going on with the Dhaliwals," she said wiping her eyes. "You remember them? We met them once at that over the top Diwali do."

"OMG, total snobs of Chesham Rotary. Awful people."

"They got the town square closed off and hired performing elephants. It was outrageous but no one said a word to them, not even the animal welfare people or the Council. I suppose they didn't want to get accused of racism. The Dhaliwals have got money growing out of the hairs of their ears. I'm not sure what he's up to but he keeps hanging out with them. And he's very shifty." Mum narrowed her eyes. "Something going on there, I wonder what? Oh I love this song. She's French. What's it called Shaani? Melted? Twisted? The video is really arty."

"Arty, yes. Oh so listen mum this is funny. It happened in Paris last month. So there was this art thief, right? Ok but mum, before I tell you, do you know the names of the French Impressionists?"

Chapter 8

Our trip to Margate was successful. It was sunny, we sat on the beach and we bonded. Mum had been right, it was what we needed. We sent a postcard to Mitch because we thought he'd appreciate that instead of a Whatsapp message and we bought back a stick of rock and a Kiss Me Quick hat to give to Princey who found everything English exotic and weird. We mimicked Princey clapping her hands over her ears and going *hai hai hai* when we had told her what a black pudding was. On the way back I discussed my course with mum, pointing out that Bio Metrics and Sports Management were regarded highly in a lot of professional fields now and most important, it would give me a qualification that I could use abroad.

"But you're not going abroad are you?" said mum anxiously.

"I don't know. I want the option. We'll see."

Ash came home the next day and we knew better than to ask him the deets about Mitch, but suffice to say he was upset and typically clammed up about the whole thing and spent all day in his room reading. The next day was Princey day and we all looked forward to it. Princey is a Christian lady from Mumbai, India who does several Indian families in Barnet. She refuses to call it anything other than Bombay. Mum met her outside St. Marys Church in Kenton where all the Indian Christians go and where you can always find a maid, so that's where mum went and waited till the service was over on a Sunday and they started chatting. I was aghast when she told me this stranger was coming to do.

As it turned out Princey has became our rock in the past seven months. It goes without saying that she's half the price of a normal agency cleaner, which is true for all cash in hand people. It isn't that mum needs so much help with the housework, it's because Princey makes us all feel protected, cushioned. Personally I think Princey is a version of an older sister that mum never had, but needed badly. Even when the British government suddenly banned the Alphonso mango being imported into the UK due to some EU regulation, she still managed to source them and the joke in the Indian community was , 'don't ask, don't tell'. Even Manish put in an order and he's scrupulous. Indian people with their mangoes are like English people with their dogs; they'll never give them up.

She's 5 ft nothing, wiry with a smiling round face and she wears a huge red bindi on her forehead like a target and a small silver cross around her neck. She puts down her bag and her head starts lolling as though she is having a little conversation with herself and nodding assent, ticking off the jobs done. I've never seen her write a physical list; it's all in her lolling head.

"Dollysister wants shoulder and keema but I won't go to *that one* anymore. They have bom bedd my neighbourhood in Bombay."

Ash and I exchanged glances. What she means is an extreme Islamist terrorist group has bombed her neighbourhood of Malad in Mumbai. Whenever this happens (and it seems to happen quite frequently), she goes off all Muslims for a while and says rotten things about them like they are blood thirsty and dirty and mad. She hasn't lived there for 12 years but it's still her neighbourhood.

When me and Ash reprimanded her, saying 'That's crazytalk Princey, you're being an Islamaphobe, all mozzies aren't the same and Islamists aren't real mozzies anyway,' she dismissed us with "that is my feeling" and banged her chest with her hand as if she had proved E=mc2. Princey's boycotts never last long and she goes back to calling the various Muslims she interacts with on a daily basis-- the butcher, the baker, the dry cleaner, the plumber-- on behalf of the houses she cleans for, as respectfully "Jamil bhai" and "Asif sahib", Jamil respected brother, Asif respected elder man.

Until it's another day, another boycott!

Princey starts taking out her tools and putting them on the kitchen counter: apron, plastic gloves, white eraser, a small bottle of something called Khus which she adds to the water she cleans the windows with and a little clear shower cap that she puts on when she's cleaning the kitchen. I have a photograph of her in her get up holding a broom and she looks like Kali, the many hands Goddess of Destruction, only she is our Princey, the Goddess of Cleanup in Showercap and Marigolds, with it seems each hand holding a different cleaning material.

"You have to get. Go to Jamil, he has the best meat. I cook it tomorrow with mummy. And get him to give you a bundle of the hard spice for garam masala. Don't let him charge you, it is free to us. Tell him it's for Princeysister, he'll give you a free kidney too."

"See Princey? Mr. Jamil will give you his kidney. That could save your life," said Ash raising an eyebrow.

"Very funny! I already have two very super kidney. Why I should want Muslim kidneyshidney inside? It will want to pray five times a day! I haven't got time for that! Imagine how it will affect my everyday evacuations."

Ash doubled up with laughter and then rearranged his face back into new born dazed chick. He was back to "normal". Nothing, not even Mitch's cancer kept Ash down for long. He was resilient. And he seemed to have been studying although we didn't question him. 'Genius must be left alone' was the small print on the clean Genie that twirled around in the car sending happy pine needle-y smells everywhere, and always cracked me up. Something got lost in the Slovakian-designed Chinese-manufactured translation I think.

"You know what they say in India," said Ash. "You don't cast your vote. You vote your caste. It's like a Hindu mafia in the government over there. You don't agree with mozzie hating do you Princey?"

"How will you get to Queensbury?" demanded Princey ignoring Ash.

"Uber it," said Ash.

 "Walk to North Finchley, then take the tube to Euston, and get an overground? I said.

"You stink," said Ash and ambled out of the kitchen.

"No no no no. Take the bus to Edgware and then get a 114 or a 345 to Wembley. It will take you right to Jamils door!"

Princey doesn't trust the underground. In her 12 years in the UK she's never used it. She takes a network of buses and walks everywhere. As all her work is concentrated in North West London and she works all the time, I'm pretty sure she has never been to the West End or even to South London, let alone seen the Thames or the Cutty Sark or Hyde Park. She's never even heard of those places. They could be in Mumbai for all she knows. Down the road from Malad.

"Ok, but on the way home I'll get the tube from Queensbury. It's on the Jubilee line and then I'll get the northern line. And then I'll get a cab from West Finchley. It's only a fiver."

Princey disapproves of extravagance. A fiver to her is a lot of money. She thrills over making things with leftovers and she concocted a snack with the leftover cheese and chutney sarnies from Margate, mashing them up with chick pea flour, frozen peas and deep frying them. Something heavenly!

"And don't accept a free calendar from Jamil. Dodge it, because he will try to force it on you but you can not be impolite because you are a good Brahmin girl. Be clever and dodge it! We have no use for it but we can't throw it away because it is a religious artefact and we will be stuck with a Muslim calendar festering in the corner praying five times a day."

Princey logic. A world unto itself!

It took me 40minutes to get to Queensbury because I took the tube and the bus, a combination I devised. Her way would have taken me 2 hours. Time is money, Princey! But Princey like all Indian Indians has no regard for time wastage, hers or anyone else's. I grinned like a cat on the top deck thinking of how I'd shouted "You huggly" and ran out the house before Ash could come back with a riposte. It was a beautiful day and I liked sitting on top of the bus, right in the front in the right hand seat wedged up by the window, Nike Golds up on the dash. The wheels on the bus go round and round and I'm driving the bus!

Queensbury is not a melting pot or a haven of multiculturalism as they advertise London to be. It is lumpen prole Asians. Brown Chavs as Ash calls them. Mum hates that word because she originally came from Chav herself. Queensbury is Halal butchers all the way, which isn't why we go there because we don't care how the meat is killed or blessed, it's because those cuts are the best for curry. In fact ours is a Hindu Brahmin house so we're not even supposed to eat meat!

Dad's always made it clear he didn't want it on the premises but conceded that if he wasn't there we could do what we liked. My twin desires to make my family happy and to make my mother happy are yet again in deep discussion. It's to do with the promise he made his religious mum when he crossed the Black Water to the Yookay: Don't drink alcohol, don't eat meat and don't lie down with white women. I'm pretty sure he broke all of them at some point☺ I'd say dad is something I think of as "quietly" religious and "culturally" vegetarian, unlike mum who's got her little gods lined up in the kitchen alcove whom she bathes and prays to every morning. She denies it but deep down Mum believes that if she doesn't follow religious rituals she will be struck down, not just today but in all of her reincarnated lives in perpetuity.

So if you do eat meat, and you make meat curry, it's got to be 'Paki' style! Not that me or Ash use the "P" word, but mum uses it all the time. Ironically, I think? Anyway to give the P word curry it's full regal name: Mughlai Karahi Gosth. Mum learned Paki style cooking from their Muslim neighbours in Harrow in north London where they lived once for 18months and who were one family who were kind. The Maliks were liberal Muslims who also went to Old Mr. Popat the dentist who made you hold the sluicer; the Khans in the same street wouldn't go to a Hindu dentist; they'd let their rotting teeth fall out first.

Tesco don't cut the meat right because they take it off the bone. Halal butchers cut it in the right way for a curry leaving in the bone and taking off every scrap of fat and if you ask nicely they'll give you extra marrowbones which add flavour. In English food they say fat gives flavour but in Pakistani curries fat gives off something called "heek" which means stink. It's what they call 'Haram' (unlawful, unpermitted) which is everything that isn't 'Halal' (lawful, permitted)

One previous time when I had to go to the butcher for Princey (the last time they bom bedd her neighbourhood) I had a surreal conversation with the guy Old Mr. Jamil behind the counter. He came to London from Karachi in

1965, was a master tailor of leather for 10 years and then ended up in the butchery trade. After I'd got the usual order, I asked him if he had scrag neck of lamb and he cocked his head like a cockatoo and enquired 'what is that?' He'd never heard of the word "scrag". What do you do with it he asked when I explained. What is that, he said holding half a shoulder in his bloody hands, brow knitted with curiosity. A stew, you don't know what a *stew* is? No he said dolefully. What is it? When I explained he said, 'so it's like a meat curry but not tasty?'

By the time I got to West Finchley the sun was blazing overhead. It was 3.30pm. Two cabbies from our local Dollis Cars were already rounding up to the station and I leant down to see if I recognised any of the drivers. I don't Uber.

"Hey Mr. Ali, As-Salaam-Alikum can you take me home?"

"Wa-Alikum-Salaam sister," he said and then clocked the logo on my plastic bags. "Queensbury? Jamil? That fraud? But why you don't go to Hendon Halal to Mr. Hussein? I'll give you introduction. He will give you free kidney and liver. I get mine from there and my wife makes Korma that will make you twirl like an Albanian genie. Forgive me, I cannot help you. I have a previous passunja."

"Oh no worries, Mr. Ali. Here, I've got something for you."

He unrolled it and read the words appreciatively: Jamil Butcher Eid Lunar Calendar .

"What a beauty. My wife will put it over our mantelpiece," he lolled. "What kindness!"

I smiled.

They're so polite. All of the cabbies at Dollis Cars have come from war torn countries; half of them aren't legal I'm sure. They all call me little sister and tell me about the food and the customs of Sudan, Afghanistan, Syria, Ethiopia, Somalia, and a host of other countries I've only heard about as problems on the news. I asked dad how they manage to be so decent when they've all seen such untold badness-es in their countries and dad said he thought it was because they had found safe harbour in the UK. The human spirit thrives where it finds kindness. Mum says don't be so familiar, they'll get the wrong idea, you're a girl and you're supposed to behave in a certain way in their eyes.

"Try Kamaal," said Mr. Ali gesturing to the car behind him.

"Bonjour Kamaal," I trilled.

Kamaal was from French Algeria and had told me how Algerian cous cous is the only cous cous you want to bother with; Egyptian cous cous is inferior. I told him we had read Franz Fanon in World Politics and Literature in school and he told me to listen to a band called The Cure who wrote a song called Killing an Arab after reading that book. I said no, they wrote it after reading The Outsider by Albert Camus and Kamaal had said oh, my mistake sister, thank you for correcting me! I thought he'd go mad, because men don't usually like being corrected. Kamaal means Great Act in Hindi I told him. You're a class act Kamaal.

"Ca va?"

Before Kamaal could answer, a big fat smelly man pushed past me and started banging on the roof of his car.

Chapter 9

"Taxi!" he shouted.

Kamaal shook his head. The fat smelly man wouldn't accept it. Then he said the name of our street and "Puttomtom." To which Kamaal said his Tom Tom was broken and then the fat man started banging the top of Kamaal's car with his fat fist. I stepped back. Why does he want to come to our street? He must be a detective.

"I live there," I said and the man turned his full attention on to me. He was mopping his big black eyebrows with a big white handkerchief. He was wearing a suit but his stomach was so big the buttons of his shirt were popping.

"We share the cab ok?"

So we shared the cab. He looked out of the window, scowling.

"You know one Indian lady in your street called Dolly Dev?" he said turning his hooded eyes towards me.

"What do you want with her?"

"That's between me and her, where does she live?"

"She lives with me. I mean I live with her. I'm her daughter."

He stared at me.

"I got no problem with you. I need to see your mum."

"But why?"

"What time she come home?"

We were almost at the junction. We went past the cluster of shops near the Dollis Cars office; the Spar, the locksmith, the workers caff and the launderette. We sailed past our car in Lansdowne Road and I glanced to make sure it hadn't been stolen or broken into. Kamaal was looking at us in the rear view.

"She's not home. You can't talk to her," I said to the smelly man.

"Never mind," he said and settled back.

Kamaal stopped the cab and the fat man paid him and helped me out with my trolley. Then he slammed the door and Kamaal drove off. The man looked up at our house. I knew instantly this was not a detective. This was bad.

Mum came out the front door.

"Hello," she said in her Gleaming White Dental Practice telephone voice. "Can I help you?"

"I am Mortea'zar. You are Dolly?"

"Mrs. Dev. And you are?"

Behind mum from inside Princey was peeping out from the kitchen door.

"Your friend Max has disappeared. No one has seen him for one full week plus one day."

"Thanks sweetheart, take it inside for Princey."

I did as I was told and Princey took the trolley and we went and stood inside the kitchen, both listening.

"He has a lot of friends Mr. Mortea'zar as I'm sure you're aware. Maybe he went to see them?"

"He didn't go to see no one. It is you he went to see."

"He didn't come to see me."

"I say he did."

"You can think what you like. You've had a wasted journey. Goodbye."

"I have business with him."

"That's nothing to do with me. Please don't come to my house again. This is bordering on harassment."

I came out of the kitchen and stood in the hallway. The man nodded and shambled away down the road. Mum closed the door.

I raced upstairs to my room. I was quaking. I should never have let him get in the cab. Downstairs I could hear mum and Princey unloading the meat, preparing the marinade, chattering and giggling. Ash was there too, I couldn't hear him I could just tell from their tone. I had led that horrible smelly man straight to our house. He was looking for Max. I was glad they were all together downstairs and the front door was locked. Mum had dealt with him brilliantly. I was proud of her.

But why had he come?

The smell of gently frying onions wafted upstairs. The once a month laborious cooking of the Mughlai Karahi Gosth had begun. Mum's never eaten meat, she just doesn't like it but she's always cooked it because her dad and her brothers demanded it. It amazes me how she gets the salt just right. She freezes it in portions for me and Ash and although we are a Hindu Brahmin family, dad allows us to transgress. He said it's our choice. What on earth would he think if he saw the way Ash is half cut in the evening these days? If he knew what had happened?

"Shaani!" mum called.

Mum and Princey were standing at the cooker.

"Sniff," said mum putting her arm around my shoulders and bringing me in between the two of them. The oil was separating into pools and the onion paste had turned brown. Mum dipped a teaspoon in and offered it to me.

"More salt?"

"Mmmm," I said. "No."

"Princey keep stirring," mum said. "Can you give me a hand getting some stuff out of the garage Shaani?"

As soon as we were outside the house I noticed mum look around warily.

"Where's Ash?" she said.

"He's gone to the Dhaliwals I think," I said.

She was always nosing around Ash, always wanted to know his opinion and where he was and what he was doing.

Sometimes I got the feeling that she didn't like me and Ash being as close as we were.

She pushed opened the see-saw corrugated garage door and we went inside. It was a dilapidated room with our old standard lamp standing wonkily at one end, and the sofa which was too big for this house but they didn't want to get rid of because they had saved up to buy it for the house in Chesham. Lining both the walls were stacked up boxes of Miscellaneous still unopened from four years ago.

The old heavy bookcase now held books, boxes of vinyl records – dad's Neville Brothers, Stevie wonder, The Beatles and mum's Madonna, Steps, Take That (first time round), dads cassettes and mum's CD's, shoes and boots, two bottles of Johnnie Walker Black Label that dad kept for special occasions and lots of other important things that had now become stuff.

A wooden desk with bow legs and feet like claws stood upturned, the four legs pointing to the ceiling and the underside of the desk branded Chesham Reproductions. They were thinking of turning the garage into an office. It had been soundproofed by the previous owners who had obviously had the same idea. Daylight seeped in through the cracks. Mum stood with her back to the corrugated iron door.

"I have told you to never ever get into a cab with a stranger. That's a given. Shaani, you could have been abducted. I shouldn't have to tell you these things."

"How did he know where we *live*?"

"I'm never going to see Max again," she said quietly.

If only she knew. A part of me wanted to blurt out "Who cares about him, he's dead! He's dead!"

"I'm sorry he frightened you. If you ever see him again call the police immediately ok?"

I nodded dumbly knowing I would do no such thing. I wished I could stay in that sealed garage forever. Dragging Max's body into the Brook and watching it slip down into the mud was an image I did not want to think about ever again. We came out of the garage to bright sunlight. Mum put her hand on the back of my neck and rubbed.

"Anything I can do for you today?" she said with a smile and she was back to being mum. "I'll be going to Tesco around six."

The postman came and handed mum a blue airmail letter. We looked at each other excitedly. She handed it to me and I liked holding it. We would read it tonight, the three of us when Ash was back. I propped up the airmail on the mantelpiece under the big mirror. Mum went upstairs, Princey got the Hoover out and I went for a stroll.

It probably was illegal to have got rid of the body, I mean **definitely** it was, I supposed I was an accomplice but Ash hadn't killed Max with intent, it was an accident. He must have had a heart attack or a seizure or something, because I'm sure a fall like that couldn't kill you. Anyway it was done. Ash hadn't meant to do it, he'd be horrified if he knew what he had done, and I knew Ash.

That big 'I am' going out to push the gypsy burglar with a stick wasn't him at all; in his own way Ash had been trying to protect us. Maybe he was scared about the burglaries and felt he had to do something and he'd taken his Dutch courage...If he had an inkling of what had actually happened he'd go and give himself up to the police station today. He was scrupulous about things.

He denounced mum for paying cash in hand and if he knew Princey was illegal (I still didn't really know if she was or not) he would forbid mum from employing her. He often had arguments with mum about how Asians bucked the system. He wouldn't even ask for a discount in shops. I can't tell him. I can't let him give himself up. He'll ruin his whole life. And I'll be an accessory. I started thinking no one is going to miss Max. When they find the body even if they connect him to mum, so what, she met him twice? Even if they put him in Lovers Lane. People went missing all the time and given his connections they'd put it down to some gangland killing, collateral damage.

I didn't care. It was finished. I wasn't going to feel bad or guilty about it, what was the point? Max was a bad lot, they wouldn't waste their police time going after him. For all I knew the police were quite happy that scum like him died or were murd—met with unfortunate terminations. And Ash hadn't meant to do it. No, I'd definitely done the right thing. It was over.

That evening mum was at Tesco and Princey was ironing and I was upstairs in my room listening to music on my headphones. Ash was still out. It was 6.45pm. There was a knock.

I opened my door and Princey stood there with an impassive expression.

"Man is there."

"Who is it?"

"Man.."

"Is it the same man from before?" I whispered.

"No, not same. I didn't let him in."

"Good."

I went downstairs calculating that mum would be back by 7.30 at the earliest and Ash would be late back or might even stay over at his friends house.

The man outside our house was not Mortea'zar.

Chapter 10

He was young and tall with a raincoat, neatly cut hair, black and thick. He had dead eyes. There was a polite formality.

"Good evening. I'm sorry to bother you. My name is Victor Sahayle. I've come to meet with a Mrs. Dolly Dev."

"Not in."

"Nevertheless."

He stood patiently. I noticed the raincoat was a good one. Burberry. Smart shoes, not trainers. Trousers not jeans.

"She's not in," I repeated still standing in the doorway. I knew Princey was behind me peeping from the kitchen doorway.

"I must meet with her. I think she will want to see me."

His voice was low, unassuming. I folded my arms and closed the door behind me, forcing him to step back into the path.

"You should go. This is bordering on harassment," I said with my nose in the air.

He looked up in surprise.

"I am not harassing you. I am very polite."

I just stared at him.

"So if you could please ask her to –"

I made an impatient gesture. "What d'you want her for? I'll pass it on."

"Alright. You see she has a close relationship with one of my associates. And now he's gone missing."

"So what?"

So this guy was one of the gang or whatever. The horrible stinky one had sent him.

"This associate of mine. He borrowed money. But now I need the money back and he's nowhere to be found. Or contactable."

"So?"

He hesitated.

"Are you her daughter?"

 "What's your name again?"

"It's Sahayle. Victor Sahayle."

He was maybe twenty five. Fair skinned but the black hair told me there was some kind of Asian in him. I looked directly at him feeling superior. Who's heard of an Asian guy called Victor? And the Indian surname is pronounced Sohail, you've mangled it up! You can't even say it right. You don't frighten me. I kept my arms folded and said nothing, staring him out. He pressed his lips together and then produced a phone from his pocket.

"I'm sorry you have to see it."

I looked at the screen. Vile porn. No faces, just a female genital close up. Two fingers opening up a labia.

"What the.."

And then my heart literally skidded like a dodgem car. It was an iPhone S and needed only a nano touch to scroll the picture. The next one was mum pushing her tits together. I knew because of her ring. And the next confirmed it, and was somehow even worse. Her lovely face in a full frontal expression of pornographic ecstasy. I dropped the phone. I felt physically sick. I actually thought I would be sick. He picked it up off the ground and put it in his pocket almost apologetically. I knew he'd copied the pictures. I could have smashed that thing to smithereens it wouldn't matter.

"Sorry. You see why I need to meet with your mother?"

"Can you p-please erase that?" I could hardly breathe.

He looked at me patiently with those dead emotionless eyes. "These were sent to Max and he's kept them for a purpose."

"Please.." I said helplessly. "I don't understand what you're talking about. Please erase them now."

"Yes of course," he said "I'll get rid of them for you. The price is seven thousand pounds."

My brain wouldn't work. I was standing on my doorstep and I couldn't think. And then I thought: He doesn't know Max is dead. What's he going to say when he finds out? And what about Mortea'zar? He had seven grand in his pocket to lend Max and now he wants it back. Who are these people?

"Haylo haylo beti how are you ok?" a familiar voice boomed.

"Hello Mr. Singh uncle," I said.

Sahayle stepped aside politely but he wasn't going anywhere.

Mr. and Mrs. Singh came strolling up our garden path single file, grinning widely. He was fit for 78, tall and thin in his usual joggers and t shirt with a badly wrapped turban green today, and straggly beard. And the Mrs. in her regulation dowdy shalwar khameez and transparent dupatta covering her head, following behind him. He had introduced her like this: 'Mine is a good cook but also very religious.' In the four years since we'd met them he had given no more information about her.

"Sorry shall I shift the car? I thought you weren't coming back till -?"

"Not to worry. My car is with son in Tooting. There has been a shooting in Tooting. He is fortunately safely in the good part. Tooting has some good parts and is coming up but there are too many Indians there still, so Tooting must wait a while. Haylo haylo young man?"

Mr. Singh looked Sahayle up and down enthusiastically. Like all Indian Indians he had no problems staring at people. The sun was hot overhead and I had to get my brain to work.

"These are our neighbours Mr. and Mrs. Singh. Err…This is Mr. Victor Sahayle."

"Haylo haylo" said Mr. Singh shaking Victor Sahayle's hand like he was welcoming him to the neighbourhood the same way he had done to Dad.

"Pleased to meet you sir."

Blackmailer! You bloody blackmailer. Standing there polite as anything with that gross phone in your pocket, calm as a cucumber.

Behind me Princey opened the front door.

No! no! no! no!

"Can you give us a cup of chai, sorry to bother?" said Mr. Singh.

Indian code was the opposite to English code. An English person would never ever come to your house and demand tea, they would kill themselves first. For Indian people to do it meant they wanted to include you as they would a family member and so how could I say no, go away from here!

"Of course uncle, we were just about to have a cup of tea!" I said with a bright smile, which is what I'm supposed to say.

Princey looked at Sahayle and blinked. Something passed between them but he stood his ground. Bomb in his pocket.

"Come in come in uncle, auntie...err. Mr. Sahayle?"

"Mr. Sahayle?" said Princey.

Mr. Singh came in and Mrs. Singh followed. Then Sahayle.

"I will make tea." Princey disappeared in the kitchen leaving me to host.

We all sat down in the front room that Princey had recently hoovered and aired. A vase of two cut roses from the garden were on the mantelpiece next to dads letter. Mr. Singh took up residence on the large chair that dad usually sat in and Mrs. Singh sat down on the edge of the sofa. Sahayle waited for her to sit and then sat down next to her with a suitable amount of space between them. How does he dare to enter the house? But I was glad he was polite and I could see Mr Singh appraising him.

"Mr Sahayle is an ex student of dad's. From Chesham Uni. He's a.. teacher himself now."

"Arrey what what? Another Teacher? The most important job in the world. Dev saab is in the Middlesex University I know, it is a funaaastic place, so big. Ah very good you are too a teacher," Singh sighed happily.

Sahayle was sitting on our sofa, comfortable and relaxed, his legs crossed, listening intently.

"So how was India uncle?" I said. "We would love to see the video sometime."

No we wouldn't!

"My sisters daughter got married." said Mrs. Singh and lolled her head at Sahayle. "A very nice wedding."

Sahayle nodded and raised his eyebrows a little.

"A very expensive wedding," said Mr. Singh to Sahayle. "We are Punjabi Jats, wastage of monies is what we do. And where are you from? Kashmir?"

I felt my skin crawl. I knew he had said that because Sahayle was tall and fair. Indians were openly obsessed with skin colour. They judged you on Fair, Wheatish, Dark on top of Caste and Class and I didn't want anyone to think that our family was like that. Not that it mattered what a blackmailer thought of us!

"No sir, I was born in Kiev but I left there many moons ago."

"Ah yes Jaipur has very good onion cachoris!"

For some reason Mr. Singh saw and heard everything as Indian, even when it wasn't Indian. His turban brain converted everything the way newly arrived immigrants converted pounds to rupees so they could tell the real cost. But he'd been living in the Yoookay for over 50 years!

"Mine can make good ones but not *as* good," he added and lolled.

Mrs. Singh who had been looking at the carpet keenly suddenly cocked her head and a little tremor came into her eyes. The *not as good* rankled.

"He is Russian!" she spat out.

"Technically Ukrainian, but neither actually," said Sahayle. "My mother was Russian, my father from India. There was a love affair between the countries once."

"Oh dear, a mixed marriage. You are not a Muslim as well are you?" said Singh.

"I was born a Christian," said Sahayle.

"Nobody's perfect," said Mr. Singh and turned his attention to me with a big smile.

I looked up in desperation. Princey set down the tea tray. She had done it all in mugs. Mugs were good enough for these neighbours. And a blackmailer.

"Lovely cuppa char," said Mr. Singh and slurped his way through the tea. "I am a Tetley man. What do you teach Mr. Sahayle? My grandson will not study at all, he runs about and she spoils him running after him with the food in her hand."

"I teach, err general studies mainly," said Sahayle looking at Mr. Singh respectfully.

"Hmm. Ooooo? Good, good. Hmm," said Mr. Singh.

He's clever enough to know that Singh can't distinguish between a university and a school subject, I thought.

"In fact, I was wondering if you might take me to see the campus of Middlesex university tomorrow?" said Sahayle turning to me casually. "I'm thinking of applying for a job there."

I stared at him. Unbelievable. How can he say that in front of everybody? And now he knows where dad works!

The front door slammed.

"Prin-ceey!"

Please tell her to go away Princey, right now.

"Namaste uncleji, auntyji," said mum bustling in, the Indian Hostess smile on her face, hands in Namaste.

No Mum! Go away, get lost.

Mum started prattling on about the wedding and the Singhs lolled their heads indulgently, and then she came and sat down looking with interest at Sahayle.

"Hello there," she said with a smile.

"Hello," he said and casually lifted a pleat on his smartly pressed trousers.

"Princey can I have a coffee please?" said mum smiling at Sahayle.

"Pinis," said Princey from the doorway, holding the tea towel as though it was a mop she would like to stick into Sahayle's face. I blessed her silently. Somehow she was on my side.

"Oh well," mum shrugged and threw back her head and laughed.

Sahayle looked at mum for a moment and then looked away. I couldn't bear for him to look at her, not him, not with what he had in his pocket. My throat was dry and I gulped down my mug of tea and drained it.

"Shaani!" said mum. "Manners! Are you going to introduce your friend?"

"This is Mr. Victor Sahayle. He's an ex student of dads."

"Oh that's great. How nice of you to visit us."

"I was hoping Professor Dev would show me the Middlesex campus but apparently he's away.."

"He's got a job there na!" shouted Singh flicking his fingers.

"I am thinking of applying for a job there," said Sahayle carefully.

"Yes, but Shaani can show you. It's not far."

Mum!?

"That would be great. I must go now. May I come tomorrow around 11? Will that be all right?"

For what? Getting you seven grand?

"Shaani?" said mum raising her eyebrow.

"Yeah sure, I can do it. I'll see you then."

"No need to see me out. Very nice to meet you all. Goodbye"

Mum and the Singhs turned their heads to see him walk out.

"Nice looking boy," said Singh and half lolled his head at mum who just smiled enigmatically. She even lolled her head back at him which she does when she is in the company of Indian Indians, just like she starts talking in paki English. Why do you *do* that mum? She laughs and says she doesn't know.

"Who is he Shaani?" she said with a smile when the Singhs had gone.

"Like he said. Ex students of dads. Why?"

"Oh right. Ok. He's a nice looking boy Shaani."

"Excuse me I just need to go to the bathroom."

I raced upstairs and locked the door and put my head against the cold tiles. Then I threw up in the sink and turned on the tap. How could you mum? How could you send those vile disgusting pictures? Who are you? I can't look at you mum. And she thinks Sahayle is a boyfriend I've kept hidden away, when all the time in his pocket, sitting in front of you he had those... It would be funny if it wasn't so unspeakable.

I put my head under the tap and rubbed the towel on my head. Tell her. I can't tell her. It'll break her. It'll change everything. It's too late. Max is dead. I put him in the Brook. Whatever she did, doesn't matter. A lack of judgement. She said it was something for herself. Why *that?* I don't want to know why, I don't care. Sahayle doesn't look like a bad guy. He knew how to behave with the Singhs. He was dressed nicely. Maybe you can reason with him? Maybe he didn't really mean it about the seven thousand?

Of course he meant it, this is happening Shaani. But how can he think I would just give it to him? He's a blackmailer, that's what he does. He might not look like it but that's what he is. But where would I even get seven grand? If I had it I'd give it to him. But he'll just ask for more, that's what they do. I've got to get mum away, I've got to get her away from here somewhere safe. First of all, I've got to get her away. I can do this. I don't care what I do and how many lies I tell.

Chapter 11

"Chinese or Pizza?" said mum. She never liked to cook when Princey had been because the house looked so perfect. I watched her getting the menus out of the drawer and studying them. In the corner of my eye she seemed like someone I didn't really know, and that made me feel strange, dislocated, scared. 'Excuse me for grieving. Maybe you'll find out what it feels like one day and then you won't be so quick to judge.' I thought back to when I'd seen her in the window of The Green Dragon. Kissing a stranger after drinking on her own in a pub on a tab that her boss had paid for. But Max had not been a complete stranger. He had been her lover. To whom she had sent...

"What about Ash?"

"He's out with the Dhaliwals. At the Indian Gymkhana Club of Mayfair. It's really high class."

"How can he get in there?"

"They're members apparently, or they own it. Just you and me tonight kiddo."

She'd started using perky phrases picked up from American TV shows. It's like she's a construct, a whole collection of cliché phrases and stuff that I don't recognise. She isn't the sort of person that is my mother in my community in my life.

"Ashi's good at cultivating people," she sighed. "I wish I was. Anyway, now there's this potential big problem over our heads. I can't bear to think about it, it's just more bad luck. I'm telling you this star that follows me around, I can't catch a break."

"What?" I cried.

"Calm down, it's just the guttering. Singh said if we don't get it sorted soon it'll collapse the drainpipe. It'll come down on our heads. Things are growing in it. But I think he's being a bit dramatic. You know what these old school Indian Indians are like? He just went on and on as though I was a negligent householder. I just don't want to think about it. It's another bill."

Mr. Singh had assumed the mantle of the male elder with us, which in Indian terms was a kind gesture but I felt acutely embarrassed by it. We were without our head of the family and therefore to be pitied and so it fell to me to bridge the gap. I suppose it should have been Ash but he was too young.

I immediately went outside and looked up at the gutter running across the top. It had clods of green grass growing out of one open end and the gutter was attached to the vertical drainpipe. The drainhole on the ground was covered with leaves so I took a stick and pushed the leaves away. It was full of gunk. Was that normal? I looked up at the guttering again.

When had they last been looked at? I have no idea what needs to be done, I thought, but I'm not going to bury my head in the sand the way mum does about these things. The drainpipe was old, made of iron. That means at least it won't crack. If it was plastic it would be worse. But then, maybe they could replace it easier. I noticed five or six bees circling it. Were they wasps? Was it a nest inside? Then what happens, do they come out of the tap? Oh I don't know! I'll look it up.

"Where did you go?" said mum with her hand on her hips. "Don't just walk away when I'm talking to you!"

"What did he say, exactly?"

"Oh I can't remember. If it breaks or cracks, it'll flood and the home insurance won't cover it. Which reminds me the alarm system needs to have the annual check otherwise they wont insure for the next year. Anyway there's a big list of things that need doing on the house, it's not my priority."

"I'll call them mum, give me the numbers."

Mum started writing the number off her phone on the back of a Tesco receipt. She's always doing that. It's so annoying. I've told her she can just forward the number.

"Ash said Barnet Hill area's been dubbed Kill Hill," said mum with a laugh. "Yes there's been two other murders in the Borough of Barnet in the last year! And it's such a sedate suburb. I suppose this is where it all goes on.

"What?"

"They found the body of a girl in a suitcase a month ago. In the woods near the station."

"I didn't hear that."

"Oh yes, it was even on the national news, and in the local paper. Grisly. I put it up on my Facebook. I got 50 likes and two hearts!" Mum hooted with laughter. "A friend commented "Is that your excess baggage?"

"Mum you didn't..!"

"It's just a joke Shaani. I know you young people don't have a sense of humour, too woke—"

"No one does Facebook anymore."

"Well, *we* do. Facebook to me is just like being at a party and gossiping with your friends in the kitchen that's all. I think I'll have mixed Chinese vegetables. Behind the twitching net curtains, a la Desperate Housewives. You can choose whatever but I'm not having carbs."

Sometimes mum's attitude to life in general seriously alarmed me. She takes everything either really intensely or totally lightly. She's all over the place. The reaction to everything is to run away or put it up on Facebook or.... *Stop it, stop being disloyal.* Even in your head. It's mum. *That's my mum.* She's so much more than that. But I don't know her. It feels as though I don't know her.

"Did they find out who did them?"

"Got to be Eastern Europeans. It's always Eastern Europeans these days isn't it? Apparently the poor girl had only been in London for a year. She was from Slovenia and her boyfriend, who has conveniently disappeared was also from Slovenia. Or was he Russian I don't remember."

"And the other murders?"

"I think Ash said. Some gangs. Maybe the same gangs who go around burglarising. That's a dad word. I don't think that's a real word is it Shaani? It's one of those Indian English words, like *pre pone* and *thrice* that no one uses in England. Ash said the Borough of Barnet is the highest for burglaries apparently." She smiled indulgently. "Ashi's got it into his head that he's got to keep the house safe. Have you seen the Swiss Army torch he's bought?" Mum hooted with laughter. "I know its crass to say it about my own son but he's so precious."

"I don't want anything mum."

"You can have some of my veg. There's no point in ordering if you won't have anything, I can just have a yoghurt are you ok? Shaani?"

"I'm fine mum."

"Not on a diet are we?" she raised her eyebrow with a women of the world insinuation. "Are you going to take Mr. Sahayle to the campus tomorrow?"

"I said I would didn't I?" I said and stomped upstairs.

I closed my eyes. The hours dragged. I just lay there thinking tonight I want it to rain and rain and rain but tonight it's clear. You're going to meet a blackmailer tomorrow. I could see the shaft of moonlight coming through the window, so pure and lovely. I lay there for hours and hours listening to the desolate sounds of the street ebb and flow until I heard a key in the door and I went downstairs.

"Did you have fun?"

Ash was giggling taking off his coat. I knew he'd be half cut. Something to do with the news of Mitch had unsettled him.

"Where's the leftovers?"

"You stink!" I said.

"You huggly."

"How much did you drink?"

"A lot. Dhaliwal owns that club, the barmen know his tipple and bring it before he's even sat down. He is so smooth. Like a capo. That's Power up close. He's definitely got that Casino rigged too, because I won like three times and I'm rubbish."

"They have a casino inside?"

I was surprised the Dhaliwals had let Ash drink and gamble openly. He was 15. The rich play by different rules Shaani, Ash had said some months ago. People like the Dhaliwals have what's known as Fuck You money. Fuck You with your Rules, I can do what I like. Do you respect that Ashi? Of course not, it's laughable, but it's fun playing with their toys.

But drinking and gambling? Wouldn't happen if Dad was here no way. I suddenly thought of mum framed in the steamed up window of the Green Dragon. How pathetic it was, to do that for a posh meal in some fancy restaurant with that creep Max. Especially when she didn't even eat carbs.

But then, the very few are courted like Ash who seemed to have been elevated to celebrity level.

"All do these private clubs. During the day the housewives gamble while their husbands are out getting laid."

I started laughing.

"Shaans you should have seen it. Old Dhaliwal has his eye on me for his dumb blonde daughter right, and by the way she really does have blonde hair, Asian Beyoncé I don't think so. He makes it so I'm a "winner" so she and everyone else, his associates etc., all think oooo what a prize, what a guy. Alright listen he actually said "Ashish you and me we are having chemistry. And that is wonderful because you are *doing* Chemistry. I said Physics and he said yes. He doesn't even know the difference! That is surely a new level of thick right? It's all Science to him, or should I say Greek?"

"You are a prize. You're going to Princeton."

"That's no reason. A persons character is what's important." said Ash. "Oxford. You can't drink on the street in Princeton."

"How much did you win?"

Ash took out a wad of notes from his trouser pocket.

"£500. That's how much Dhaliwal spends on a round of drinks. There you go."

"For me? Why?"

"Why not? You can say you've living off immoral earnings. Basically he's paid me to be his bitch."

I looked at the wad of notes.

"No, it's yours," I said and put it on the breakfast counter.

"I'll put it in the kitty," he said.

"But so do you like her?"

"God no! She's the worst kind of girl. Totally obsessed with her looks."

"Why'd you go then?"

Ash shrugged. "Something to do."

I felt proud of my brother. Whatever his faults and flaws, no one would ever pull the wool over his eyes. Even when he was a baby I knew we would have each others backs.

He was opening and closing the fridge door and the cupboards.

"We didn't order in the end. Listen Ash," I lowered my voice.

"I know, I know. Mum's asleep. I won't be noisy. Starving, there were all kinds of nibbles there but no actual food. I don't think those anorexics eat anything. It's an extremely skinny family."

"So you know that guy?"

"What, your boyfriend?"

"What?"

"Sahayle?"

"*What?*"

"Mum texted me he looks like an accountant. You can do better than that Shaani. Is he really your boyfriend?"

"Shut up, of course not. Not *him*. I mean you know. The other night?'

"The burglar?"

"Yeah so. It *was* a burglar. Mr. Singh said there's been reports in the area."

"Kill Hill. I know"

"Yeah yeah, Kill Hill. So......I don't think you should say anything to mum about it."

"Ok."

"Ok, coz..don't want to freak her out."

"Ok. Starving now?"

"Yeah. So because apparently that guy, the one you saw off the premises, apparently he's part of. Gypsy gang. And they've been doing burglaries in the neighbourhood. But don't say anything. The police or whoever, they don't like civilians intervening do they? Yeah?"

Ash yawned.

"I've told you all that already. Old news? What's the police got to do with it?" he said.

"Right. I'm off to bed then. Don't make a mess. Princey only cleaned it today and we can't afford her every week."

"Yes off you go to Bedfordshire little mother." He waved me off, his head inside the fridge.

In the morning, mum went off to work as usual at 7.30 and as usual Ash was still in bed. If it's Kill Hill and there's burglaries and killers everywhere and they're doing reccies all over the area they're bound to find Max soon. How long before they find him ? It's been over a week. How much longer? Maybe they've already found him? How soon do they put it out on social media? Or the local newspaper? I had to handle myself properly with Sahayle today. As far as he's concerned Max has just gone AWOL and that's good. It gives me leverage.

But not really. Seven grand. It's a ridiculous sum. How do I even know it's the sum that Max borrowed? Sahayle could be making it all up. Random. But then, why has he got the pictures? Somehow, I don't know how, my brain kept swerving those photographs. They had became something to sort out. The problem to solve. I couldn't visualise them. I didn't want to. They were toxic.

I went to my wardrobe and took out my one pair of non jeans and a short fitted jacket that I'd bought for the christening of Bo's baby, the first teenage pregnancy in Chesham senior. Years ago Bo had been my 'bestie beastie' and she would always say 'Shaani, you're so trad girl, even my mum don't be a domesticates like you, will they let you go travelling with a slack *gori*?' and I said, "Nah, it's just normal Indian conditioning, I'm no trad! When we're on our world trip we'll just be gone baby *gone*…" But our world domination had got shelved. I hadn't seen Bo since the christening. She'd turned into another person. That baby must be almost five now and her mum looked after it while Bo left school and did bar work, the father having disappeared.

I laid out the clothes carefully on the bed, smoothing out all the creases. Then I left the house and walked to the gym and did just 30 lengths but quickly. It felt good to be slicing through the water. Shame I didn't have a bestie anymore. I wasn't very good at making friends. I'm a bit lonely sometimes; maybe mum is right I shouldn't rely on Ash, I should go out and make friends. But Ash isn't my friend, he's my little brother. The ceiling sparkled diamonds in a crystal white sky. The water clung to my arms like morning dew on a leaf. I could see whole worlds reflected. Such an ordinary thing I'd seen a hundred times and suddenly it seemed the most precious thing.

When I came out of the turnstiles with my bag, hair still slightly wet, I saw two men by the desk.

Chapter 12

I slowed down to listen but they moved away. I gave a nod to Troy .

"Feds mekkin'quirees," he said.

"About what?"

"Missing gang person. He was member at Pumping I-inns, and that's the same peoples owns this gym so..."

"Same people is it?"

"Yeah I know. That place is a cesspit."

"What did he do?"

"Probably killed someone innit?"

"Innit," I said.

I walked home fast. Everything was a blur except the bit about "He was a member of Pumping Iron." They're going to find him soon. I went upstairs got changed quickly and came down to make coffee. I had to be perfect today.

"Job interview?" said Ash who was sprawled out in his manky bathrobe at the breakfast bar, the three boxes of cereal lined up.

"I do wear jackets sometimes."

Ash shook his head. "You stink!"

"Shut up, it's only body spray. I'm supposed to be taking this guy to show him the campus," I said with a frown.

"So he *isn't* your boyfriend?"

"Why do you keep saying that?"

"Mum said… anyway so…why do *you* have to take him? Who is he anyway? I need to vet him. We can't have you out n about with any tom dick and harry. I hope he's a good Brahmin boy, if not we'll have to kill him. By the way, you *stink!*"

"You huggly," I said dispiritedly.

I sat down at the breakfast bar. Maybe I was too dressed up. What was the dress code to see blackmailers?

"What's he like?"

I shrugged. "He's just one of dads old students and now he's a teacher. Princey's left us a gobhi curry and chapattis for lunch today."

"I'm out. I'll probably be out all day. Save me some for dinner. Do not finish it."

"Where are you going?"

"Dunno yet." said Ash and poured his mug of coffee on to his Shredded Wheat, Sugar Puffs and Muesli combo. "I should put this on YouTube, it's such a tasty meal."

Sahayle arrived at 11 in a pair of chinos and a white shirt and jacket. I thought he had shaved because his face looked smooth.

"Hello," he said. Just as if we were regular people and he'd come on a visit.

"We can get a bus there," I explained. "To the university. Ash this is Mr. Victor Sahayle. This is my brother."

"Alright," said Ash and Sahayle nodded and thankfully we left.

We walked in silence for a few minutes and then he said "Have you got the money?"

"I couldn't get it so quickly. It's impossible."

"I need to have it."

"I know. I just need some time."

"Because things have obviously changed now that Max's dead."

I stopped and looked hard at the pavement. "What?"

"Keep walking," he said, cool as a cucumber. "They found his body last night. Near the marshes in Woodside Park. That's around 10 miles from here. There's a stream or some sort of tributary that ends there, so he could have been killed anywhere close by. They haven't released the details I expect because they have some leads."

"Why do you think he was killed?"

"No one commits suicide by impaling themselves to a bank with a branch."

My heart was racing. "Is that how he was killed.?"

"That's how he was found. They don't know yet the cause of death."

We walked a bit further in silence.

"And how do *you* know all this?"

"We have a friend high up in the police force. He's no friend of mine, he's a friend of Mortea'zar. Tazers poodle they call him. They go back a long way. Once he slayed a man who had crossed Mortea'zar. He cut him from ear to ear."

A car zoomed past. It was a busy and noisy main road. I looked at Sahayle sideways. I took a deep breath and kept walking.

"Not that anyone will revenge the death of Max. He was not liked," said Sahayle.

I don't care about Max, I don't want to think about him. I want to erase those pictures. Had Sahayle left the phone at home? Where did *he* live? What if someone else who lived in his house got the phone in their hands. And saw those pictures of my *mother*. Why wasn't it under lock and key? Safe from anyone's eyes.

"Will you please erase the pictures?" I said miserably. "It's not who my mother is."

He looked at me and pressed his lips together.

"You're an odd girl. You should not be taking care of these matters. It should be your mother. It's not what you should be burdened with. I should be talking with her."

"What do you know about it? What's it to you?" I said. "I don't want you talking to her!"

He nodded and we kept walking.

Suddenly a door flew open on the opposite street. Two screaming Chinese women in long white aprons burst out with their hands shaking above their heads. They were screaming, stumbling down the road, waving their arms like blind women. Then a small red ball bounced out of the open doorway and without thinking I tore across the busy main road just in time to grab the grinning toddler that emerged from the staircase in the door way. Her fat little arms outstretched looking for the ball. The women who were half way down the high street now doubled back as though they were in an Olympic race. The older one scooped up the child, hugging and soothing her in her language, but the other one just crumpled and collapsed at my feet, shrieking.

I was genuinely shocked. She was shaking uncontrollably. A passer-by stopped and patted her on the back saying, 'it's all right, your baby's safe now,' but the mother couldn't get up or speak or even touch her child. The fear had made her a gibbering wreck. The grandmother was calm, holding the bemused toddler tight but the mother lay on the pavement writhing in agony.

The red ball was still in the road when I carefully crossed back to where Sahayle was standing.

"Jesus," he said staring at me.

"I think they must have been cooking and the kid was hiding somewhere and they must have thought it had got out," I said slowly. "They must have thought it was dead."

"You acted fast," said Sahayle looking at me.

The incident had made me remember how mum had been when I'd pulled Ash out of the pond. She couldn't speak, she just kept sobbing uncontrollably. It was guilt she was riven with. Horror at having taken her eye off her baby boy for a few seconds. All of her feelings had passed me by back then. Diving into the pond to get Ash out had been my natural reaction and I think it would have been anyone's natural reaction to rescue a child. I had never considered how deeply it had affected mum long after. She couldn't stop sobbing. Being a mother was so huge, limitless. It was an ocean. It had never occurred to me before. Belonging wasn't only ideas of land and religion; It was biology.

"Excuse me Mr. Sahayle. Do you mind if I just text my mum to let her know I'm all right?"

"Why wouldn't you be?" he said with a crease between his eyebrows. "I haven't done anything to you."

"No. She's just like that, she likes to know where we are. Also, there's this problem with the drainpipe. I've got to sort it out before it comes down on our heads. It can crack any minute. And I think there's a wasps nest inside. I think they corrode the pipe."

The fact is I suddenly needed to know my mum was all right. I sent her a text. Sahayle didn't know what he was talking about. Being a parent and being a child, they weren't two different things, they were all the same thing. I couldn't help worrying about mum just as she couldn't help worrying about us. We were all part of the same body, the same blood and fear pumped through our veins. I put my phone back in my jacket. My hands were clammy.

"Thanks. Sorry."

"What's wrong with your drainpipe?"

"I don't know. But I'll figure it out."

We walked on and then he turned to me and said:

"Makes it worse for your mother of course."

"How could it be worse?"

"They're bound to get her in for questioning when they arrest the perp."

"If they catch him."

"Oh they'll catch him."

"But what if they catch the wrong…"

"True. There's plenty of guys that would have happily done it. They'll round up the usual suspects but it's a question of evidence."

He smiled for the first time, a nasty criminal sort of slow smile. He just kept looking ahead. I was thinking :You're a low life. You're a bad seed. You bloody blackmailer!

"What if it was an accident?' I said.

He didn't say anything. You're asking too many questions, you're giving too many opinions shut up shut up. We walked on and then he stopped. I stopped too.

"This place looks like they do good fish and chips. It's called the Golden Plaice, not very original. Do you feel like having a small bite to eat?"

I was taken aback. "Umm, thanks. But I've got lunch at home."

"Fair enough. When do you think you could get the money by?"

"Monday. I can get it by Monday. Definitely," I said recklessly.

We were standing on the road by the quadrant, with cars whizzing past, a fish shop, a Jewish bakery, an old furniture upholsterer, a hairdresser and a bench under a grey sky. There was nothing to see except traffic. A dull uninspiring street where I just happened to be standing next to a blackmailer.

"The thing is I wouldn't bother you about the money but it's just that the man I'm in partnership with, he won't let it go."

Oh yeah that old trick. I'm bad but my associate, he's much worse.

"I would write it off, but he won't let it go. He'll come back to your house."

"…Back? You mean your partner, is it Mortea'zar?"

He nodded and smiled.

"I *hate* that guy!"

"Do you?"

"He's so rude!"

"I owe him my life."

I stared at him. "What do you mean?'

"It's a long story." He was from another world, another planet.

"But…Aren't you scared? This life you lead."

He pushed out his bottom lip, considering it.

"It's not in my personality."

What is in your personality I wondered. Being a blackmailer. I wondered if he'd killed anyone. I bet he has. And you've disposed of a dead body Shaani.

"…I'd better go home. They'll think it's weird that I've been out so long. They expect me to be at home. You see?"

"Your family. Yes. They worry about you."

"It's not that so much. I've got chores. I've got to stay in for the alarm person. And I've got to find a man for the gutters. And my brother, he's already suspicious..well you see it's a pain. In a family."

Why was I telling him all this?

"You're like a little mother. Busy all the time, no time for yourself."

I blushed. "No! Not at all. It's just that I took a year out and so I've got to pull my weight."

"A year outside of what?"

"I deferred my place at university. That means I postponed it. For a year." I felt a bit bad as it came out so patronising but how would he know about university procedures?

He nodded. "Alright. But you must try to get the money by Monday."

"Thing is, I don't know how to get it. I haven't got that much, if I had it I'd give it to you."

"You'll find a way," he said. "People always do." He paused "He wants his money back but also because he's going to use it to pay me. I'm going away. To Mexico in fact. So I'll need it. Do you think you could definitely get it by Monday?"

"Yes. Definitely. Monday. I'll see you on Monday then. "

As soon as he turned the corner, I took out my phone. *People always do.* Yeah, you'd know, wouldn't you?

Chapter 13

"Hiyaaaaaa! Yaouw alrooight bab? I was thinking bout yaouw. Me miss yu."

"Listen Pushy, yaouw've got to do me a favour blood," I said, lapsing irresistibly into her 'Brutois' = Brummie Patois, the language all young Asian girls spoke in Sparkbrook.

"Oh hello, no text, no Instagram, no commiseration for your favourite cousin? Sad day for the men of Brum innit, Missy Push P hoff de market."

"How much your dad pay him?"

"I know right he goes *"but dowry is an antiquated and demeaning system of transaction rooted in patriarchal privilege,"* she said in a BBC voice. "To which me kiss me teet and say dadd, me *want* dowry! Don't be shy to add value to your daaarter! Flat, cyaar, Caribbean holiday, cyaash, gold bars, all acceptedd with grace. Fact is Shaans, I'd rather enjoy it now while me husband still got juice in he bokkle."

"So listen.."

"Can you believe? Arranged marriage to raas. Me! I'm so retro. Honestly Shaans, I can't get over how good we clicked. He is, get this, like a better looking version of me dad. From the same *see eee* with the same surname!! I had to make sure we weren't actually related. I said to dad, we're not *Muslims* dad, I aint gonna marry me cousin am I?!"

"So listen Pushy, please please can you ---"

"BTW ow's Uncleji getting on? He's been there for what like a year now? WTF?"

"Seven months."

"What's he doing it for? Why im a chase peesa land that belong to he mum? It's not like you can sell the land to developers and make a good money right? Me mum says when they was little, you know they were five sisters, they used to go to your dad's house in Lucknow to see him for holidays, him being their cousinbrother an all?"

"Yeah yeah yeah I know—"

"And she said they went one summertime to see this land in Chayaa that belonged to his mum's people? Mate, it was pure dry desert *then,* it beyond worthless now. Peeps are saying 'im abandoned you fora handfula dust ....Dem 'ole injuns, dem try recapture dem purrfek childhood wot they never had, in dem purrfek India that never was. Laard have a mussy me a nuh him a getting 'ole...but is he getting doolally as well?"

"He's 55! He's not old!"

"You know me love you. But it de community be talking. Yuh mum's got to put she foot down. Man cyaan't stay away so far, so long from him family. People gwine talk nuh true?"

I took a deep breath.

I knew she didn't mean malice; it was in her family culture to be direct. Pushy had pulled down her knickers in the drawing room one time to show me her appendicitis scar, utterly oblivious of who else was in the room. Dad's mum might have been from a village, but she could read and write and she knew how to behave correctly. She had a degree in her suitcase! And yet it was his dad's side that had flourished in the world, grown strong in number and stealth. Five paternal aunts had married and multiplied, and so we had family spread out across Dubai, Australia, America like massive fishing nets. The Devs were a force of nature and none of my paternal aunts had given up their surnames so Pushy's lot were the Dev-Sharmas of SparkBrook, Birmingham.

In their own way they were intimidated by dad because he was a humble lecturer (not a professor, but I'd let Sahayle use that term and I know mum liked it) who had done a PhD entitled "Postcolonial, Transnational and Global Literature and Theory with special interest in Empire, India, and the Upper Province." and by Ash, the genius who they couldn't comprehend as an entity. But like Mr. Singh of Lansdowne Road, the Dev-Sharmas took every opportunity to assert their world view as superior.

I don't know if they exactly looked down on us, but they considered us Devs an oddity for sure. We were not rambunctious and rustic, we were sedate and quiet and anti-social in their eyes because we did not have minimum 20 people (all family) in the house at every weekend as they did, and we didn't buy meat and rice and flour in massive quantities to save money by distributing amongst family members. Yet the funny thing was, despite these divisions I knew Pushy loved me and was always asking me to join her in this or that group holiday.

She'd do anything for me and even though she had lots of actual cousins, she thought of me, her second cousin as her soul sister. And her mum practically worshipped Dolly who she saw as a glamorous film star because of her voice and hair and eyes and figure. The Dev-Sharmas knew nothing about mum's origins; they had only known this Gorgeous Young Creature who had lifted the Professor out of his loneliness and into Heaven, like in the movie My Fair Lady.

"Pushy listen, shut up, my bars are going down. Listen, please please get Anuradha *buaji* to beg my mum to come for Henna and the Sangeeth this weekend?"

"She already asked her innit, she said she had some work thing?"

"She's lying! You know what mum's like, she needs to be begged. She needs to feel special."

"Ah I see what you do."

"What?"

"U want the house free for de weekend innit? Got yourself a sweet bwoy coming?'

"No."

"Girlfriend! Why yuh nuh tell me? It's done."

"I want her gone by tonight Pushy. Tomorrow morning at the latest."

"Alright chill. You know I can get me mum to do anything I want. Do you know what she made me promise once I was married to my MFI? Man from India innit? She goes please Pushpa stop talking like Black People, do me this one favour. You know what racists Injun peeps are Shaans! I said yuh is a bumboclaaat I mean yeah I'll dress up in my Injun gear, yeah I'll do the Indian tings but don't ask me to not be *me*, yeah? No one teks SparkBrook out d gyaal. Don't worry. My soulsista, we cool. But you are gonna come to the wedding though yeah? In your diary?."

 "Of course. Cheers Pushy."

"Word," she said.

"Word," I said.

When I got home there was a pile of junk mail by the door as usual that no one had dealt with. I picked up the local newspaper, scanned it quickly and then chucked it in the bin. No news of Max. Maybe it had been reported too late for the newspaper, but it could be on London South East tonight. I had to prevent her from finding out that Max's body had been found and the Henna and Sangeeth in Birmingham was perfect cover. None of that lot watched any news except Indian News on NDTV which was piped via cable 24/7 in their house.

Mum was sitting in the front room staring into space.

 "You'll never guess what just happened Shaani?'

"What?"

"Anu literally pleading with me to come for the Henna. I'm indispensable apparently."

Wow Pushy works fast, I thought. It had taken me just over an hour to get back home.

"You'll have to go now, you can't offend dad's side!"

"Not going," she said.

"But why?"

"They just want me on parade so they can pity me!"

"What rubbish."

"She's all alone without her husband. What's he really up to over there? And what's *she* up to home alone? No, I won't go to be judged."

Mum looked at me and bit her bottom lip. Even she could see the irony of this. I took a deep breath.

"That's exactly why you should go. Do the Henna. Lead the Sangeeth. Prove them wrong. Show them who's boss. You're worth fifty of those gossiping fishwives. Remember them cooing and swooning over your designs at Shilpa's wedding?"

"Well…"

"We know we're good. We know we're better! Small minds will always think small things."

She looked at me then with her doe eyed beauty, welling up.

"You really are an extraordinary girl Shaani. And to think I made you. How did I do that? I'm so lucky to have you."

"Don't start! Mum honestly don't get all soppy now. And don't come and sniff my head. It's gross!"

"Alright. You're such a hard nut. I dunno, young girls today."

"What you waiting for? Pack!"

Mum stood rooted to the spot.

"If you're worried about us being on our own.."

"No, I know you're sensible. Anyway I'll always be checking in by text. You can look after yourselves. The thing is I haven't really got the right *clothes*…I can't go looking wrong because before you know it it'll be all over the jungle drums from Birmingham to the Devs in Nairobi and Perth and New York and Toronto and your dad will hear about it in guest house in Chayaa, never mind how bad the electricity is, bad news will get through and there'll be a big drama because I wore the wrong sari. I haven't got the right…"

"Of course you have. Come on lets go and pack. Hurry up! You should definitely go but tonight!"

"Hmm," she looked at her watch. "Trying to get rid of me."

"If you go in the evening you'll avoid the traffic. You know how they always stay up till way past midnight watching Bollywood Films on DVD, especially in this 'auspicious' period. You'll probably get there just in time for dinner ha!"

"Well.."

"And you know how you love night driving."

"I do."

"Come on Dolly. It would be rude wouldn't it to snub them?"

Mum nodded. "I suppose..."

So we went upstairs to her bedroom.

"Check this out, get us in the mood," said mum and put her iPhone in the hub. Wedding flute music filled the room.

"It's called a *shehnai*, they play it during the time of weddings. You've heard it before haven't you?"

"Yes."

"Beautiful isn't it? I love it, it reminds me of when I got married. I had a very modest wedding mind you, your uncles were drunk and got into a fight, what a surprise. But still it was the best day of my life. I'm sitting there and I'm so tired and starving because the lead up's been going on for days and your dad lifted the sari pallu from my head and looked into my eyes. Our worlds converged. You may laugh Shaani, but it's an important memory for a woman. A rite of passage. And I was convinced we would live happily ever after."

"Yeah yeah yeah."

"No one really listens anymore," continued mum, talking to herself because I certainly wasn't listening. "Yeah, yeah yeah. What they mean is I'm bored, tell me something better. Well you know most of your life when you're middle aged is just that, yeah yeah yeah. It's all over. When you're a mother and your kids don't---"

"Dolly!" I said impatiently. Infamy infamy everyone's got it infamy! FFS.

I took down the suitcase from the top of her wardrobe and laid it on the bed. It was the suitcase where mum kept her Indian clothes that she'd had washed and ironed when she was last in India. There was a big choice; all fancy stuff with gold embroidery and bright colours and silks. It was very important to be dressed correctly not just at the wedding but at the engagement events too. You couldn't wear cotton or black, it was frowned upon. You had to wear wedding bling. I started taking out her saris and shalwar khamees all perfectly folded and super-starched, something they called *charak*. Amongst the clothes was a small bulging cloth bag.

"Are you going to wear Naani's jewellery?" I said.

"No, its horrible. Bless her."

I knew she didn't look at the jewellery from one year to the next because it was too gaudy and orangey but she kept it in the old cloth bag for posterity because it had been part of Naani's dowry. She had been talking about getting a box at the bank for the last four years. In Chesham they had put it all in the local Metro bank but the one in Barnet didn't offer the same facilities and you had to pay yearly. Mum didn't think it was worth it.

I could sell it, I thought wildly. I'm sure I could get at least 4 k. Maybe he'd be happy with that? Would it be worth that much? I had about £600 in my savings account, possibly

£680. If I gave him £5,000 surely that would be enough. Enough to go to Mexico or whatever he wanted with it. After all Mortea'zar didn't *need* the money, he just wanted it back so he could pay Sahayle.

"Maybe I'll sleep on it. I'll go tomorrow," said mum suddenly after we'd packed up her little overnighter.

But why? I want you to go tonight.

"They'll think it's so cool if you rock up tonight, like a film star. They already think you look like Katrina whatshername. Half of them can't even drive, they let their fat husbands do it."

"Oh hardly! She's size zero. But thank you my darling," said mum and squeezed my arm. "I feel like hanging out with you and Ash tonight, if he's home."

But what could I do? I couldn't force her. But I had to act fast. I felt impotent. The same feeling I'd had when I'd gone to see Max. Powerlessness. I had no power in this house. Or authority. How could I? I didn't earn money. I wasn't at Uni I was just floating around. I couldn't effect any change. And yet, to my mind I was the only one around here with sense. I had to get her out. Then I could get that jewellery and sell it and destroy the photos and keep Mortea'zar out of our lives forever. The doorbell rang. It was 5pm.

It's the police. I know it's the police.

Chapter 14

Ash was talking to someone at the door. He closed it, and looked up at us on the landing at the top of the stairs.

"It's some bloke sent by Sahayle."

"Sent him for what?" said Mum raising her voice over the shehnai blaring out of her room.

My heart leapt. Another one. There's a whole gang of them. Max, Mortea'zar, Sahayle and now what? Why was he doing this to us?

"Sent him for *what*?" demanded Mum from the top of the stairs.

Her phone rang and she took it, automatically walking towards her bedroom because for some reason there were dead zones on the upper landing where you got no reception. I seized the opportunity and raced downstairs, pushed past Ash and opened the door.

A big white man with rough skin and furry eyebrows stood on the doorstep. He had a thick angry scar across his face. OMG he even *looks* like a criminal.

"Yes," I said folding my arms.

"Mr Sahayle sends me."

"We don't want it," I said vehemently. Go away, I thought. I'm in my house; you can't do anything to us.

"I do," he gestured pushing two fingers upwards.

What does that *mean*? He's going to shoot us?

Ash pulled the door further so he was standing next to me shoulder to shoulder.

"What do you want?"

"Nothing, he pays ok."

"Sorry?" I said.

The man put up two fingers again and I saw he had a ladder leaning against the hedge behind him.

"Peep"

"He's come to fix the guttering," laughed Ash. "Nice one Sahayle."

Ash walked into the front room leaving me to deal with the man.

"Really?" I said. "Can you do it? You know what the problem is?"

"Sure, no war is" said the man with a beaming toothless smile. The scar didn't look angry anymore, just part of his strange foreign face. "I start now. I must go long way thraaaffic. In East London. My home. I start now. OK?"

He made a sort of half bow.

"Did you say he's already paid you?"

"I do other jobs for him. This one I do for him Regalo. No, no. Geschenk? Cadeau! Cadou? Mi Inglish very bad." He shook his head mournfully.

"Gift, you mean? A gift?"

"Geeft. Okayokokay"

"Ok," I said in a daze. "Thanks very much Mr…."

"I am Mischka Illya Gavrilovich thank you," he said bowing to me. "But you can call me Messi. Like Lionel Messi."

He toddled off to get his ladder. Another white man popped up from behind the hedge and together they began to extend the mechanical ladder against the wall of the house, chattering away, giving each other instructions. He can speak French and German and his own language I thought as I stood in the doorway watching them. His English is shit though. Across the street was the entrance to Lovers Lane, the dirt track along the fence of the golf course, with the No Balls Allowed sign in the playing area where no one played. It was empty. The light was lovely, dappling through the trees.

I went out and stood behind them, watching. I wanted to make sure he was going to clear the gutters just as he said. Just in case. You never know. They could be burglars for all we knew. But no. I was being paranoid. The assistant was holding the ladder while Mr. Messy was going putt putt thud thud putt putt on the gutter. So Sahayle sent you? What sort of blackmailer was this guy?

"Shaani!" said Mum opening the door.

"What?" I said irritably. "You made me jump sorry."

"Shaani…! Come inside, come inside quickly."

Why wouldn't she go tonight, oh why did she want to make an early start? What was wrong with a late start tonight? Once mum was out of the way I could think. It was as though a bomb had started ticking in my head ever since Sahayle had said "it'll be worse for your mother". I've got to keep things at bay. I don't know what I'm *doing* but I just need time.

Mum went into the kitchen just as the TV news was switched on in the front room. I went into the front room where Ash had left his trainers and bag.

"Ash!"

"Quiet!" he shouted with his hand up like a policeman. "It's the news."

"Shaani, I just spoke to…" Mum grabbed my arm and pulled me back into the hallway.

The front door was ajar.

In walked a familiar figure. "Haylo haylo. There is a dirty white van parked very badly on the corner of Ashley Gardens and Lansdowne and two dodgy looking *goras* hanging around. Hey Shaani girl, you know what is *goras*? Whitey! I wonder if you know anything about it? These *goras* they are most wily, they pass undetected among the English *goras,* and perform criminal activity," panted Mr

131

Singh. He was in his usual wrapped in a hurry turban (navy today) and jogging trousers. "This is not Chesh-haam, this is London and fool of wolverines."

"Hello Uncle, please come in," I said gritting my teeth.

Please go away!

Ash turned off the TV, jumped up from the chair like a jack in the box sticking out his hand. "Hello Uncle how was India?"

"I think the white van belongs to."

I looked at the front door hanging open. It was still light outside. A pale lavender light.

"Please sit," said mum with her 'telephone voice' smile. "Thank you so much for letting us know. We'll attend to it."

Mr Singh sat down happily on the sofa in the lounge, his hands on his knees. I must go and shut the door, I thought dully. But there's such a nice breeze coming in from outside. The hallway drenched in that gorgeous light at the end of a summer's day. The slow thud putt of the men clearing the gutter overhead and the shehnai streaming out from mum's room. It's ok to leave the door open if we're in the house, I thought. Mum went into hostess mode.

"Come, let's have a cup of tea together. Shaani help me in the kitchen please."

"Oh yes I have bought for you a packet of Daalmote. From Agra," Mr. Singh said apologetically, producing a grimy looking polythene package from his trouser pocket. "This is. My reason for coming."

"Thank you Uncleji, how kind. Daalmote from Agra. It's the best," said mum and took the package from him with one finger and thumb.

Why we *all* called him uncle I did not know, only that it would sound weird for me and Ash to call him granduncle.

"Want to go for driving practice tomorrow?" said Mr Singh and Ash nodded "yes please uncle," and then, "Mum I'm going out tonight don't bother with dinner for me."

"So tell me is it true you are going to the Arks Bridge two years urlee? I heard one Indian boy went when he was five, what about that?"

Mum steered me into the kitchen.

"Shaani, I just got a call from a friend at work. Max is missing. She said he might be *dead*."

I looked at her. She was distraught.

"This Daalmote is rancid," she said. "It's out of date."

"Let's put it out anyway. I'll get the tea bags."

"Shaani, if it's true…"

An unfamiliar male voice was talking in the front room.

"Make the tea mum," I said hurriedly.

A man in a grey suit jacket and dark trousers was standing in the middle of the room with his back to me. He turned as

I walked in wiping my hands on my jeans. Caucasian. Short hair, pleasant smile, middle forties. Not unattractive but a stranger.

Everyone just walks in, I thought.

"This," said Mr Singh as if he had invented him, "Is Inspector Hustings. He is making house to house calls."

"Hodgkins sir. Hello. Yes is Mrs Meenakshi Dev here?"

"Yes, I'm Mrs Dev," said mum behind me, her hands lightly on my shoulders.

"Hello, good evening. I'm DS Gary Hodgkins from Barnet CID." He flashed his card.

"Please do sit down Sergeant," said mum.

"Thank you, I won't take up much time."

Ash was leaning forward intently.

"What's it about?" said mum

"We're investigating a recent incident of homicide and due to various leads, we have been making house."

"to *House*!" said Mr Singh. "Good old Fashioned English police work. They are touring all the Asian houses, for obvious reasons."

"Sir, not at all. This is a routine investigation. This is not racial profiling," said the policeman immediately.

What obvious reasons did Mr. Singh mean, I had no idea.

"No no no no no of course not. Anyway, we don't mind. We Asians don't mind. We are not like the Blacks. Come and search my house, I have nothing to hide, and neither do my good neighbours the Devs. I, Balvinder Singh can vouch for them."

Hodgkin's smiled but with a certain distaste. He's definitely filf, Pushy would have said, spot the racism under the tablecloth of tolerance. Although Mr. Singh would test anyone's tolerance.

"Who's been murdered?" said Ash.

"Ash!" said mum. "None of your business."

"No it's fine Mrs Dev. It's a man by the name of Pietr Maximillian Kalnikoff."

"Not Sukhvinder, Sukhvinder is a Punjabi name! He was not a Punjabi," said Mr. Singh to the room. "Thank God he was not an Indian!"

Yeah. Because there was only 1 billion and counting, we didn't want to lose any. I wondered if Mr. Singh was actually deaf.

"---Have any of you, not you Mr Singh you've already been *most* helpful---"

"Most welcome," nodded Mr Singh and sat back with satisfaction.

No wonder he'd come running to our house out of breath with the Daalmote and the white van was just an extra bonus. Anything to get in to see all the fun at the fair at the Dev house.

"Have any of you heard of or know this individual?"

We all shook our heads. I prayed silently for mum to keep her cool. I didn't dare look at her.

"Hiiiiii," came a shrill voice from the hallway and everyone turned to see a tall skinny supermodel tottering on kitten heels. The kind of girl that made grown men's eyeballs stand out on stalks and produce sound effects like boooiinoinoiunoiggggh. She had golden skin, dead straight blonde hair and a Kim Kardashian bum in a tight dress. "Am I too early? Soweeee."

The girl stood in the middle of the room now while everyone was seated. "Hello Aunty, so lovely to meet you at last."

"Hello," said mum helplessly.

Hodgkins opened his mouth to speak when the gutter guy walked in, followed by his assistant, both of them red faced, and smiling, wiping their filthy hands on their filthy trousers.

"I kill it. Job darn," said he. "Hello, I am Messy and I kill it."

"OMG that's so funny!" said the girl.

"You killed him?" said Mr. Singh pointing his finger. "On my god, you people."

The girl tittered and tottered on her heels with the confidence that only the very beautiful can muster.

136

"Wrong time Giselle. Get lost," said Ash curtly and the girl looked crestfallen, crumpled ballerina.

OMG!

Jaswinder Dhaliwal, 15 years old, granddaughter of the Tata-Khanna – Dhaliwal dynasty, known simply as Giselle, one of Model 1's top featured Fresh Faces in line for a major cosmetics contract because she was 'worth it,' was being asked to vacate the premises by my spotty oik of a brother.

"Just a minute. Please everybody, just stay where you are," said mum raising both hands for order. "This is Detective Hodgkin's from Barnet CID. Now please go ahead detective. How can we help you?'

"Oh," said Giselle and tried to raise an eyebrow. Mr. Messy and Mr. Messy assistant shrank back, jaw dropped.

"Thank you Mrs Dev. It's just preliminary enquiries at present. I can see you're busy so I'll just leave my card. Call me if you have anything to report. " He put his card on the mantelpiece where dad's airmail was still standing, unread, forgotten.

"The deceased we are investigating also went by the moniker Max," said Hodgkins and left. A great gust of wind tore into the house.

The front door slammed shut.

Chapter 15

"What are you doing mum?"

"Nothing nothing.."

She was sitting in her bedroom with the laptop on her lap, hands shaking.

"Mum. Calm down."

Ash had gone out with Giselle. Mr. Singh had gone home. The two guttering men had slipped away back to East London in their dirty white van.

"Do you know how to delete things on Facebook?"

"Just press delete. What do you want to..?"

"No! I mean delete forever. I mean erase it in the FB memory."

"What's the matter mum?"

"Max is dead!"

"Well so, what's it got to do with you?"

"I've got to wipe this stupid post I put. About the girl in the suitcase."

"What's that got to do with anything?"

"Because I. Because Max might have been killed by the same man who killed that poor girl. And. And."

What she was really freaking out about were the photos she'd sent him on the phone. But she couldn't talk about those to me. She couldn't erase those. The fear and panic on mum's face was awful. It was the same as when I'd seen her lose it at the door when she couldn't go out in the storm to meet Max.

"Mum, it'll look much worse if they find out you tried to erase something. It was a joke, like you said."

"Oh stop it Shaani, you don't understand! You don't know what you're talking about!"

Of course I did! But I couldn't tell her I knew. That's why I didn't care about paying Sahayle the money, and I didn't care if he came back for more because I wanted those photographs gone. I never wanted to talk about them with my mother.

"Listen mum. Calm down ok?"

"Yes, you're right. I'll have to tell him. Hodgkins. I must tell him straight away."

"Tell him what?"

"That I was…that I knew Max. He'll find out anyway. Maybe he already knows and that's why he came to our house. Oh God, he's been murdered for Gods sake and all I'm worried about is how it'll look for me."

"Just breathe mum. Take a breath. Think it through."

The only thing that could link her to him were those photographs. Unless they had been seen together and I'm sure they hadn't, the police might not make the connection. But it hadn't taken me much brain cell to figure out she was having an affair with him, I'd put two and two together and so would the police. But I couldn't have her tell them. Not yet. Not until. Not until I'd got rid of the photographs. Got Sahayle away from us.

Mum was shaking her head. "I'm going to call him right now. I have to come clean about it. And also about Mortea'zar coming to the house looking for Max. I have to tell him everything."

Mortea'zar!

"Ok I'll get the card," I said and went downstairs. It wasn't on the mantelpiece, or on the carpet. I looked around but I couldn't find it. I went upstairs and mum was staring into space.

"I can't find it. But it's almost 9pm. Why don't you take a pill. You've got to make an early start tomorrow."

"Are you mad? I can't go now!"

"Why not?"

"Because I have to…confess."

"For Gods sake mum. You had an affair with him. Not even a proper one. You didn't kill him. Having an affair isn't illegal."

"But I'd be withholding information."

"No, you just call him on Monday and tell him then, tell him it was too delicate to discuss in front of your children and

141

you were scared to say anything. You're not a suspect mum. For Gods sake!"

"Did he say he thought it was related to the suitcase murder, a gangland killing of some sort? Or did Ash say that, I can't remember can you?"

Her nails were drumming on the table nervously.

"You should go to the Sangeeth. It'll be good for you."

"I don't know. But I'm going to sleep now. Take a NightSleeps. I'm so sorry about this my darling. I feel terrible. I don't want you to have to…"

"Don't worry mum. Just sleep. Everything will be better tomorrow.

I went downstairs thinking about the receptionist at Pumping Iron. Would she have told them about me? I didn't think so. Like Troy she was underpaid and had no loyalty to the company and like Troy and everyone else I knew, she didn't trust the police and wouldn't help them voluntarily. And I was willing to bet her boss had told her to make like the three wise monkeys in face of any police enquiry; deaf dumb and blind, because Pumping Iron was indeed a cesspit of all sorts going on. If Hodgkins knew I'd been to see Max and the reason why, then he knew it all, so why not just wait for him to do his worst? But if he knew anything he would have said something. He wouldn't have just left it like that. It was a routine enquiry that's all it was.

I took dad's airmail down from the mantelpiece and pressed it close to my heart. It felt good to have Dad near even though he was thousands of kilometres away. I tore it open.

It was tiny handwriting wall to wall. Dad it was your presence we all missed most. You were the centre of good. Our centre was missing and we were bereft, spilling out everywhere. I put my hands over the words. I could feel the indentations of the biro.

My own Dolly,

First of all, I miss you very much this hot and clammy evening. I've been wondering what exactly I'm fighting for. Someone once said the past isn't over, it's not even past. And is that what I've been doing here, circling some lost past, determined to resurrect it? Land won't make any difference to the kids and in fact they'll end up having to deal with it when I'm dead. Selling it, or renting it out or building on it or simply maintaining it will entail Herculean will. After jumping through endless hoops and filling out yet another form, this Kafkaesque maze makes me wonder what legacy I'm actually leaving for them. How would they begin to know where to start with the paperwork over here? They might even end up hating me for it. I'm sorry I've left you all alone. I'm sorry I've been so remote. I can't do the Skype thing because simply it'll be too strong, I'll see your faces and I'll come home on the next flight. But I need to stay here just a little longer my love. I need to see this through but I need your understanding. I re read Shaani's letters yesterday, all three of them! I was remembering how we had been discussing Terrorism in the world today and Islamophobia (I know you don't like her getting chummy with the Muslim taxi drivers but she's curious and I'm proud of her for engaging with these issues, it's her world and she should have an opinion about where its going) and how extreme things seemed and I'd given her one of my favourite poems to read and we'd talked about it especially the lines 'The best lack all conviction, while the worst Are full of passionate intensity.' Whatever Shaani ends up doing in life, I feel she has a great urge for self-expression. She has so much passion inside, even though she always purports to eschew feelings. She wrote something for my birthday, which she said was inspired by seeing the leaves outside our house on a rainy day when she was thinking about me. I think it is actually a poem. A good one too. Here it is, I want to copy it out for you. Don't tell her you read it ok? Don't tell her I wept with pride when I read it.

The Leaf

The Leaf unobtrusive, does not announce itself.

A placid citizen in heady bush and heavy branch. So still in it's leaf-ness.

A shoulder and rest for us glittering bubbles. It lets them shine and show off. It holds.

The sun comes out, the drops disappear out the door, consumed with the busyness of their lives.

The leaf knows each personality.

And soon we become few and further away.

And on and on the world turns.

Silent. Strong. Unannounced: The leaf is everywhere, in other leaves, interleaved.

The memory of leaf sparkles inside the raindrops forever.

What tenderness each drop of rain receives! What enriched heady life!

The news you send of Ash and Shaani is great, I'm glad they are working as a team. I think the pressure of the scholarship is harder on him than he lets on and he is (secretly) more driven, more ambitious than anyone I have ever known. What I worry about is whichever one he gets into, he'll push himself to be in the creme de la creme of the crème and will accept nothing less of himself. I think this is what people who change the world are made of, but I wonder. Sometimes his mind frightens me, because excellence can be ruthless, devoid of compassion. But I am an old man and I worry about these things. The world is changing. As you said, he'll always be fine, he knows how to navigate the world. Oh and talking about navigation, my God the drive to the court every day in that three wheeler has given me permanent bruising in the bum. And I have a constant sore throat because of the pollution. Court goes on, day-by-day, interminable documents are read out in Hindi and in English and nothing seems to move further. My lawyer has to translate the jargon for me. It's all in the most archaic English you've never heard in England. He says we have a chance. Another week and we should see a breakthrough. That means at least the end of August. And then, whatever happens, I will come home. I give you my word. Seven months is too long to be away from you. I think you should get this letter in a week so the promise stands my darling girl. Please write to me. Absence makes the heart. You know the rest. Your own Vinod.

I folded up the airmail and put it in the drawer in the kitchen on top of the blister pack of batteries. I felt exhausted suddenly really tired and as soon as my head hit the pillow I was out. The first thing I thought of when I woke up was I had to see if Mum would go away. Until she went away I couldn't think straight. Once she was gone I would take the jewellery and go to Wembley to one of the jewellers there. Maybe I could get a loan on it? How did that work, I didn't know. I had my ipad and a kindle but I didn't think I'd get much for those at Cash Convertors, but I could try. And maybe for the platinum bracelet I'd got from mum and dad for my 16th. It was in its velvet box in my wardrobe.

"Mum," I said knocking on her door.

"Come in Shaani."

I walked in with a cup of coffee.

"Thank you my darling. Oo in a cup too how very porsche."

"How do you feel mum?"

"Like I don't want to get out of bed. Ever. But I know I must. I've decided to go to the police station and lodge my request, even if he's not there which I suppose he won't be as he's a detective and I suppose they don't work weekends. If they'll give me his mobile I'll call him. I'll tell him what I know and I'll tell him I'm going to Birmingham for my niece's wedding event, but if he doesn't want me to go, I won't go."

There was no point in talking to her, her mind was made up. She sounded so paranoid, as though she was under arrest. It's guilt, I thought. She feels guilty about sending those porn pictures and she's ashamed. She's stuck on that feeling. I felt for a moment like an eagle soaring above the clouds seeing the situation in pure form and structure, what had to be done, now weighted down with unnecessary emotions.

I didn't care anymore about judging her for the pictures, it was only important to disappear them. And as for Max I felt nothing. I was sorry he was dead but I couldn't get myself worked up about it. Maybe she wouldn't actually go through with it. Maybe Detective Hodgkins wouldn't be home. But in any case, she had to be handled properly. She was on the edge.

"That's good. That's ok. Are you sure?"

"I have to Shaani. I can't pervert the course of justice. And as you said, I haven't done anything wrong. Well, not legally, perhaps morally."

She said it wrong, like "a pervert" not "pervert," but I was in no mood to laugh. The sun was streaming into the room. We were both early risers up by 6am but it was 8.30am now and she snuggled down deeper into her bed.

"I'm going to have a lie in. I need it. The pills made my head woozy."

Ash came running up the stairs and pushed open the door.

"Why you still in bed? Get up mum!"

"Oh Ash stop telling me what to do the whole time!" she said rolling her eyes.

"Mum, you've got to go downstairs and meet Giselle's mum."

"What for?"

"Because she's come to meet you!"

"Its not even 9am and it's Saturday!"

"Well, they're going to the country. And we're on their route. And they want to say hello. Well she does. Dhaliwals already gone with the brother. Its just Giselle and her mum and anyway. So come on!"

"Suddenly so keen," said mum arching a theatrical eyebrow.

"Not at all. I just think it's rude of you to not meet her."

"Cant you say I'll meet her another time, I'm so happy and cosy in bed," said mum.

"Mum are you seriously kidding me?" he said.

He was actually sweating. I started to laugh. For a brain box he was so easy to wind up.

"Of course I'm kidding you. I can't think of anything nicer. Tell her I'll be down in ten.

Chapter 16

Mum went for a shower.

"Turn that music off!" said Ash. "Sounds like a grotesque carnival!"

"It's Indian wedding music! What's your problem?" I said.

"Indian weddings are a crime! Ostentatious displays of wealth, gaudy women dripping gold and diamonds. I hate those things! They're just a way of laundering money. They make me sick!" He was really cross now. "Why are you both not down there?"

He had his palms upturned as if to say what's happened to this family? The mother's still in bed and the sister isn't presentable and we've got *guests*.

"Alright," I said.

I've always known that underneath it all Ash is totally conventional. He likes order and tradition and a certain correctness. Whatever he really thought of the Dhaliwals, it was important to him that they saw us as a decent family. Maybe especially because dad wasn't here. And maybe, despite myself I felt the same way. A realisation came flying into my head like a dart hitting bullseye: He really hates it but he knows he'll have to submit to it because the Dhaliwals would do nothing less than OTT wedding.... Oh, he wants to marry Giselle!

My frown simply turned upside, I couldn't help it. The way mum said she couldn't help sneaking a quick sniff of my head (gross!). We were connected. We lived for the good of each other and our failures and successes were shared, celebrated. We were little raindrops, reflected in each other. We were family. Oh it was like mind reading! I had decoded his behaviour not because I was a good detective, but because I knew him. I'd known him all his life. I had saved him from drowning when he was 3 years old. I owned him.

How long before I can tease him about it…?

My phone kept vibrating.

"Come downstairs," Ash hissed. "Take that mentally ill grin off your face"

I answered the phone.

"Hello?"

"Hello it's Sahayle"

"Just a minute please," I said and wiggled my fingers at Ash to go away.

"You," Ash said pointing at me. "You should present yourself properly. Get changed. You can't meet them in your jim jams!"

"Oh shut up!"

"No, Shaani you've got to learn how to behave. You're part of a Brahmin Indian household. The older sister. You've got to know the codes."

"Take your codes and shove them."

"And don't swear," said Ash holding up his forefinger. "Not ladylike."

"Just a minute – Just a minute please. Ash I'm coming I've got to take this. *You* shouldn't keep *your* guests waiting, go downstairs."

"What's so urgent?"

"Just go downstairs, please?"

"You are going to get dressed?"

"Ash, stop being such an asshole."

Ash shrugged and went downstairs. He was all talk. The truth was he didn't know how to do Indian hospitality; he left it up to the family. He's such a typical Indian boy I thought, and yet it didn't make me angry. It made me love him the same way mum did. I got angry when she indulged him but I indulged him too. Indian boys were treated like Gods, it was a terrible truth. He wanted everything neat and nice but he didn't want to do anything towards it because he didn't see it as his job.

And despite all his better judgement he was in love with Giselle. He didn't look happy about it at all. I had never thought that's how people could be when they were in love. Maybe he thought she would distract him from what he was going to do in his life? No. Ash was going places; anyone he married was going to be a passenger and a happy one at that.

I looked at the phone in my hand. Go away! Unavailable Number. I felt sick. He's probably got a string of burners. All criminals had them. Where was the phone he had the pictures on? Somewhere safe or was it lying around? I just kept looking at it. I imagined Sahayle on the other end, standing in a street, or in a room. Wherever he was I felt like he had me on a leash like a dog that couldn't escape. I walked out slowly to the landing and saw the bars go down immediately in the dead zone. I looked at the phone and felt like flinging it out the window.

I can't bring myself to talk to him. I've got to have the weekend to think about how to get the money. Why is he bothering me? It's not fair…if I could only, if I could only stand here and get cut off. I imagined standing on a street and pushing Sahayle in front of an oncoming bus. But if I didn't take this call it would be like sinking into quicksand. I don't want to talk to him, I don't want to! What's he going to demand now? He was waiting on the other end. I had to talk to him. No, I don't want to!

I shoved the phone into my pocket. I went back into mum's room. The shehnai music was like being swathed in swaying silk. It almost lifted my heart and I looked out of her window at clear blue skies. I looked down and saw Ash's shoes and I picked them up and went out and put them outside his room. The painting in the hall was at an angle and I straightened it carefully. The picture hook was almost half way out and I thought the painting could fall and there'll be broken glass everywhere, so I took the painting down and pushed at the nail with my thumb. The phone kept pressing against my thigh. I hung the painting and made sure it was secure by pulling it slightly. Yes, perfect. The phone seemed to be nudging me, a lump in my pocket.

OMG, shut up, go away Sahayle.

I strode into my room. Immediately the bars came up to maximum. I put the phone down on my chest of drawers next to my teddy bear. I straightened out the creases on my bed spread until it was perfectly smooth. It was as though he was in the room, waiting quietly, lifting a crease on his trousers, watching me as I avoided him. *You've got to talk to him.* But I kept pressing out the creases on the bedspread. I must have developed OCD in the last week, I thought crossly. On top of everything else now I've got behavioural issues! The bed needs to be completely perfect. I can't answer unless it is.

I could hear voices downstairs in the hallway. Just take them into the front room for God sake Ash, I thought. The bedspread was wonky. I pulled it off and started again. I'll just smooth it out and tuck in the corners. It's got to look right. If you leave your bed made badly it sets the wrong tone for the day. Oh stop it, stop being insane!

I immediately stopped being insane and picked up the phone.

"Hello, sorry I just had to."

"You're out of breath. Finish what you have to do. I can wait."

"No it's - sorry," That's nice of him to say, I thought. He had already been waiting for quite a while. "Just family stuff."

"I've caught you at a bad time."

"Shaani," mum's voice came from her room. Her door opened and the shehnai came flooding out. "Put the kettle on when you go downstairs. Ash won't think to do it."

"It's all right. Hang on. Yes, ok, I'll just be a minute mum"

"What are you doing?" said mum, her voice muffled.

"Getting changed," I said opening my door and putting my hand over the phone. I didn't want to shout in case they heard us from downstairs. Then I closed my door and took off my pyjamas and pulled on my jeans and a t-shirt. Then I sat down on my chair again looking out at Lovers Lane. I wished I'd never gone to see Max. But what was the point of regret, it's what old people did, count their regrets, but shouldn't-haves didn't change anything, they just made you miserable. You're in it now girl, you're in it up to your neck. So deal with it.

"Hello, sorry."

"I heard the flute. Was played very often in the streets behind the orphanage where I grew up."

I knew he'd be an orphan. He had that haunted look about him as though he had lost people.

"It's more like an oboe. It's called a shehnai. They play it at weddings. My cousin's getting married and weddings cheer people up, everyone in the family gets carried away. It reminds them of past weddings. Well anyway."

I was rambling and I knew why. It was to make it normal. I was talking to a friend on the phone, about stuff, as if it was all normal.

"It made me think of an open truck on a bumpy dirt road with all of us packed in like happy clams going to the circus. It makes you nostalgic for the old country."

What did he know about it? He wasn't properly Indian or British Asian. He wasn't properly Russian or Ukrainian. I doubted he could speak any language other than English. He wasn't anything. He didn't have a family and he was a blackmailer. Or maybe he was married? Maybe he had a wife and children? Somehow I didn't think so. He was a lone wolf. Only he was connected to that vile Mortea'zar and God knows what else?

"I suppose you can speak the lingo can you?"

"Ye--es. Hindi not Urdu. I can understand both. Why are you calling me?"

"Can you talk?"

"Not really. You said Monday was all right."

"Yes but I needed to talk to you before Monday"

"What for"

"Mortea'zar. He's not happy about waiting till Monday. If it was up to me."

"So you keep saying," I said angrily.

If he'd only stop repeating those words maybe they would just fade away and not be true anymore. But he kept talking like I was some imbecile who hadn't grasped the point.

"The money is Mortea'zar's money but I'm collecting it for him, do you understand? It's what he'll then pay me with. I've led him to understand it's your mother I'm dealing with – if he knew it was the daughter, well…he'd come there for sure. He wouldn't have any faith that you could get the money."

"But I can!"

"He's annoyed because it's taking so long. Because he says, well your mother could just go to the bank and withdraw it and she's deliberately delaying payment."

"Who can go to their bank and withdraw seven grand? He's mad."

"He knows there is a fund. An account your father opened in the bank after dissolving an investment."

How did he know about that? Because mum told Max and I bet Max blabbed about it. How could she have been so stupid?

"He thinks… Anyway he's got something against your mother. He thinks she's playing him. He. Hates people like that. I'm calling to say, perhaps you *should* let your mother handle it. It's not your problem you know?"

"What does he mean people like that?"

There was a silence and I could imagine him pressing his lips together, his eyes squinting a little, trying to put it politely.

"Mortea'zar hates rich people. He thinks they're wily. He says rich people always look after their own comforts; they don't give a damn for anyone else."

"But we're not rich. Is that what he thinks? We're not rich. We're just middle class."

"He says he can tell from the way she spoke to him. Dismissed him like a fly. He says you can always tell."

"It's her telephone voice! She's a receptionist in a dental surgery. And my dad's just a lecturer not a professor, he doesn't even have tenure. How are we rich?"

"He wants to blow up the rich, do them harm. I don't know the reasons behind it. But I wanted to tell you. I can go to her. And your mum would probably be able to lay her hand on the money a bit easier. I don't see why you don't."

"Oh you don't see, you don't see! You don't understand because it's not your mother. You don't have a mother so you don't know! Please…" I said. "Please don't go to her. It's complicated. Let me deal with it. I'll get you your money and you'll delete the photos. That's all there is to it. Alright?"

"Alright. Relax. I'll wait. I just thought."

"We had an agreement Mr. Sahayle."

"It's not for me."

"Yes yes yes, the money's not for you so you keep saying again and again. It's him, you don't care about the money. Only you do because you want your payment. But you don't care about the money. You're such a saint aren't you?"

"I don't care about the money," he said quietly.

Liar! You want the money. You said so, and now you're trying to make out you're so good. I hate you, I felt like screaming at him. I felt like kicking him. I was terrified of Mortea'zar's threat. Mortea'zar can't come near this house, he can't come to mum. It'll all come out about Ash and Max and me and I can't have that.

I heard mum going downstairs and I could hear them talking. I needed to be there. I just needed to be there in case. I don't know what in case. And I had to make sure she went to the Sangeeth. Mrs. Dhaliwal was holding things up.

"Look I can't talk anymore. I'm...I'm sorry for shouting. It's just so difficult for me. There are these, family obligations. I'm. We've got guests, I've got to go downstairs."

"Ok then will you definitely have it by Monday."

"Yes yes."

"Alright. You'll have to give me only 6,500. I've already given him 500 and told him it's from your mother"

Oh great thanks that's big of you, I thought. As if.

"Alright," I said. I just couldn't bring myself to say thank you. Thank you for what?

"Shall I come to you or."

"No! No way!"

"Alright. At 12 in a pub called The Good Friend, off Tavistock Square, where the famous statue is."

"Yes, yes there."

What statue and where was Tavistock Square I had no idea. I just had to get him off the phone and go downstairs.

Chapter 17

I rang off. I was furious, my head in turmoil as I ran downstairs. All I had was today and Sunday to get the money. I'll sell the jewellery and my bracelet and my ipad. Mum must have told Max about our fund, and Max told Mortea'zar. How could she? Forget the loan on the jewellery, you won't get that much. I'll go to Ealing Road; there are loads of jewellers there. Ok, ok I can do this. Something was whizzing around in me like a whirlwind and I had never felt like that in my life. This is what it feels like to be utterly trapped. A trapped rabbit in the headlights. A rabbit with its foot caught in a trap more like. Shaani, Shaani tell someone! Ask for help. Don't try to do this alone. But who was there to trust? Who's judgement could I trust? Certainly not mum's.

"Hello aunty, nice to meet you" I said and mum put her arm around my shoulders.

"There she is. My first born lovely."

"Hello darling," said Mrs. Dhaliwal smiling at me.

She was mum's age and mum looked very good but Mrs. Dhaliwal was photo-opportunity ready. Fine crafted features, plumped up skin and heady perfume around her like a cloud. Wrapped up like a Christmas present in her lovely heavy shimmering sari (at least 26 'weight').

162

Diamonds and gold sparkling off her. Fuck you money for true, as Pushy would say.

"I've heard so much about you Shaani, it's an honour to meet you."

Rich people, really rich people, really rich Indian people had the combination of showing off their money like a peacock while speaking humbly like a beggar. If that ignoramus Mortea'zar knew anything, he'd have known that.

"Me?"

"Oh yes, Ash has told us about his brave sister who saved him from drowning. He said he wouldn't be here if not for you. I take off my hat to you young lady, you are nothing short of a heroine."

"OMG" I felt skin crawlingly embarrassed; it was a historical fact in our family, not something to be puffed up in public. I hated any kind of over-praise. It was so phoney. Like getting a hundred likes on Facebook. I knew what I had done and that was enough.

"She's very modest. We're not allowed to boast," said mum with a proud smile.

"Oh," said Mrs. Dhaliwal nodding and put a finger to her lips. "You must meet my son. He's a sporty type too. Tennis is his game but he has no drive. He's just left uni and is thinking of travelling." Mrs. Dhaliwal exchanged a rolling of the eyes with mum, as if to say 'you know what they're like' – "but I thought it would be nice for Shaani to – talk to him. He needs direction."

"Great idea," said mum beaming. "Shaani?"

"Ok," I said.

"So Meenakshi, I was wondering I know it's last minute, but if you're free for lunch on Sunday. Tomorrow?"

"Well, I think I am."

What?

"Great, great. It's actually a Havan that we're having, you know to spiritually clean the place and all that. The priest is a man who lives in Burnt Oak *only*," Mrs. Dhaliwal lolled her head quickly and laughed, to denote how she had deliberately gone *desi*, using the *"only"* in the wrong place as they did in India. "Quite cheap considering he's a masterji chef and priest in one. He cooks, he prays eyyyyy what's not to like?"

Dolly threw back her head and laughed like a machine gun. Oh Mrs. Dhaliwal, she seemed to be saying, you are the Mistress of accents, one second desi, the next New Joisey, so talented, so very shiny…

"Dhaliwal says it's a waste of money but I say, it's good to do the Havan. He's such a *desi*; he holds every *paisa* with his teeth. I said to him at least all your previous sins will be extinguished and lets face it you've got plenty. The amount of bankers he did the accounts for back in the 90's."

Mrs. Dhaliwal chuckled and lolled her head in the exaggerated Indian way.

"Oh yes," said Dolly lolling away like she was such a good pukka Hindu. "You must have a Havan. Drive away the evil spirits, not that there will be any," she rushed to add.

"You must all come!" said Mrs. Dhaliwal clapping her hands. "The ceremony won't last long. You're not vegetarian are you?"

"No no its ok, I can eat chicken."

Since when?

"Good. I think you'll enjoy the food. His specialty is Hariyali Chicken, from the Imperial Hotel in Delhi where he was Head Chef. There'll be about ten of us for lunch. Us four, you three and a few others. Cant really fit in too many."

"You mean the Havan isn't going to be at your house in Chesham?"

"Oh God no! Whatever evil lives there Meenakshi, is there to stay! We've been there for over 25 years! No, that's what I wanted to tell you! It's you we have to thank really."

"For what?"

"Well remember when you first bought this house and we were at that party of the Rotary, where we first bumped into you both in fact, and you said you were selling up and had bought in the Greater London suburbs. A house near somewhere called the Brook and a viaduct, all very charming. You told us how the estate agent made a point of telling you about this Brook and how it was a tributary from the river Thames and how it was environmentally protected and all that. I remembered that, the babbling brook.

So fast forwards, we decide to get a flat in London to rent out and the estate agent comes up with a selection of places and guess what, there was a penthouse in Barnet, overlooking your famous babbling Brook! Ding, I thought. The babbling brook. Only let me tell you Meenakshi, it doesn't babble, it hardly bubbles. It just lies there. Flat and dull. It is not impressive. But no matter. The flat is a good investment. We already have two flats in Mayfair but the management fees are criminal. I said to Dhaliwal this is the one. We'll rent it out for a year or so and then Giselle or Nilesh can use it as a pied a terre, if they want. Do them good to see how the other half in zone 4 live."

"Good investment," said Dolly.

I bit my lip. She's calling us "the other half" to our *faces* and you can't tell.

"Yes, and I'm so pleased that this business is over. Because it's no good for the property prices."

"Business?"

"Well that man who was found dead? In Woodside Park. They've arrested the murderer thank God. Code G! That's what they say for arrested, isn't it great?"

"Murderer?"

"Oh yes. A well known murderer to the police."

"Who was it?"

"A man called Jacek Wojcik. A Pole. And the dead one is a Romanian I think. They all sound the same to me these people. White people, they all look the same to me in the light!" said Mrs. Dhaliwal and tittered.

"Hahahahhahaha, funny, good one," said Dolly.

"Anyway so. And the girl that was found in the suitcase, she was a European too! I think they were all mixed up in something. Sex trafficking or drug dealing, you know what these Eastern Europeans are like. But this Wojcik character sounds very shady, he's got a finger in every pie, even back in Poland if you please. And to think the EU allowed him to stroll in to the UK. I mean think of it Meenakshi, how *our* parents worked so hard to get on in this country."

"Taking the insults," said mum nodding.

"Turning the other cheek" said Mrs. Dhaliwal.

"Working all hours with no benefits or holidays."

"Being spat at and called names, yet still they dug in."

"My parents had only the clothes they wore when Idi Amin kicked them out," said mum. "My dad was turned away from every job he went for. What could he do? They broke his spirit."

"Mine too darling, mine too. But they didn't crumble. They didn't resort to drug dealing and murder did they?"

It was a script that Asian immigrants recited so often it was almost a litany. I glanced at Ash. It was what we termed "The olds bonding over the hard luck stories". We had heard it so often in drawing rooms. Only Mrs. Dhaliwal had landed on Rich airport bagging a distant relative of the Tata-

Khanna empire, a self made chartered accountant from Kenya, and mum had married a strict Indian Indian Brahmin vegetarian teetotal much older university lecturer. Presently on unpaid sabbatical.

"They picked him up within hours but I think they kept it on the down low, you know the Q T." Mrs. D laughed at the jargon coming out of her mouth. "Listen to me," she said. "I love CSI"

"But how do you know so much?"

"Well," Mrs. Dhaliwals eyes shone.

Chapter 18

"We can't stay talking in the hallway, come and sit down, please have some tea. I'm so sorry to keep you in the hallway..." said mum.

"Well just for a minute. But no tea. We must go! Dhaliwal expects me to be there by lunchtime. It kills him to defrost a curry from the freezer. 25 years in the UK and he won't go to the pub for lunch like a normal person, it has to be home cooked Indian food."

We all moved into the drawing room, which smelled musty because it hadn't been aired since Princey had last come. The roses had wilted.

" I know, Vinod's just the same. Alright then go on," said mum. "Go on then what?"

"Well, a week ago Dhaliwal and the kids had gone to the country as usual and I had to stay in London for a hair appointment, so I decided to stay in the flat. I always think it's good to stay one or two nights in property you're going to rent out."

Mum was nodding knowledgeably. There was no stopping Mrs. Dhaliwal wittering.

"Anyway so I stayed there but I just couldn't sleep. It was a terrible day, like a night, do you remember? A week or ten days ago. They even had a news item on it: *The day that was night.* There hadn't been one like it since the summer of 1942 during the war! Anyway the rain was lashing down and the flat felt so gloomy."

"Oh is it one of those flats set up on the hill opposite the Brook? There's about five of them, three stories high, set on a gradient?"

"Like a zig zag yes. They call it Accordion Mansions. Well please, they're hardly mansions. We've got the top one. They've very cleverly designed, because from the street you can't see them but from the flats, especially ours you can see the road and the Brook and the trees and the woods. You can actually see the London skyline, the Eye and the Gherkin and St. Pauls on a clear day. They've won an award."

"I heard about that," said mum.

"So I come out to the balcony. It's heated and covered you know, there's a lovely glass roof and you can sit and have your breakfast there. So I sat down thinking what a strange day it is, like a night! There was such an unholy racket, the rain on the roof like a thousand needles. I thought it was going to smash! Unsettling really. But I sat down looking across the tops of the pines. And then what do I see but two men pull something out of a car and deposit it into the Brook! Two men."

"No!"

"Yes! I didn't have my lenses in and it was raining very badly and I couldn't imagine why anyone would be out in the rain, and I forgot all about it. But then when I heard—actually

Ash told us the other night—that they were investigating this homicide of a man impaled on the banks, well I wondered if…perhaps…I mean I know it's quite a distance from Woodside Park…"

I kept looking at the floor at the interesting pattern of the carpet that we were going to change once we decided on whether to have a beige one or to go for another pattern. I cursed Ash silently, I couldn't help myself even though it was totally irrational. You're out smooching with Giselle while I'm here in hell and you told her, you told her about the police coming to our house.

"…I'd been studying the route of the Dollis Brook and I saw that it went through Woodside Park. You know? How sometimes two things just come together in your mind? I suppose that's how it is for detectives, don't you?"

"Really? Yes.'

"So I told Dhaliwal what I saw and he just says oh you can't see a thing without your lenses in, but I'm sure I saw *something*, you know? I mean shouldn't I report it to the police" Mrs. Dhaliwal bit her bottom lip. "Dhaliwal said don't talk to the police when you don't have to and I said for God's sake this isn't India, you don't have to be frightened of the police. I want to be a good citizen. I want to do what's right."

Mum was nodding away, Mrs. Liar in full flow.

"Dhaliwal grew up in Kenya and India, he's not a Brit like us, and so he *expects* the police to be corrupt. But of course you know, don't you, because Vinod grew up there too.

Funny that we have that in common. Even when we got married I remember telling him, you know you're going to have to realise I'm a British girl, and he said yes I'll be British soon too. But he isn't. He isn't British yet! He got the passport but he still thinks like an Indian. It's not like that here I told him."

You want to put your nose into everything I thought. You want to be at the centre. But you didn't have your lenses in did you? Why don't you stop gossiping? What did you see? *What did you see?* They knew us for years in Chesham and they never invited us and Mrs. Dhaliwal never made any comparisons between her marriage and my parents. But now, because Ashi's turned out to be a bright spark and they've got plans for him, suddenly she's mum's best friend. And mum was lapping it up.

"But then I thought maybe Dhaliwal was right. Giselle of course just told me the police are pigs, you can't trust them, but that's Giselle, she doesn't know anything, she just repeats what she hears her friends say."

I kept looking somewhere in the middle distance. Go away you horrible woman. You liar! Why won't you stop talking?

"Then Nilesh says it doesn't end there. If you report something to the police as a witness, then they can invite you to go to a *line up* and all sorts of things. Oh no I thought. I'd die if I had to pick out two criminals from a line-up, I mean what if I got it wrong and they came after me or my family? Well I thought, justice be hanged, my family is more important. Right?"

"Yes," nodded mum. "It's us mothers who have to think of everything. I don't see how it's any different than single mothers, it's still women doing all the work!"

"Husbands? *They* don't get any criticism from the kids. They're always golden. When we make plans we factor in our kids because we have to; *they* just make plans for themselves, just like they did when they were bachelors! Oh Dhaliwal says, I work, the home is *your* arena. Oh yes, the home and the kids and the million and one things running a home entails….he doesn't think that's work! Well *you* know, what with your husband away and all..."

"Would you like some Daalmote auntie, it's from Agra!" I said and pushed the plate under her nose.

"No, no, I don't eat anything fried. Anyway. So in the end, I took the advice of my family and said nothing. I shut up, that's what I'm supposed to do isn't it? I'm only a mother and the wife! What do I know?"

She pushed out her bottom lip theatrically.

"But then," her eyes lit up and mum leaned forward.

"I discovered I *knew* one of the policemen on the case!! I don't actually know him, but he's married to the…well now *divorced* from…the daughter of an uncle of a cousin of mine. So I called him up and invited him over for tea!"

"Wow you're so bold Sharmilla. Who was he?" said mum.

Mrs. Dhaliwal snapped her fingers.

"The one who came to your house! Hodgkins. Gary. We went to his wedding! Can you believe it? And a year ago, we met him socially and he told us they were getting a divorce and we said keep in touch."

"Wow," said mum.

"He's only the lead detective on the investigating team! I read it in the local paper! What a piece of luck. But then, nothing happens by chance does it?"

"Can you just invite a policeman for tea?" said mum.

"Oh Meenakshi! Don't be so bourgeois. They're just ordinary people. I took him out to the balcony and pointed out the Brook. As luck would have it, it was a lovely sunny day. I asked him if he could see it, and he said sure he could."

You could hear the glee in her voice. I was careful not to move a muscle.

"Then what happened?"

"I told him about that awful day that was night. But also about me not having my lenses in. And the rain."

"Was he interested?"

"He said it was unlikely that the incident—if it was an incident—had anything to do with the case but thanked me for my vigilance," said Mrs. Dhaliwal wrinkling up her nose. "I got muddled once he started quizzing me about it. Your memory and the evidence of your eyes is not really as reliable as you think."

"That's why I always write things down."

"Well exactly so do I. Anyway so nothing came of it, but I've invited him for the Havan. He's newly divorced, and he lives alone and I thought it'd be nice for him. And its good for policemen to observe different cultures isn't it? It's almost an educational thing for them. What do you think?'

"I suppose."

"And it's good to know a policeman isn't it? He's a detective now after all. All right he's not the Inspector, but apparently these days the inspectors are like CEO's of companies, they just do all the questioning of the suspects. Gary's heading the team that brings the suspects in. Quite edgy, don't you think? Oh and he told me he was a *lawyer* before he went into the force, so he's clever, very clever. I think it's great to know a policeman! It's like knowing lawyers and doctors. I tell Dhaliwal, no one wants an accountant at their party, they're too boring. Boring and rich, he says! No class, honestly I shouldn't say it about my own husband but I ask you?" She paused for breath and looked up. "Oh hello, when did you get here?"

A tall good-looking guy with long hair parted in the centre, wearing a cool bomber jacket, half denim and half something else.

"Sit down, where've you been? And where is Giselle, we've got to get going."

"My mother is obsessed with grisly cases. Hi aunty, hi.."

He had a cut glass accent. Private education, private everything.

175

"This is Shaani."

"Hi Shaani. I'm Nilesh. The one who hasn't got himself a job yet."

I laughed.

"Take a seat Nilesh *beta*, do you want a drink?"

"No I'm fine aunty," he said and sat down on the edge of the sofa, in the same place Sahayle had been. But Nilesh was a different breed. Pure class. Mrs Dhaliwal put her hand on his arm proprietarily for a few moments, the same way mum had put her arm around me when I'd come downstairs, and continued. "I asked him what's the one thing you've learned from being a detective."

Mum laughed. "You were interrogating him. You're terrible!"

"Yes, it was great fun. Anyway so he said what he had learned in 20 years was that you couldn't predict how human beings will act. People do things they never thought they would. I think that's very true. After all I married Mahesh Dhaliwal!"

Mum and Mrs. Dhaliwal tittered and Nilesh rolled his eyes at me. He was used to a mother who liked being the centre of attention. She seemed so certain she had seen two men. I silently prayed she would keep to that story if she decided be a witness, which seemed improbable. Even the policeman had told her to get lost.

"Anyway look, enough of my prattle." Mrs. Dhaliwal sent a text. She shrugged, "It's the only way I communicate with my kids now. I emoji them! We'd better get going, we're meant to be in Suffolk by lunchtime. It was wonderful to see you after so long Meenakshi. I'm delighted you'll all be coming to my little Havan lunch. And Shaani, I'm so honoured to have met you darling."

Ash and Giselle came into the room, studiously not walking in together. Giselle came in first and sat down and Ash stood.

"Mum, you know that's not a peach. That's a *bum*. God!" said Giselle.

"Accordion Mansions. You have to drive to the other side, into Church Street, as there's no entrance from the Brook side. Ash knows. Around 1pm Sunday? The blessing will be around 2pm. We won't eat till 3ish. It'll be fun Meenakshi." Mrs. Dhaliwal turned to her daughter. "Why would they have an emoji of a bum, that's disgusting Giselle. I'm sure mine is a peach, have I got an older iPhone model? Maybe it looks different, let me see yours…"

She was like an unstoppable hovercraft thundering through the water. She left imperiously with her children in tow, all of them talking at once and Mrs. Dhaliwal swishing her expensive heavy 23weights silk sari, oblivious to all the things she had got wrong, expecting, demanding that everyone and everything bend in her direction like weeds in the wind.

I said "But mum you're going to the Henna and Sangeeth and you're going to stay the night."

"Yes but I can come back tomorrow."

"But mum…"

Ash was listening to the conversation without saying a word.

"It's fun," he said flatly.

"What is Ashi?" said mum.

"Being with them. Something is always going on. It's a bustling rowdy crowdy family. The little brother Jody is a musical prodigy and he's always playing the piano. Their house is brimming with energy. It isn't the money. They have lots of different kinds of friends; someone's always dropping in. Nothing happens in our house."

"Ok," said mum.

"So you've got to go. And you. To the Havan. I'll be out for dinner tonight."

Ash left.

"He can be so mean sometimes," said Mum tearfully, and I put my arm through hers.

"He blames me for dad being away. He blames me for us not being a proper family."

"Ashi's an idiot."

"Don't be horrible about your brother Shaani. He thinks I should be a society hostess and give parties and have people over. But I've never been any good at that sort of thing. I've never been good at making friends the way he is. But don't be horrible about your brother Shaani. He's a genius."

I sighed. Talk about male privilege. Indian boys got away with everything.

"If you step on it you could get to Brum for lunch.'

"You know Shaani, if they've caught the man who did it, maybe it's not important for me to tell that policeman about me and Max? I don't think I could face it."

"He'll be there tomorrow. And you'll have to face him."

"I'm not going to tell him there! Oh God, and now we have to go. We promised Ash. It's a mess Shaani."

Mum hung her head and stared at her shoes. I knew how she felt. She had messed everything up and she didn't know how to make it better. If she only knew how bad it actually had got! All she wanted was to have this lovely religious lunch and forget about the world. She would get to play the mother of the future groom. Respectable and valuable. This lunch was important for us as a family. The Dhaliwals had their eye on Ash and this was all the lead up to what would probably end up being the wedding of the year, covered in all the Asian society pages.

Of course no proposal or anything formal had happened but just like job interviews, the process had begun even before the deals were made. We the Devs all had to be on our best behaviour from now on. For all I knew we would never have such a lunch again. I didn't want to think about that. I didn't want to think about what might happen after Sunday to me, to Ash, to us the Devs of Ashley Gardens if I told the policeman what I'd done.

"Do you feel bad about what's happened to Max?" I needed to know.

Mum put her face in her hands.

"God forgive me but I don't care. I know I should, it's a human life and I knew him for a while, but I don't *care*. He was nothing, it was nothing. It was the biggest mistake of my life. It's not fair! I just don't need any more bad luck. I'm human I made a terrible mistake. I shouldn't have to pay for that should I Shaani?"

"No mum."

Others may have to pay I thought desolately.

"They've caught the guy, case closed."

She brightened.

"Yes, case closed. So what are *you* going to do today my lovely?"

"Oh nothing just hang around. But they'll be expecting you for the Sangeeth mum…"

"Yes, yes. Shaani they'll be expecting me. One day we might be part of the Dhaliwal family, but today I'm a part of the Dev family. I'll go to Birmingham now. I'll be back tomorrow."

Once mum had left I went straight to the kitty and took out the £500 and shoved it in my pocket. Then I went upstairs and got Naani's jewellery and then I got my bracelet and my ipad, kindle, iPhone and gold Nikes. I shoved everything into my swim rucksack. I took out the Nikes; I could have ebayed them but there was no time now, I didn't think Cash convertors would take them and it was too much to carry. She didn't see two men. She's such a *liar.* I breathed slowly, one thing at a time. Get the money today, go to the Havan tomorrow, pay Sahayle off on Monday, and delete those photos. And on Sunday just brazen it out if the policeman's even there. They've caught the guy, case closed. Only it wasn't case closed. They had caught the wrong man.

But what's the point of thinking about him? You've got to do your research. I counted off all the London boroughs of Asian populations in my mind. Where there were Asians there was gold, and where there was gold there was buying and selling.

The Boroughs of

Hounslow

Harrow

Hayes

Brent

Newham.

All brown.

Tarrantino calls the neighbourhoods of New York 'cities' as in the City of Compton but these weren't cities, they weren't even towns, they were villages. But they weren't 'urban villages' with farmers markets and espresso coffee shops and home made gluten free breads. The Asian villages of

London were proper villages, where everyone had their nose into everyone else's business.

Where had I been before?

Wembley,

Ealing Road,

Highbury,

Queensbury

Southall.

Go where you've been before, it's safer. Southall in West London was the obvious choice but it was probable I'd bump into someone we knew. Even when we lived in Chesham people would drive to Southall to get wedding clothes. And I didn't even know how to get there by tube. Upton Park in the East End was another place where Asians thrived in an area called Green Street where apparently you could still get a chicken curry and rice for £1.50 and on Saturdays this same area was over run by lively white West Ham fans and the Asians stayed behind closed doors.

Wembley? Ealing Road? But that would take two buses...and what I remembered of the place was that it would be too busy. Asian ladies would be out in force buying food to feed the five thousand *i.e. their family!* Queensbury was good for meat but no good for jewellery. Tooting. What about Tooting? "There has been a shooting in Tooting. Tooting has some good parts and is coming up but there are too many Indians there still, so Tooting must wait a while," Mr. Singh had told us.

Tooting Broadway. I looked it up. Hmmm. It was on the Northern line. Yaaaaasss! The map showed at least 7 jewellery shops all with Indian names. I knew it! I switched to Street View. Good. I'll go to three and compare the prices. Hahhahaha Shaani Kumari Dev, you're *such* an Indian, trying to get the best price. Was that part of the Indian DNA? And as for the kindle and ipad, there will be a Cash Convertors in that area as sure as eggs.

I didn't need to consult the Street view. I'd only been in London for four years but I knew there would be a crappy market selling cheap stuff. Just as there would be a betting shop and a Fried Chicken Shop. Tooting might have good parts and might be coming up, but it was still a fairly trashy area where poor Asians lived. And where poor Asians lived, there was gold to sell and buy. I hitched my bag of loot over my shoulder and opened the door.

A man I hardly recognised was standing in the pathway.

Chapter 19

"Hey honey, how you doin?"

"Hello! How lovely to see you come in, please come in," I said automatically, hiding my shock under manners. At first glance he was painfully thin, his skin sagging, his clothes hanging off him like a scarecrow. But immediately I saw the Stetson still jaunty. His piercing blue eyes still beguiling. He was still Mitch. The same shy diffidence, the shuffling gait.

"Mitch!" I cried dropping my rucksack to the ground and rushing out to put my arms around him in a hug. My joy too, was automatic. We stood in the pathway hugging as we always had, even though I could feel his bones. I held him lightly; I didn't want to hurt him. And yet in the absence of my father, Mitch was the next important man that I respected in my whole life. It was good to see him, so good. Mitch was like a lamp burning bright in a window. A little cancer could never change that.

He followed me in and we went directly to the kitchen where we always sat when he came to see us, before he went out with Ash to talk or took a walk down to Barnet Fields. Five miles was nothing for him, he walked that every day and was a serious hiker too. Without asking I started to make Darjeeling tea, properly in the pot and with the extra pot of hot water.

"First flush," I said and he sliced the air with his palm as it to usher in good times.

I knew you wouldn't mind me raiding your secret stash dad. First flush wasn't given to the likes of those who couldn't appreciate excellence, but this was Mitch.

"I got real thin," he said at last sipping the tea, as if he had only just realised. "Sorry, I keep forgetting I'm a sight for sore eyes."

So typical of the man to be sorry for freaking other people out.

"How's the treatment going? Ash was completely tight-lipped when he got back, he didn't say anything and we didn't ask him because. Well, it's Ash." I rolled my eyes.

He laughed loudly and nodded.

"So, the drugs don't work anymore, the chemo just makes me sick. Maybe it works, but I don't want it. When the oncologist says 'you're welcome to try palliative treatments, you kinda know it's over,' said Mitch without emotion. He sipped the tea and nodded appreciatively.

"It's not over, till it's over Mitch," I said. "You can't say that. They don't know anything."

He smiled and nodded.

"Yeah, I still believe in miracles," he smiled.

"Me too," I said. "We're all tiny miracles. To quote a certain Harvard professor."

Mitch groaned and started laughing hard and shaking his head. His lovely Father Christmassy beard was still thick, and the hair on his head was still strong, white and wavy. It must have resisted the poison. His hair was hope.

"Honey, I've been trying to reach Dolly but is there something wrong with her phone? I left her a coupla messages too but no dice."

"Yeah yeah, her phone broke. She's getting a new one. Maybe that's the reason. I can give her your message," I lied.

I knew exactly why mum wasn't answering his calls. She couldn't bear to talk to someone with CANCER, it terrified her. She didn't even want to hear the word. It was so stupid.

"Ah, ok. Maybe she'll be home from work soon? She works Saturdays right?"

"Mitch she's gone to Birmingham for my cousins thing, it's a wedding related event, a ladies evening, and yes usually she does. I'm so sorry you've had a wasted journey. I'm so sorry you got tired out."

"It wasn't wasted, I'm delighted to catch up with you Shaani. You look wonderful as ever and I know you've been using your gap year to full---" He couldn't finish, because he started to fight for breath, and turned his head a few times as if he was trying to release something in his windpipe. Then he coughed, clearing his throat dramatically. I waited.

"That's not the ---it's just because I get tired, you know, it affects the entire neurological system. Disregard my manners," he said ushering away with his delicate hand.

Something I had observed in people who were sick was that they were so concerned about the others, the people around them. Given that human beings were apparently selfish and base, I'd always thought that was a funny thing for sick people to feel. Maybe it was a last stab at being human, because in our last hours we would only think of ourselves. In our very last hours when everything else had fallen away, we thought only of ourselves. The McMillan nurse in the hospice that Naani had been transferred to had told me that.

"Did you come by to talk to mum?" I said suddenly. "Is it that important?"

"I'm combining," he said. "I have to be in London for a few days, some inevitable medical appointments in Harley Street, and a coupla other things which I'll get to in a minute as they are related. Yes, I thought I'd come see you guys. Taking the chance that Ash wouldn't be here."

"I'm so glad you did---hang on what, what did you say?"

"Ash is pissed with me. Very very angry. From the moment I picked him up to the moment I dropped him off at the train station, he alternated between screaming at me and giving me the silent treatment. Ok I get it, he is furious that I won't go for new treatment, and he won't accept that it's my choice. Ok, it's a common reaction amongst friends and relatives, that's not what concerned me so much."

"He never said a word. He never even ---"

"I wanted to talk to Dolly about his, I guess you could call it disassociation. He's putting too much on himself and it's not healthy. And he won't accept my cancer, he won't allow it. It's feeding into his insatiable desire to be the best. Perfection doesn't allow failure, your own or anyone else's."

"Yeah, I think dad thinks so too."

"Right. In fact Vinod and I discussed this a while ago, but it was more of a general conversation, although I guess we both knew of the implications. I don't know if the cancer's given me some kind of far sight, but I see it, I hear it, I sense it completely in him now. He's really tensed up the whole time. He's acting. Underneath he's coiled up, stiff, and intense. I can see it. It's not healthy. There's a lack of joy. What once was a joyful thing to him, numbers, solutions, problems, they've become a sort of grindstone. I wanted to speak to Dolly about it."

I stared at Mitch. It was like he had X-Ray vision, and dad too, because all I saw was Ash just being his usual normal abnormal normal.

"What do you think we should do?"

"Nothing much. Just be aware of it. Make sure he sleeps."

"He's always drunk! Then he's up all night playing video games."

Mitch shrugged. "That's a kind of self medication, he's unconsciously trying to calm himself down. It's pretty common. Studying helps, it's a focus and I know he's studying. And there's a girl too?"

"Yeah."

"He said something odd about this. He said 'if I marry her which they all want, we can move on with our lives.'

"What is that supposed to mean?"

"I have no idea."

I could see Mitch's eyes drooping.

"Mitch, why don't you come through to the lounge and lie down for a bit? We don't have Sky Sport but the computers connected to the TV and you can watch something good on ----"

"I am so sorry about this."

"Why? What's there to be sorry about? You're just tired. I'll get the blanket from ---I'll get you the spare duvet. Go on."

"But you were going out?"

"No, it can wait. You better do as you're told Mitch."

"Oh yeah. I know how bossy you are missy."

I went upstairs and dumped the bag on my bed. I can't leave Mitch alone. He needs to sleep and recover his energy but I've got to be here when he wakes up. It reminded me of when I would take care of Naani. She liked to sleep all day and then she was up all night watching QVC and in the morning she thought mum was her mother and I was her school friend. It helped if one of us was there when she woke up, to ground her. Her delusions were nonsensical and sometimes we used to think she made them up but we were lucky, she never frightened us. She didn't outstay her welcome. She died before she got really bad and mum had said at the eulogy "my beloved mother never took up too much space in the world."

I smiled at the memory. I didn't want to think of her dowry wrapped up in a sweatshirt shoved inside the bag, but everything just became stuff in the end didn't it? Whether it was shoved in the garage or in a jewellers safe. I took the duvet and a pillow down to the lounge. Mitch was lying down on the sofa with his eyes closed and I tiptoed around him and draped the duvet over him. And then, for no reason I knew I put my hand on the top of his head. And I thought of you dad, lonely student in London waiting for your mothers letters. And I thought of how fragile and alone we humans were on this earth and the peace that came from the touch of another human being. And if it was the touch of a person who loved us, the peace increased immeasurably.

I could hear the clock ticking from the kitchen, the day was slipping away and I walked over to the chair and sat down. Mitch was sleeping deep. He'd be up soon, I knew. Chemo took it out of people and they often needed to sleep. Five of my school friends had parents who had suffered cancer and we had even had an assembly about it and we had had countless school sponsored runs and bake sales in partnership with Macmillan.

When he wakes up I could tell him I thought suddenly.

He was a pure scientist but he had first said the phrase "The unexamined life is not worth living" to me. Mitch had been in psychoanalysis for years back in the States and he wasn't fazed by emotions. I could tell Mitch everything. How it all happened and how it had gone out of my control and the straits I was in. What blessed relief it would be to unburden myself. And Mitch would understand, he'd sit and nod with his Stetson on, listening. I closed my eyes because I thought I was going to cry with the relief of it. I need to tell someone. I need to clean my soul. I can't go on with it otherwise. I don't even know what I'm doing. I can't do it; I can't sell Naani's jewellery and take the money to a pub for a blackmailer. I can do it physically, but can I do it?

I heard the key in the door and I got up quickly and mouthed hi to Princey, telling her Mitch was asleep.

It had been a nice dream. I couldn't tell him. I couldn't beg him for 7k. I couldn't tell anyone about pushing the body in the Brook, and those horrible pictures and the mess I was in. I had to go on with it alone.

"You ok?" she said. "You look tired, let me make you some of my special *kara*."

"Yes please Princey," I said and sat down at the breakfast bar, stroking the feather on the side of Mitch's Stetson.

There was something good about being *attended* to, looked after, taken care of, even if it was just a small cup of tea or a *kara*. The attention that someone took over it meant everything. It was glue to the bits of us that were coming unhinged. As she set about boiling up ginger and honey and cloves for a special warm tonic for me, I told her about Mitch. She nodded smartly, understanding everything and started to clear away the tea things. She could take it, she didn't frighten easily.

The information about Ash I kept back. What was the point of telling her such an abstract thing? Maybe Mitch was over reacting? If Ash had in fact gone there and shouted at him and given him the silent treatment it was because as Mitch concluded, he was sad about the cancer eating away Mitch's existence. I wasn't surprised that my brother had such an extreme reaction. Mitch was important to him. I wasn't sure if I trusted Mitch's diagnosis about Ash, because to me Ash was the same as he ever was. Happy go lucky. Above it all. Resilient.

Maybe Mitch was projecting his own over heightened emotions on to Ash? Maybe it was a guy thing, and boys related differently to men. I wasn't even sure what 'disassociation' even meant, some kind of ADHD, or autistic thing? But weren't all science-y boys a little bit like that? Someone had once told me that 80% of the boys at Oxford University were on the spectrum.

"Mr. Sahayle," Princey said. "Is he a bad person?"

I was surprised to hear her mention his name.

"I don't know. I don't know him. He's an...old student of dads. Why?"

"I have seen him in Church. But that doesn't mean anything."

"Your church? He goes there?"

Now I'd heard it all!

"He came there once. I only saw him once. He lit a candle for his mother. I know because he asked me how much the candles were and I had one spare and I gave it to him and he insisted I take the money. I told him don't be a silly boy."

"How long ago was this?"

"Maybe one year. He said he was going to Mexico, it was his dream and he wanted to say goodbye to her. She died when he was a baby and he couldn't remember her but he just wanted to get her blessing. He was going to start a new life. That's why I was so surprised to see him on the doorstep."

"Why did you ask if he was a bad man?"

"Because that other one is bad."

I looked at her inscrutable eyes. She had made the connection between Mortea'zar and Sahayle. Nothing much slipped Princey's gaze. She was tough as old boots. *Can I tell her?* Can I tell her everything and be rid of it? But I can't tell Princey. I just can't, it's crossing a line. I can't tell her about the photographs, I don't want her to think badly of mum. She'll judge her in the worst way, she won't be able to help it. And mum loves her so much, they have such an easy gossipy friendship. It'll ruin that.

Telling it won't help the situation. You have to get the money. The clock struck 4pm. It was too late today.

Mitch woke up and phoned for an Uber. He said he'd check in to his flat in Cavendish Street, which was close to Harley Street where he had an appointment at 8pm. I was surprised to hear that consultants saw patients that late but apparently private medicine was a world unto itself. His daughter who was an academic in Minnesota had taken out an extensive expensive private health plan for him five years ago when he had been fit as a fiddle going on weekly hikes around the Peak district.

On hearing his diagnosis she had sent him a Jewish healing prayer to read every day with a note "It's never too late to davven effectively." Mitch showed me the piece of paper with the prayer written on it. It was short. I suppose she knew Mitch wasn't the praying kind but if it was short he might do it.

"Do you do it Mitch?" I asked.

"I've gone over to the dark side," winked Mitch but I think he meant the private medicine, I couldn't be sure.

I waved goodbye as his car turned right. I watched the car drive away. I'll see you again, very soon I said out loud to someone or myself, perhaps some unnamed deities. You're not going to die yet. It's not your time yet. Ash isn't ready for you to die. You've got to stay alive until he's at Oxford or Princeton, till he's married, till he's had a family. And I knew in some way I was thinking of you too dad, about when you won't be with us anymore and about Naani who hadn't outstayed her welcome but we wished she had. These awful malingering thoughts of death, thoughts I had never dwelt on before.

Princey finished up and patted my shoulder and lolled her head and turned left to go to the bus stop. She wouldn't get home till late, as she had to get two buses. I stayed standing in the doorway looking out at the fading pale summer evening wishing I could press pause. Not a single sound could be heard.

It was the first Saturday evening I spent watching TV but I couldn't keep my mind involved. I kept getting up. Ash and mum wouldn't be home till late. The house was lustrous and I didn't want to disturb it. I went to bed. I closed my eyes. I've got to sleep. I thought I would dream of Mitch's kindly face or dad's gentle words, calming sweet dreams but all I dreamed were racing demonic questions, a furious torrent of organising and cataloguing whirring in my head.

I should just tell the police. But if Sahayle finds out he could release those photographs on the Internet; Mortea'zar definitely would. Even if I tell the police nothing will get solved and Ash might still get sent to prison, and maybe me as well. And there'll be scandal. Imagine the field day Mrs. Dhaliwal will have. But that man they'd arrested. I can't bear to think of him, I can't bear it. Jacek Wojcik. He's innocent and I know it. He's innocent and I'm letting him stay in police custody.

Abruptly I got up to go to the loo. I walked past Ash's room and I knew he wasn't there, still out. Sometimes at night when I went to the loo I heard the tiny tweets and pings of the video game he liked playing. And suddenly the thought of Ash not being in his bedroom next to mine was unbearable. I can't tell the police. I can't. I've just got to try again. I can't do it tomorrow. I'll have to do it on Monday.

Online on a tube map I obsessively read all the names of the stations trying to commit them to memory, as if I had to remember them for a test.

Kennington,

Oval,

Stockwell,

Clapham North,

Clapham Common,

Clapham South,

Balham,

Tooting Bec.

I felt unreasonably aggrieved: If I'd done an A level in Journey Finder I'd have got an A star. Ok, now stop it Shaani, that's enough revision and research. Go to sleep. Tomorrow be cool and enjoy the Havan. On Monday the reckoning. I'll have to do it early morning. And then go to meet Sahayle at 12pm in The Good Friend near Tavistock Square where there is some famous statue.

It's definitely not ideal but that's just how it is. That's what I've got to do. When I came out of the loo I heard the letterbox, but it didn't bother me. I knew it wasn't the police, because the police were going to be at the Havan tomorrow. I lay down. I've got to sleep. I've got to calm down. I've got to get through the Havan lunch tomorrow.

Go to sleep my little angel, go to sleep I crooned to myself, but my voice wasn't a patch on mum's.

As soon as I closed my eyes pictures of a man came into view. A man they were beating up in the interrogation room. A man whose family was back in Poland. A man behind bars shouting I'm innocent. A man shouting for help but the warden ignored his pleas. *Shut up you slag. Eastern*

European scum. Undercutting British workers. Anything could happen to him in there. What if he killed himself? I opened my eyes. What do I care? He's a low life scum. That's what Mrs. Dhaliwal says but what does she know? She probably gets her information from the Daily Mail.

But Wojcik is a criminal; she got that from the police. Even if he didn't kill Max, he's probably killed plenty. But I couldn't shake the image. They've arrested him for something he definitely didn't do, and I know he didn't do it. He probably has a family. It's not right Shaani what you're doing. Withholding information that would free him. Something about it made me sick in my stomach. It's the sort of thing you'd never be able to forget. It would haunt you forever. Whatever else I had done that was wrong or illegal, to let an innocent man take the blame for something I know he didn't do was just another level of wrong.

I'll have to tell the policeman tomorrow. No I'll tell him on Monday. I've got to get the money and pay Sahayle off first. If it all comes out I can't have those photographs mixed up in it. I don't want to think of them. It makes me think differently about mum and I don't want to think of her like that. *It makes me think differently about her.* And this frightens me. If I keep thinking differently about her then I'll lose respect for her and if I lose respect for her I won't care about her and then. And then nothing much will matter. I can't. I've got to erase them forever.

Something deep inside me was looking forward to this Havan. Perhaps on some level I thought if they could clean the flat of evil spirits, maybe I could piggyback on it, and get some spiritual cleaning of my own conscience. I knew it wasn't that simple. But wasn't religious ritual exactly that? A comfort. A sense of order. A breathing space. Reassurance. But the Prayers for Healing probably went First Class straight to the top floor while the Prayers for your Conscience, they were like envelopes without a stamp, that even if they reached their destination, would arrive torn and tattered and illegible. Those Prayers probably went right to the basement into the slush pile.

Could it make a difference if an array of gods and goddesses were actually looking down on you? Perhaps they could show mercy. Maybe they could change things, the way the Greek Gods and Goddesses did? Maybe things only went wrong in the world because the Gods and Goddesses weren't paying attention, pre-occupied with other distractions, busy enjoying themselves but maybe when we prayed hard it poked them, reminded them we were down here and in a mess and in need of their help.

And the other reason for looking forward to the Havan was that Ash was right we don't have fun and it'll be nice to be around people who have fun all the time, more normal. We are a normal family and we should be like other normal families. Noise and food and music and conviviality and religion and community and gossip and nothing serious. A normal life. Great. How normal could we be? Dad's away on a wild goose chase, mum had an affair with a low life and sent him porn, Ash killed him by mistake and I disposed of the body!

It was laughable. How idiotic and ludicrous it all was! I just want tomorrow to come and I want to have this lovely day with the Dhaliwals I thought bitterly. Something's going to happen and we'll never have another day like it. Maybe something will happen to me. The thought, abstract as it was came like a cloud that covered over a sunny day. I'll tell the policeman everything. I've got to take responsibility for what I did. I think Ash's too young for them to put him in prison. But whatever happens, let's have tomorrow, let's just have fun and be a happy family. Let the Gods look benevolently on us and let us be cleansed of evil spirits.

Just for a day at least.

Chapter 20

Accordion Mansions had a doorman and original paintings in the lobby. The lift flew us up so fast we gasped. Mum took both our hands for a second and then let us go. She looked amazing in a white and pink silk shalwar khamees and a golden dupatta. It was one of her special outfits that were always kept carefully ironed in the suitcase. A waitress in black and white opened the door. The flat was large and sunny with high white walls. In the through lounge were three large butter leather sofas, sumptuous sheepskin rugs on the polished floorboards and white units with large white bowls on them. It smelled heavenly.

"Welcome, welcome to our humble abode," said Mrs. Dhaliwal shimmering in a diaphanous yellow sari and a bold contrasting red blouse, her diamond bracelets blinding us as she raised her arms in greeting.

"Who says 'humble abode???'" said Ash under his breath and I supressed a snort of laughter.

"Meenakshi you look adorable! And you drove back from Birmingham this morning? What's your beauty secret? I want his number and price list!"

Dolly giggled.

"Dolly, please," she said and gave Liar Dhaliwal a big hug.

From stab-in-the-dark speculation "something's going on there," mum had somehow seamlessly crossed over to future Mother In Law status, a leap as incredible as a reality star morphing into world leader. She thought she wasn't any good at cultivating people like Ash was, but it wasn't true; she was a natural.

The flat seemed to go forward and disappear into the sky because the door to the balcony was wide open. The balcony with the glass roof where Mrs. Dhaliwal had gone on that terrible day that was night. A part of me was desperate to go out there and see what she had seen, but I couldn't bring myself to do it. I was frightened. What if I give myself away? I don't want to stand where she stood. I don't want to *see* the Brook. I don't want to see it ever again.

"Shaani, manners!" said mum. "Don't stuff those samosas in your mouth like they're going out of fashion. You've had two already! That's not like her at all, she must have skipped breakfast! I'm so sorry Sharmilla."

"They work them off, don't worry," said Mrs. Dhaliwal. "They eat like horses and they don't put on an ounce. Mine are just the same. She has a healthy appetite, it's a good thing."

I stared at Mrs. Dhaliwal and painted on a fake smile, which was difficult with a mouthful of food. It was all bullshit. Anyone who ate *food* was an illegal immigrant who should be deported as far as Mrs. Dhaliwal was concerned. Scum in other words. The entire family as Ash had said were very skinny, and that wasn't genetic. Regular operations in Swiss Clinics were performed on them, blood transfused, stomachs tied, fat sucked out, faces lifted, eyelids undrooped. Regular columns in the Asian Age were devoted to them. They had a chef who cooked all their meals and Mrs. Dhaliwal *socialite extraordinaire* counted every calorie and fat unit and famously, chopped an almond in half for a guilty pleasure. They were strangers to carbs. No wonder mum had bonded with Mrs. Dhaliwal immediately. They'd have great times going out to dinner eating fresh air off of silver platters.

It was a fairly intimate gathering. Us three, Mr. and Mrs. Dhaliwal, Giselle, Nilesh, a little boy of ten or eleven, two elderly people and a man in a suit who all seemed to be something to do with Mr. Dhaliwal, possibly clients. According to Mrs. Dhaliwal the policeman wasn't sure if he was coming. The priest was wearing a suit but he had religious white and orange daubs on his forehead. He was standing by the altar checking all the bits and pieces. Thick bunches of tiny white jasmine flowers were set in a bowl. The auspicious fire had already been started and the flat smelled vaguely of sandalwood and other spices.

I sat down on one of the sofas feeling relaxed and happy. It was a purpose built apartment, with everything sleek and modern and the smell of new. Nilesh sat down next to me and started telling me about his travels. Mum and Mrs. Dhaliwal and Mr were standing to the side chattering away. Giselle and Ash were out on the balcony and the little kid was running about but not annoyingly.

My eye became drawn to the only painting in the room. It was strange. A beautiful woman with black hair wrapped in flowers but her body was not a body. It was a system of grotesque splints and metal bars and bandages. The more I looked at it, the sadder I felt. And yet there was something in the woman's face that made me question my sadness. Her face was proud and her eyes were like a tiger, burning bright.

Nilesh had an easy manner about him and I nodded as he talked about the painting, how a big art dealer had urged them to buy it, but none of them liked it, it was too depressing. The problem was they couldn't leave it in the flat when it was rented out because it was too valuable and his mum didn't want it and so they were trying to sell it on but the price had gone down and so it had become a millstone around their neck like the brace around the woman's body. Nilesh laughed and apologised for the First World Problems of the Dhaliwals. I kept staring at the woman in the painting and she seemed to hold deep unimaginable secrets. All this carnage in her body, yet there was such hope and defiance in her eyes, the human spirit survived. There was something impossible about it. And yet. The unimaginable was possible.

I supposed I should go out to the balcony and verify what Mrs. Dhaliwal might have seen…but it was so pleasant listening to Nilesh's friendly easy voice chattering next to me, and the yelps of the little kid who was some sort of musical prodigy. He told me what his little brother's name was but I'd forgotten and it didn't matter. The smoke from the Havan filled the room and my senses. I could easily stretch out and go to sleep like a cat. It was such a lovely atmosphere. Peaceful, with Nilesh's voice like a soft crackling fire to the side of me. He was the sort of boy I could marry one day. Kind, well bought up, decent. He was the sort of boy I would marry one day.

When I went to the kitchen mum accosted me. She had a glass of wine in her hand which I thought wasn't allowed at religious events but it seemed that Mr. and Mrs. Dhaliwal weren't all that religious yet like a lot of people insisted on going through the rituals like the purification of a house because…I really didn't *know* why, just that most of the people we knew did it. Maybe they thought that if they did it, and donated large amounts to the temple, all their sins would be forgiven and then they could carry on committing them. But I couldn't bring myself to be angry with Mrs. Dhaliwal that afternoon for being a liar, because something in the atmosphere of that flat was so comforting and important.

Giselle and Ash said they were going out. Just as they were leaving, the policeman arrived.

"Sorry I'm late," he said to Mrs. Dhaliwal who waved away his apology with "What can I get you Gary? You're not on duty now."

"Orange juice if you have it."

"Oh," she said disappointed and looked at mum who raised her glass demurely.

Please don't flirt with him mum, I thought. She had had two large glasses already.

"Good job I'm driving," I said cheerfully to the policeman.

"You're Shaani, is that right? Lovely name," said the policeman. "Sharmilla told me you've taken a year out. My daughter's thinking about doing the same."

"They're all at it these days," said Mrs. Dhaliwal bringing him the OJ. "I don't see the point."

"Well, they want to have a breathing space before getting on the treadmill. I'm not against it, but."

"But *you* have to pay for it," said Mrs. Dhaliwal.

I could see mum enjoying Mrs. Dhaliwals slightly inappropriate behaviour. It was always enjoyable to see super rich Indian people still trying to save pennies; it gave you a sense of democracy. You could scorn them as well as admire them.

"What was your reason dear?" asked Mrs. Dhaliwal and the policeman smiled and sipped his juice.

I had my answer down pat because every single one of my parents' friends had demanded it. Taking a gap year was still considered an expensive and pointless waste of time in the Indian community, in other words "what white people did."

"I wasn't sure if I really wanted to go to uni because I didn't want to be in debt and I wasn't sure of what job I wanted to do and if the degree would help and I didn't know if I could do the work and pass exams," I trotted out the list. "All the advice you get, it can get confusing."

"It's hard being a teenager," said Mrs. Dhaliwal. "They don't have the full toolkit. They're always so incredulous aren't

205

they? It's *shut up* to everything. They can't cope with real life."

"You don't know anything about the world, that's the thing. You only find out once you're married with kids." added mum.

OMG could you all be more patronising? Especially given how mum had grown up, and yet she had reinvented herself for the Dhaliwals and perhaps for the world.

What I wanted to say was, it's *none of your business.* The truth was I had known exactly the degree I wanted to do, at which university and for what reason, but I had made the decision to stay at home while dad was in India but people understood the flakylazyteenager model better. For some reason people thought a 19 year old couldn't take decisions, when it seemed to me that was the one time you were free to make decisions for the purest of reasons, because you weren't bogged down with a mortgage and a job and kids, regret and loss and failure.

The policeman nodded. "Yes my daughter says the same thing. It's such a shame. When I was at uni it was a very different idea. There were grants for one thing."

Both mum and Mrs Dhaliwal looked at him with admiration. A policeman and educated.

"Did you always want to be in the police?" said mum getting in on the act.

I was itching to slip away but I was trapped in the circle of adoration.

"No. I started off thinking I'd be an architect. I loved if you can believe it, town planning. The way cities are organised."

"Ohhh," said Mrs Dhaliwal.

"Wow," said mum.

She just embellishes everything, I thought. She told us he was a lawyer before he became a policeman.

"I didn't have the temperament for being an architect. So I had to find another vocation."

"What d'you mean the temperament?" said Pathological Liar Dhaliwal

"I think I was lacking. The creative gene. The thinking out of the box. I preferred order."

"And the police work offered you that?"

"Yes. Police work is about systems and procedures."

"Oh," said Mrs. Dhaliwal. "Yes. Inspector Morse and Midsomer Murders, they're not realistic, that's why I prefer CSI."

"Well Sharmilla, *they* always catch their criminal. And that doesn't always happen in real life. Most crimes aren't the evil work of a Moriarty. They're bungles and muddles."

"Bungles and muddles!" shrieked Mrs. Dhaliwal clapping her hands but only the finger tips. "I love those words, they're so English! So there are lots of unsolved crimes then?"

I could see a kind of envy creep into mum's face. Mrs. Dhaliwal had the self-confidence of Fuck you Avenue.

"Many. Even in CSI," he smiled.

"So tell me this," said the unstoppable Mrs. Dhaliwal. "What have you learned from being in the police force? Aside from that anyone is capable of anything."

"That's easy. Murders are usually committed by a friend or a spouse"

"Oh," said mum putting her hand over her mouth.

"So this man …Wojcik, was he a friend of the murdered man, found in Woodside Park?" said Mrs. Dhaliwal with glee, clearly delighted at having "trapped" the policeman into talking about the case.

"As I said, it's often what happens," said the policeman.

The women waited but he had nothing more to say so they moved away. I was about to move away too but he said, "I wonder if I could ask you something Shaani?"

My heart started to beat faster.

"I don't want Chloe to just laze around, I want her to use the time constructively but it's impossible to tell her what to do. Being a weekend dad and all. Any tips?" he smiled.

"Well…" I said "It is good to have a plan on your year out"

"Did you have a plan?"

What did he mean by that? A plan? Was it a trick?

"What do you mean?"

"Your plan for your year out"

"Oh yes so. So I decided that I'd make a solid structure for myself. You know, waking up at the same time every day, going for a swim, and my chores and then the gym and Tai Kwan Do twice a week."

"Excellent," said the policeman. "I should join a gym myself. I should practice what I preach. Are Virgin any good?"

"I'm with Barnet Community Leisure Centre"

"I like to do weights mainly. Do they have good weights there?"

"Not bad."

"What about Pumping Iron? Have you been there?"

"Yeah once, but it's not really my kind of place."

"Right," said the policeman and turned his attention to the view from the balcony.

He knows I went there to meet Max and he wants to know why.

Chapter 21

Mum was honking with laughter and clapping her hands at the tips. Our kitchen table had a gingham tablecloth on it, serviettes, placemats and a basket of croissant and pain de chocolat as well as a cafetiere of coffee. She had folded the serviettes in thirds just as they had done at Mrs. Dhaliwals. Who for? There were only two of them.

"What's all this?" I said hitching the strap of my swim bag over my shoulder.

"Mum's gloating," said Ash and bit into a croissant, his bathrobe open, his long legs sprawled out.

"Like the table Shaani? I don't know why we don't always set the table nicely. Do you want to go shopping? We can go to Brent Cross for your chair?"

"I've got things today."

"What things?" said Ash.

"Those ones that are none of your business. Gloating about what?"

"Yesterday. Mrs. Dhaliwal and her perfect Havan. Degenerating into farce."

"What?"

"The priest. He scarpered. Didn't you notice the purification process was not concluded? Now they've got to live in a filthy Godless flat like the rest of us."

Mum started clapping her hands at the fingertips and laughing. Ash shook his head with a big grin on his face. "She loves it. She loves it. She's like a chimpanzee."

"Ashi, don't be mean to me!" said mum.

"Why did the priest…?"

"Giselle thinks he's an illegal or he's on a false passport. Whatever, he changed colour soon as he realised it was Old Bill. He didn't even pick up his payment! Anyway, it was all Very Embarrassing for Ma Dhaliwal and now she's under mum's obligation or whatever."

"No, no Ash. I'm not like that," crowed mum.

"You're exactly like that," said Ash. "You know what was really funny? We were out when it all kicked off. So she emojis Giselle right? And Giselle is like, mum that does not mean we are 'praying,' that means high five!"

Mum snorted with helpless laughter. "Oh that Sharmilla, she's so not down with the youth."

"What have you got in that bag?" said Ash.

"And where are you going all of a sudden in such a hurry?" said mum.

"Mitch came yesterday. To the house. Looking for you. You haven't answered any of his calls. Because he has cancer!"

"No, no that's not true!" said mum. "I've lost my phone!"

Ash looked up.

"And you haven't answered his calls either. Because he has. Cancer!"

I felt furious. It was nothing to do with Mitch. It was all the lies.

"No no, that's not..." said mum waving her hand.

"It's true in my case. But not because I'm frightened. Because I'm disgusted by his cowardice," said Ash. "I'm not talking to him. Serves him right."

"You're crazy," I said. "Which by the way is what he thinks too!"

"What's that supposed to mean?"

"It's my phone Shaani, I can't find it anywhere," wailed mum but neither of us were listening to her.

"He thinks you're off your head and he wanted to talk to mum about it."

"To me?" said mum with surprise.

"Why didn't you tell me he was here? He must be at the Cavendish Road flat. I'll go see him. I can't keep up the silent treatment, it's boring and it's not working. I'll try another tactic. Brute force! Animal aggression. I'll just pick him up and drag him to Chemo, I can totally do it. You should have told me sis. He looks like shit doesn't he?"

"I didn't want to spoil the Havan," I said quietly and Ash nodded.

Then he said, "Didn't need any help from you! Ma Dhaliwal's got a lot of grovelling and face saving to do now. Imagine if the reporters of the Asian Age get hold of that. Asian billionaires employing illegals. Bloody Asians! Always after a discount."

"But they're your future in laws!" said mum. "We couldn't do that, even if we secretly wanted to."

"You should leak it mum," said Ash and started giggling.

I shook my head. "You're both out of your minds."

"Ohhhhh," said Ash and Mum together.

"We just want to know what you're doing and where you're going and who you're meeting. That's all."

"That's all," sang Ash.

"Seriously, stay with us today. We're feeling…triumphant. The Triumph of the Devs!" said Mum and then. "I know it isn't a competition. I know that other peoples misfortunes doesn't…"

"Oh yes it is!" said Ash as if he was at a panto. "Success is not enough. Others must fail."

"Shut up Ashi. Is it awful of me Shaani?"

"I've got to go."

"What's the matter with you? Got your period or something?" said Ash. "You're in a trance."

"Shut up Ash. Don't be such a sexist."

Tell them! They're both here, they're happy, tell them. We can all sit around the table and work out what to do together. You won't have to handle it alone. Do it, say it now, this is your very last chance. But I couldn't speak. I just couldn't do it. I didn't even know why anymore. I couldn't say the words. In some weird way I had *groomed* myself into the situation of secrecy. If I didn't tell anyone, then there was a small possibility that once I'd finished it, paid him off, got the photographs deleted, that it had never happened. But Max was still dead and I had put his body in the Brook and the wrong man had still been arrested. What could I do about that? All I knew was I was taking Naani's jewellery to sell it and to give the money to Sahayle.

"What a diva!" said Ash turning his attention to his phone. "I'm calling Mitch."

"Go, then, go!" said mum flicking her hand at me. "Leave us all to ourselves. Go!"

The two of them grinning from ear to ear like cats with cream around their mouths.

I can't crow about the priest running away and spoiling Mrs. Dhaliwals Havan. I haven't got the headspace to. I don't even want to think about that Havan. I know that policeman trapped me, he tricked me. He knows I've been to Pumping Iron. Well if he knows and he suspects me, why doesn't he haul me in for questioning? He was at a party. At a religious party. He's not supposed to be working. But everyone knows policemen are always working. Does he think I killed

Max? I just can't *think* about it now. I've got to get the money and get to Tavistock Square.

I got out at Tooting Broadway and turned left. I couldn't believe it! There was a long line outside Cash Convertors and I thought about how much I would actually get for an old kindle and an ipad. Not much, move on, you can't be late. It was already almost 10.30am. Surely the jewellery would reap me enough. Maybe if I got 4k it would be enough? He might let me off the rest; he'd already paid 500 to help me out. No time to get comparison quotes. Just go to the first one that looks ok. I walked along the street and passed one jeweller, it looked too small, then another, it looked too big. And then, Vinod Jewellers. That's Dad's name, I don't want to go there. That's superstitious, don't be silly, just go in.

I pushed open the door of Vinod Jewellers and saw a hundred un-nerving images of myself in the floor to ceiling mirrors reflecting each other. Two men sat behind the counter. I imagined hills of money piled up in the rooms in the back.

"I want to sell some jewellery. Please?"

"Ok, come through dear," said the man and I went through the shop into a small back room. "I'll just get my eye glass."

There was a small table with a folded red cloth on it. I sat down and took out the jewellery and put it on the cloth. He came back and sat down.

"Why are you selling this?" he asked casually picking up the necklaces.

"I need the money, I mean my mum she needs the money. For my sisters wedding. My dad can't get enough loan from the bank."

The man lolled his head.

"I understand the situation," he said.

He unfolded the red cloth and rolled the stuff around on it. It shone in the light and was heavy. I didn't have any feelings about it now, I just wanted the money. I felt good, as though I was almost at the finish line. Well, at least half way through the race. Then he picked up one of the necklaces and frowned.

"But this is a mangal sutra."

I sneaked a look at the clock on the wall above his head. It had been 10 minutes but I felt I'd been there at least an hour. I was sweating. It's just one lie on top of another...

"What sort of woman would sell her mangal sutra?"

I looked at him in confusion.

He leaned forward. "Are you sure your mother sent you?"

"Yes."

"I am very sure your father does not know about it."

"Why, what's the problem?"

"Are you Indian?"

"Well British Asian but—ok yes, I'm Indian. Of course," I said.

"Don't you know a mangal sutra is a woman's bond of marriage? It is given to her by her husband and she must wear it always. It's the equivalent of a wedding ring. What sort of an Indian are you, if you don't know that?"

I looked at him helplessly. Naani hadn't worn it for always. Naani hadn't worn any of her wedding jewellery, ever, even once she had lost her marbles. She had bundled it all up in a bag and forgotten it. And mum had worn no such thing that I could remember…A mangal what now?

"Well, she must be some sort of twisted individual to sell this. I will not take a woman's mangal sutra. It's bad luck. She may as well break her bangles in front of me. No baaba, no thank you."

"But…"

He brought his hand down on the table.

"No," he said. "Not that one," and pushed the thin necklace towards me.

It was black beads and a few gold beads anyway so I thought ok. As for mum breaking her bangles in front of him…I had seen this exact scene in a Bollywood film where the wife is so grief stricken at her husband's death, she smashes her glass bangles on the sink and ends up bleeding to death i.e. her husband was dead and therefore so she may as well be. The good wife is a dead wife. What was it supposed to mean all this self-sacrifice? Here we were in today's London, but I'd walked into some other time and space. Some other century.

"What about the rest?" I became completely business-like in that small room. I had no time to argue the odds or feel bad.

"And she wants to sell this lot for a wedding of your sister. Because daddy can't get enough of a loan from the bank?"

"Yes uncle," I said lowering my eyes.

I wanted to say "FFS why is it any of your business, just give me the money," but I sensed there was Indian code you had to adhere to so I just kept looking at the cloth, hanging my head in shame. Shame was hard currency with Indians. Like bitcoins the system was peer to peer and transactions took place between users directly without an intermediary.

He took out the eyeglass. "Alright dear, I can give you five hundred pounds, possibly £550."

"What? But it's not enough."

"Not enough, not enough? But did your mother think she can *fullee* finance a wedding with these few jewels? It is a wedding in a village in India yes, not in the Yookay?"

"It's just not enough."

I knew I sounded desperate. It hadn't occurred to me that the value would be so small. It was gold after all, didn't that count for anything? Wasn't it…. antique or something?

"It's gold uncle," I said.

He shrugged. "Indian gold. Third class stuff. There is always *millavat*. Every time they boil it down, they add metal. Same as they do to milk, they add water. And this one, from long ago, even more millavat, mixing you see? No standardisation in those days. Half of it is metal."

"Are you sure?"

He sat back in his chair and eyed me like a lizard.

"£550 is a lot of money. Take it or leave it," he said moving his index finger like a metronome.

"Alright. I'll take it," I said feeling miserable.

I took it. I felt wretched. It's gone, those links are gone. If it was a Bollywood movie she'd be saying I'll get them back for you one day Naani, I'll get them back for you mum, may God strike me down if I don't! But I knew I wouldn't, I knew I couldn't. With the £500 I had in my hand and the £550, it was £1050. Couldn't that be a good enough deposit? What if Sahayle won't accept it? He has to accept it. I can't get any more. I haven't got time to queue up at Cash Convertors to sell the kindle and ipad, which will get me nothing anyway.

I could see them all, the judge and jury, my grandparents, my mother, my father, Mrs. Dhaliwal, Mr. Patel the pharmacist, Mr. Popat the dentist, even that phoney priest at the Havan...their heads looking down at me from the clouds, shaking their heads

My heart started hammering. I've sold Naani's jewellery. She never wore it and mum never wore it and it was ugly, but it was still Naani's wedding jewellery. Mum had kept it. It was a link to her family, her past. Now it's going to be melted down to make earrings for some silly girl in Southall. What if you've done entirely the wrong thing? What if it's all a mistake? What if a policeman catches you and demands to know where you got this money?

I stopped by the side of a shop and tightened my grip on the handle of the plastic bag. I regulated my breathing and forced myself to watch the street and the world go by. The money was in wads secured with a rubber band. I hadn't counted it after seeing him count it out, so professional so slick, I remembered his practised hand laying out the used notes on the red cloth. Then he had put them in a brown paper bag, patted it and given it to me to put into my swim bag. He had taken out a Tesco plastic bag and told me to put my swim bag in it. Thieves don't think about stealing a plastic bag. Thieves I said? Bag snatchers, pick pockets, you've got to be careful. And this area, everyone knows Indian ladies are walking about with cash and jewellery in their handbags. I tell them, but they don't listen.

"You'll be all right dear," he had said with a kind smile.

It occurred to me that he had concluded we were poor and had to hock the family jewels to pay for the wedding and suddenly he had felt sorry for us, for me. When I'd walked in he might have thought I was a thief or a careless girl out to get some money for kicks but he had changed his opinion about me and now he felt sorry for me and I was grateful for his pity because I pitied myself.

"Now hurry home to your mum. I'm sorry I could not give you more. Gold is low. Be careful of danger. My best wishes to your family. August is an auspicious month."

I lifted the Tesco bag up and down like a weight and stared across at the unknown street. It was full of Asians. Different from Queensbury. There were Sikhs here, Hindus, Muslims, Christians, all sorts I thought dully. Any of them could mug me or stab me or shoot me. What did it matter? To English people we were all the same. It would be called a brown on brown killing. It was only £1050. Yet it had cost me so much. There was no danger here in this street of strangers. The danger was all in the pub where I was to meet Sahayle.

Chapter 22

In Tooting Broadway it was summer and 25minutes later when I came out at Euston station it was autumn. The wind was chilly and the clouds dark and threatening. I hopped on a bus and it dropped me at Tavistock Square. A group of people were putting flowers at the foot of a statue of a bald man and it made me think of you dad, not because you're bald but because for some reason it reassured me. I realised suddenly it was a statue of Mahatma Gandhi. Everything is going to be fine, I told myself.

I found the pub The Good Friend easily. The doors were really beautiful with the glass etched in a lovely pattern and the dark wood gleaming and the handles polished brass. I pushed the door open and the smell of darkness engulfed me. It was the smell of old beer but I wasn't familiar with the smell and I thought it was the smell of darkness.

Sahayle was standing at the bar. He was wearing a long coat. It was smooth and shone dully at the creases like the sleek fur on a cat. It covered most of him and I noticed again how very straight and tall he stood. His hair was tidy and combed neatly. He was reading The Mirror folded to the sports page. On the bar was a tall glass of pale liquid, barely touched.

"Hello," he said and his low melodic voice seemed to tone with the place as though he and the low lights and the warm glow of the wooden tables and the fetid smell of darkness which had already faded into a warm fug of smells, were part of a great painting or a city, for it felt very much to me like a city in there, a foreign place I was entering for the first time.

"Hello," I said.

"Thank you for coming here. I think you'll be more comfortable in a private room. I'll take you there, don't worry."

It seemed ludicrous but he reminded me of a doctor who had come to visit Naani at the house in Chesham, the same kind low tone of voice, the same slow delivery. If he hadn't been a blackmailer I might have thought I can trust you, you're good. But perhaps like Mitch, I was projecting my own anxieties and solving them by making Sahayle kind. I realised with a jolt that the pub was actually quite full.

I saw hunched figures in booths and snugs, sitting with glasses, murmuring, a steady chatter, teeth flashing, a tinkling of laughter and a sweep of sunshine passing over them from the windows from time to time as if the Earth itself was being swept by golden dust. I could hear the murmurs and yet everyone in that pub seemed to freeze into still figures. The walls were made of wood panels, same as the floor and the tables and booths. They were darkest honey.

I followed Sahayle as he walked through the pub, which was far bigger than I had realised. We walked past the booths into the back room where there were three round tables laid with napkins and tarnished cutlery, opaque etched glass lights hanging above them making circles of yellow light. Even though it was daylight outside, it was night in this room of no windows but a night that would yield conviviality and laughter.

And through there I followed him to a door that he opened easily and led me up a narrow flight of steep old wooden stairs, and then into a small room with a table and a painting on the wall. There were just two straight back chairs at the table and a large leather armchair in the corner. Something panicked inside me. I was in a private drawing room with a stranger and £1050 in a Tesco bag.

"The pub's an old inn. Built in the 19th century," he said and pointed to the wall that was panelled in dark blood red wood. "It hasn't changed since then."

I stood by the door.

"It's all right," he said. "Come and sit down. I thought you'd be more comfortable here, you looked so scared when you walked in that I felt sorry I'd asked you to come here at all."

"Why do you keep saying I'll be more comfortable?" I said. "How can I be?" I was still standing.

He frowned and again made that gesture of raising his arm and ushering me towards the seat, without touching or forcing me in any way. It was in a sense the gesture of a gentleman. Which was ridiculous because Sahayle wasn't a gentleman, he was a blackmailer and God knows what else. I didn't really know him at all. I remembered how he had felt offended when I said I had to text mum because she would be worried about me.

I sat down. He sat down in the other chair at an angle to me. He crossed his legs, and his coat that wasn't buttoned fell to the sides and swept the floor. I stared at him feeling the ground like the sand on Margate beach receding and leaving stumps under my bare feet. He was a blackmailer. He could have been a murderer. He was capable of anything. I could be found dead. My breathing was too fast and I tried my best to control it.

There was no window in that room, just a small central light but the shade was old glass like the etchings on the front doors and the light somehow smudged everything as though we were ourselves tiny figures in some old painting. Sahayle was looking at his feet, frowning as though he was trying to think of something or work something out.

"I've got the money here. I mean I haven't got it all. I've just. It's all I could get," I started talking quickly because I wanted to get out and away. I wanted to finish it, finish it now!

His head cocked up sharply, and his eyes narrowed.

"What do you mean you haven't got it all? How much have you brought?"

"One thousand and fifty. It's all I could get honestly. I haven't got a penny more, can you take it as a deposit?"

I couldn't read the expression in his eyes; it seemed to go through a process, changing like light. I thought at first he was going to laugh in my face and then get angry and shake me and I suppose I had subconsciously steeled myself for these eventualities, but he remained still. His eyes seemed to flicker and glow like embers in a dying fireplace. For some time he didn't say anything, then he closed his eyes and opened them again and I realised I had been holding my breath. Maybe, perhaps, he would say don't worry about it, yes it will do, it's enough. I'm sorry you had to sell your grandmother's jewellery. Mad thoughts dashed across my mind then.

"Would you like a drink?" he said.

"No of course not."

"Have a drink. Have a drink with me. It'll calm you down."

"I don't drink alcohol. Please I'd like to go home. I can't take it. I've had to do this terrible thing, and now I've come here and now you're asking me if I want a drink as though it's just a normal situation. I hate you! Because of you I had to sell my granny's wedding jewellery and when mum finds out she'll never forgive me. I hate you, I hate you, I hate you."

I stopped, shocked at myself. I couldn't help it, I didn't care. I had never been to a pub before, not without my parents. Every other 19year old in the world had been to a pub but I hadn't! It wasn't my world. I knew my world was changed, something awful had happened when I'd seen those pictures of mum and something awful had happened when I'd handed over Naani's jewellery. The very architecture of who I was had become dismantled. The mangal sutra, a thin unimpressive two-strand necklace with black and gold beads was still in my bag. I wasn't calm. Something had happened to me and I didn't know the name of it, only that like Dorothy, I wasn't in Kansas anymore. I was inside the tornado.

He nodded and he looked down at his feet again. His shoes were black leather and shone with pride.

"Have a shandygaff. Or a largertop. It's not hard liquor. It'll relax you."

"Ok, I don't even know what that is!"

He smiled. "A shandygaff is just the word they gave to a shandy in the 19th century. It's what you'll know as a shandy."

"Is that meant to be a joke?"

He looked hurt.

"No. I just thought it would make you more comfortable."

"Why d'you keep saying you want me to be comfortable? What d'you want to do to me?"

"Keep your voice down," he said and suddenly the blackmailer, the sinister dark stranger was there again. Menace. Invading our house. Trampling on the mat that Princey had recently brushed and cleaned so meticulously. How dare he come and smash our lives like that? I clenched the plastic bag handles.

He leaned forward and put his hand on the table next to me

"You see, it's not enough," he said gently as though he was explaining something to a small child.

"But it's something. Can't it be a deposit?"

"Mortea'zar doesn't work like that. Debts don't work that way. Not in this line of business."

"What line of business?"

He shrugged. "Best you don't know."

"Why is it best I don't know?"

He began inspecting the floor again. Then he lifted his head and looked at me with an expression of pity, the sort of pity that wasn't about feeling sorry for five minutes for a homeless person, but compassion, deep felt compassion. It sounds phoney written down but I felt it. It was a ray of light upon my face.

"You're a good girl. I can see that. You shouldn't have to be doing all this. I'm sorry about it, I truly am."

"Can't you tell your boss to accept it and stop bothering us? Please. You said he doesn't even need the money. And he could pay you anyway couldn't he? Please. He owes you. And you could go abroad, like you want to? Couldn't you? You could."

I was close to tears. Something in his intense gaze had undone me and all I had left in my arsenal was to beg and plead and lay myself down to his mercy. He was the only person in the world who I could ask to help me, and he was looking at me with so much benevolence, kindness. It felt so strange as if we were in another dimension.

"You see it's not that simple. It's true that Mortea'zar has plenty of money, but Max owed him that money and he's mad as hell at not getting it back with interest. He wants it, he doesn't care how he gets it."

At that moment the door opened. Sahayle looked up sharply.

"Hello Ruairi," he said. "Yes thank you. My friend here will have a half of shandy. Yes?"

I nodded. After all I didn't have to drink it. And with the entrance of the barman I knew without being told that whatever was going on, whatever transaction there was going to be between Sahayle and I, to the barman we had to present a united front. This pub, this room, it was used by him and his associates and everyone was watching him, just like any neighbourhood. Instead of twitching curtains and aunties telling aunties, there were flashes of an eye, conduct was noted, deals recorded. All this I don't know how, but I knew *automatically.* Whatever transaction there was going to be. Maybe I've misjudged the entire thing. Maybe he's going to do something here, with the door closed and downstairs no one will have seen or heard a thing. Is that how it happens? They always say it isn't a man who jumps out from behind a bush, it's someone you know.....

"And a packet of crisps please Ruairi. What flavour do you like?"

"Cheese and Onion. Are they Walkers?" I said automatically excited. "Yes please!"

Ours was a low carb household, especially white carbs, but who could say no to Walkers cheese and onion crisps? Mum's weakness, she wouldn't have them in the house and even forbade me and Ash to eat them in the car because she knew she'd smell them and want them and gorge on them.

The last things on my mind were crisps and yet I blurted it out. It was familiar, it was normal, it was home and the car.

"Two cheese and onion please Ruairi. And why not bring us a cheese sandwich as well? Toast it."

I opened my mouth to say no, but I supposed he had to order something because he had the use of the room. What was he planning to do to me in here?

"I'll have a lemonade without ice," he said.

"The usual," said Ruairi and smiled at us. "Just let me know if you want any lunch itself Vic. There's a beautiful gammon pie today. I wouldn't offer it, of course I wouldn't. Ah but you don't know what yer missing, the gammon is sweeter than."

Ruairi left the room.

"What's wrong with pie?" I said.

"Nothing. It's the pork. I don't eat it, it's not clean."

"What, are you Jewish?"

"I don't eat it as a sign of respect to Him who bought me up. It's *haram*. These things are important to him."

So Mortea'zar was a Muslim and Sahayle was born a Christian, but he followed those dietary rules. It was a little detail but it surprised me.

"Your name?" I said. "That's not your real name is it?"

"Yes indeed. I am Victor Sahayle."

I stared at him and he was looking at me as if from far away, concentrating to focus. His eyes were soft. He's not going to harm me, I thought. Ever.

"Princey said…she met you in Church."

He nodded and looked at the ground. He seemed to be composing what he was going to say next. He looked up.

"You see. He's a…he's a strange man. Mortea'zar I'm talking about. He's been that way ever since I've known him. He can't control his temper. …But he's the only father I've known, you see? He can be soft and kind. He found me homeless on the street when I was thirteen, off my head on glue. He took me and he raised me. From the dead really. He used to tell jokes to make me laugh when I was a boy, because I was a bit of a melancholy thing. He taught me his trade. He has been the greatest presence of my life. Can you understand?"

I nodded. Of course I understood.

"Like Fagin!"

"What's that?"

"Nothing. Go on."

"You see. Just as you have your family, I have him. There's nothing I can do about it. I've tried to talk to him about this situation, but he just tells me I'm getting hoodwinked."

"By what?"

"He says rich people—I know, I know, but in Mortea'zar's eyes you *are* rich. Educated I suppose he means and it's the same to him–he hates the educated too. He says rich people, and especially their women always get their way. They protect everything they own, their name, their money, their house, their families, even when it's all built on lies. They rather believe the beautiful lies than face the ugly truth. They think they're better than the likes of us. He says your mum keeps delaying payment because she's wily, waiting."

"That makes no sense! He's mad."

"That's how they do it he says, they make you want things, the things they represent. So-called decency and high moral values. He said I was getting dragged into the net because I asked him to be lenient about the money. He thinks I too want to have a nice house in the suburbs and mow the lawn and go to work and come home by 6pm and buy nice things and show holiday snaps. He thinks I've bought into that dream. He says I've changed. I'm going soft. He says I'm no longer the man he made and one day I'll betray him."

"But what's so bad about that dream? Why shouldn't you want those things?"

"No, you have it all wrong. I am not at all attracted to that life. It's everything alien to me. It's not a life I have ever wanted. I am my own man, and he *did* make me and I will be forever in his debt. Ah, the poor man he loses his temper. He becomes insecure and he lashes out."

"But everyone wants that sort of life. It's normal."

"No. That's not true. It wouldn't suit me. I'm more of a gypsy."

I stared at him, anger rising in me.

"So this is the life you'll always live? Being a blackmailer and having no family except your gang? That's the life you'll always live. And one day someone will knife you, or the police will come for you. Aren't you scared? What sort of life is that to live, why would you think--"

He looked away, deep in thought, not listening. Then he turned towards me.

"Stop talking now. Listen to me. You're a good daughter, I know that. I want to go away, it has been a plan of mine from long ago. I want to finish this and go. This is what I'm going to do. I'm going to help you. Listen to me. People owe me favours, I can pull in maybe 3 but no more, you'd still have to get another 2 to add to this what you have in your bag, at least you see? It has to be that way. I have to get the money for Mortea'zar, I have to fulfil my obligation to him and get him the money Max owed him. And then he will give me my pay. Do you see?"

I stared dumbly at him.

He would put in 3k of his *own money*? I was to make up the rest. But whether it was £200 or £2,000 I had nowhere in the world to find it.

Chapter 23

Ruairi came in and laid the food and drinks out.

"Only one cheese and onion Vic. I got you the smokey bacon. I don't think you mind the flavour. Billy's downstairs about the--"

"Yes I know, tell him I'll see him at the other place." said Victor looking up with a smile and Ruairi nodded and left the room.

"I've sold my grandmother's jewellery," I said.

"I'm sorry about that. Is that all you got for it?"

I looked miserably at the floor. Part of me felt ashamed. It was worth so little. I had her slippers left and that was all. Losing those small pieces that the jeweller had turned his nose up at was like losing her all over again. Oh Shaani don't *lie*. You didn't lose it, you *sold* it. My Naani, who had never had a chance to properly live, who had lost all her mind and memory, whose slippers I had slid my own small feet into. My Naani who had worn those slippers day and night and when I put them on I remembered her so well, I thought of how one day I too would be old and frail and doolally as they said in Birmingham but it didn't frighten me. Those mashed up slippers with the indentations of her feet were like my light sabre. My life force. Dorothy had her slippers and I had mine. I swallowed. No way are you going to start crying

Shaani. Don't you dare show weakness. I dug my fingernails hard into my other hand. I knew he was watching me.

He suddenly got up and walked to the other side of the room and was silent. He was thinking deeply about something. I could see the hem of his coat, and the grainy gleaming wooden floorboards. The air was still and tight and it held us prisoner. Then he turned around and came toward me.

"Give me the ticket."

"Huh?"

"The pawn ticket, or the card of the jewellery place, whatever."

"No. Why?"

"I'll get it back for you. I promise I will."

He looked at me now, so earnest. He had sensed the importance of what I had done. It wasn't about the cost, it was about the value. Somehow he knew that. And I thought: One day he'll be just like Mortea'zar and he won't know *that*. Everything that is human and here in him today will become corroded. He's good, I thought faintly. He's trying to be.

"It doesn't work like that. They won't give it back. I sold it, it isn't a pawn shop," I said gently.

"Give it to me, will you?" he shouted and I drew back. He could be frightening. This was how he was when he extorted money from people. He was standing over me and I was in his long shadow.

I took out the card and the receipt and he put it in his pocket without looking at it. He nodded and then sat down looking at the floor. He was perfectly composed.

"Working with Mortea'zar has made me. Well, lets say it's made me single minded."

"But he's a criminal!"

"Yes I am as well"

"But not like him! You're not like him."

"Yes I am like him."

"It's not the same at all!"

He smiled at me without opening his mouth.

"Yes, it's the same. When I met Mortea'zar in the park I was in a bad way. I had lost everything in my life and I was living on the street sniffing glue and anything else. I couldn't even talk a full sentence. I couldn't read or write and I was an illegal. He gave me life."

"So he rescued you but he taught you how to be a criminal. That's not…"

"I know what you're saying. It's not what a family is. Not a real family. I know. I know the difference between what they call criminal fraternities, gang families and the real thing. I do know the difference. Everyone does."

"What's he got against my mum?" I said.

Victor pressed his lips together.

"It's not for me to tell you but I'm not your keeper and you may as well know it. Simply that your mother gave Max money to pay off his debts before. She told him there was no need to pay it back."

"That's a lie!"

"The first time she got for him £2,000 and the second time £1,000"

"She did not! She hasn't got ---"

"There is an account that your father opened for her to use for the household expenses and such while he is away. She must have taken it from that. Max bragged about it. He said he had her on the end of a string. If he didn't return her call, she would ring him ten times; she would do anything for him. Max didn't request those photos. They were sent willingly. He kept them not for a romantic purpose but for this same purpose." Sahayle was business-like again, brisk and remote.

Everything in me wanted to cry out it isn't true, it isn't true, it isn't true. But it was true. I had seen withdrawal slips for large amounts; I'd thought it was for the Botox.

"Eat the sandwich. Sip the shandy. You've had a shock. I know how it is when shock affects people. I'm sorry to tell it to you. She had her reasons I suppose."

"Don't you talk about my mum."

"Alright," he said quietly.

"You're not fit to speak her name. Don't you ever speak about my mother, you don't know her."

He was looking at me with that steady distant soft gauzy gaze. I sipped the shandy and the liquid burned fire in my throat at first and then it settled inside my body like a cat curled up in a fireside chair.

"Slow down," he said and put his hand on mine on the glass. "Take it easy."

He pushed the plate towards me.

"I doubt you had any breakfast. Eat this."

I didn't know what else to do so I picked up the sandwich and bit into it. I devoured the sandwich. Then I took another draft of the shandy and wiped my mouth with the back of my hand. I hiccoughed and was so surprised I stared at Sahayle.

"How old are you?" I asked.

"Twenty six."

"Will you ever delete them?"

"Yes. You have my word."

"Your word?"

He was staring at the floorboards deep in thought. He didn't even hear the disbelief in my voice.

"Did you mean it? About adding the money?"

He nodded. "You see, because a Mortea'zar does exist. If it was just up to me I wouldn't have bothered you. I'd be on my way. I've been thinking of it for a long time. A fresh start where no one knows me. But it's not so easy. I have obligations to fulfil."

He was a terrible blackmailer.

"Take it," I said and shoved the bag towards him.

He opened it and took out the brown bag. He counted the money rapidly, like a professional, much like the jeweller had counted it out. He put it in his inside pocket. The empty plastic bag and the crumpled brown bag lay inert on the table next to the white plate and the bag of crisps. I folded them up and put them inside my swim bag.

"You'll sort it out won't you? Please don't look so worried, you'll manage it for us won't you? For me?"

"Look this is how it's going to go. I'll tell him your mother will get the money out of her household account, like she did before. But it's going to take a few days. No listen to me, don't get excited. That will keep him off your back, while I look around and look up the people who owe me a favour, and get the money, as much as I can. My plan is then to say I've been to see her and that's all there was and she, your mother, can't get out any more, not till next month. Many banks have this proviso on lump sum accounts with interest. But you see he may not accept it. I don't know if he will accept it."

"Next month? You mean this could go on.."

"It will. He will never take less than he is owed. But we'll have time, you see. But there is a bigger problem now."

"A bigger problem?" I said miserably.

"They've arrested Wojcik who's a coward. The police will offer him a lighter sentence in exchange for information, not about Max. They couldn't care less about another criminal found dead in a ditch. They want bigger quarry. Now there's a man very high up in the Met who's a friend of Mortea'zar but he can't be seen to interfere with a case. He could get Wojcik out of the way in a second if he wanted to, he's got rid of men before on behalf of Mortea'zar. He is Tazers poodle.

"Executed them?" I whispered.

Sahayle smiled. "The British police don't execute people do they? Let's leave it at that. Anyway, instead he'll *have* to let the investigative team follow the trail from Wojcik to Mortea'zar. And Mortea'zar is worried about it. You see things are connected."

"But they shouldn't have arrested him! They shouldn't have arrested him!"

"Why not?"

"What if he didn't do it?"

Sahayle looked at me.

"You said that before. What do you mean?"

"What if I told you I knew who killed Max?"

"Go on."

"What if I told you I did it? *I did it!*"

He looked at me then and his eyes softened. "No. You didn't do it. It's not in you."

"You can't tell if someone murdered someone."

"True."

"Have you?"

"I've come close to it. But I never have. I don't think I could."

Something like relief flooded through me. He took out a cigarette and walked away from me and lit it.

"Don't mind if I smoke?"

What a strange man he was. Why ask me, what did it matter?

He was only across the room but he looked at me as though I was miles away and he could hardly see me through the smoke.

 "I know what it must have taken for you to do what you did. I'll get the jewellery back for you. I will."

"I don't think it's possible…"

"Yes. Yes it is. And I'll get Mortea'zar off your back. I'll fix everything. But you have to trust me. And eat some food. Be patient. Let me talk to Mortea'zar. Now let's go. I'll take you down stairs and then I'll leave you."

I followed him out of the room and out of the pub where it was bright. But neither of us moved. We stood on the pavement looking at each other.

"You will be able to get home all right will you, how will you go?'

"On the tube. I'm nineteen you know?"

"Do you drive?"

I nodded dumbly. "I can drive."

"Could I meet you one day? After this is all over? We could drive out to the seaside? Southend or Margate."

Shoals of tourists walked past, giggling and chattering.

"Just once. Don't worry I won't come to the house. I'd just like to see you one time. Do you think that would be all right?"

"I thought you were going to Mexico."

"I am. I'm planning it. I'll go next year. Perhaps in the spring."

I nodded.

"Yes?" he said and smiled.

"Yes," I said. "Margate is lovely this time of year."

Chapter 24

When I got to Euston station, a blast of music lassoed me. It was the same song we had heard on the radio on the way to Margate. We had run on to the beach, me and mum. The sand underneath our toes, our hair fluttering in the warm breeze. The gentle whoosh of the waves, the briny smell had soothed us and made us simply happy, away from all the troubles. The song was coming from a pop up shop. A shop I wouldn't normally even notice, let alone go into. An unapologetic shop selling wild net petticoats, Lady Gaga type dresses, pedal pushers, sombreros, winkle pickers, stiletto heels, a real mishmash of styles but all very kitsch, very girly, almost like a shop for Trans People, OTT female.

It was empty except for the two assistants dressed up Elvira style with ponytails who were singing along to the song in perfect sync and I don't know why, I joined them. We were in perfect harmony off key voice wise. I saw myself in the mirror. Next to the Elvira beauties, I looked hard core Sporty Spice. My bomber jacket, USA pro trousers, swim bag. No, I thought. That's not me. Who am I?

I'm actually good

Can't help it if I'm tilted

"Want to try something? We're offering a full makeup free if you buy something," said one of the girls.

"I'll try something," I said and the girl looked thoughtfully at what I was wearing and picked out a pair of grey pedal pushers and a demure white pin tuck blouse.

"This is your style," she said but I didn't hear her.

I was whizzing around the shop bouncing up and down on my Nikes, singing along loudly and picking out clothes myself.

"What about this?" I exclaimed, brandishing a frilly pink polka dot dress with conical breasts and full frothy skirt. "And this?" Five-inch red heels with bunny rabbits on the toes. "And this?" A handbag shaped like an ice cream cone. I struck a pose.

Both of the girls started nodding madly.

"You go girlfriend!" screamed the one throwing the pedal pushers away. "Ok, I hear you, I see you. I'll get you some stuff."

"Love it," shrieked the other.

"What about this one?" I said brandishing another outfit. This one was bright yellow flared trousers and a tight check red shirt that tied up under the bust. I am bursting with joy I thought. I feel so light. I could jump up into the sky and swim a hundred lengths no problem. I don't know why I'm in this shop or why I'm trying on these totally inappropriate, crazy, colourful outfits, only that I have to, I must, I need to. Right now! If I don't put on these tight yellow flared trousers I'll explode!

By the time I had tried on the fifth outlandish outfit, the three of us were cracking up. They clapped every time I came out of the changing room, whistled and made catcalls. They adorned me with chandelier earrings, chunky bracelets, beads, pendants and acid pink scarves, as though I was a little dolly and they were dressing me up, delighted with the result. And all the time, the three of us were singing along to the next songs on the speaker. And the next song and the next song was even better than the last.

I'm in love with the shape of you.

We all knew every word, every inflection as if we had learned the songs by rote for a test and now they were second nature, and before I knew it, suddenly hoards of girls were pouring into the shop full of curiosity. I prancing around in my outlandish impossible clothes was a magnet, drawing them in. Some thought it was a private party, some thought it was being filmed for TV, some just loved the atmosphere. I had no money but the girls said this top I was wearing was *mine*, they wanted a photo of me on their walls, no one else could carry it off the way I could, worn so *cutely* over my USA Pros, it was casual super-chic.

I could hardly hear them above the noise, the shop was heaving with people. This isn't me, I kept saying and laughing. This isn't me. Is it? This is me. Isn't it? When I finally got on the train to go home I was in a daze. Was it the shandy that had affected me so oddly? Was this drunken behaviour? Or had I sort of lost my mind somewhere in The Good Friend? Was it my new face? I stared at myself in the glass in the train. Yeah the make up looked fine but I saw something I had not seen for a long time. I was smiling from ear to ear without a care in the world. I was free. I kept thinking of Victor's face. I didn't have to worry about a thing. He was going to fix everything.

I trusted him.

"The wanderer retur.... Whoa Nellie," said Ash looking up from the table, a croissant in his hand.

"Shaani! Shaani!" said mum standing by the worktop with a mug in her hand.

"No good?" I said and twirled putting both my arms out and giving a bow.

Mum and Ash had their mouths open, jaws to the ground.

"What? I have breasts. So what?"

"OMG," said Ash.

"Ditto," said Mum. "Who are you and what have you done with my daughter? Who is this? Wow, just wow."

Mum took about a hundred pictures of me on her phone.

"You look hot sis. No doubt."

I started laughing.

"You guys."

"She can't take a compliment. She's never been able to take a compliment," said mum snapping away.

"Mum stop that and don't you dare Facebook it, it was just a makeover thingybobby. I thought you'd lost your phone."

"I have never heard you say thingybobby!" said Ash looking at me like I'd grown a third head.

"Shut up!"

"It's so weird, I found it in the drawer. I have no idea what it was doing there. Shaani, wow."

"Off her head on the meds, it was right under her nose all the time," said Ash and chuckled.

"Hang on," I said. "You're both in exactly… the same places. Haven't you moved since this morning?"

"Yeah. We've been sitting in the exact same position for, oh let me consult my Dr Who watch. Oh yeah six hours. Waiting for you to bring us to life."

"But Ash, you're in the middle of eating a croissant. Check! Mum is holding a mug of coffee! Check! The..Cafetiere is *half full!!* Check!"

Mum looked at her mug and looked around the kitchen.

"What else is the same?" she said.

"Mum, don't encourage her!" said Ash getting up.

He came around the table, croissant still in hand, dropping crumbs and stood in front of me.

"…and look look the clock is the same as well!!!" I started jumping up and down in glee. "Spooky! So spooky. How can you explain that? You can't. It's sort of like magic."

"Magic does happen," said mum. "It's a fact. Years ago, the Ganesh in the temple in Southall started drinking milk."

Ash sighed and looked at me sternly.

"Have you heard of Occam's Razor?"

"No who's he your boyfriend?" I said and mum hooted with laughter.

"Right, now listen head case," said Ash putting his hand on my shoulder. He was genuinely irritated. "Occam's Razor says the most obvious explanation is usually the most accurate. So, lets look at the evidence. Mum has just got back from work so obviously she's still in the same clothes. She's having a cup of coffee, again, in the same mug. Big whoop. I was finishing off the stale croissant from this morning. And the clock as you well know needs a new battery. It's stopped. It's a stopped clock that tells the correct time twice a day. Yeah?"

"Yeah…but."

"Scientifically impossible. Your theories are boring," he said to mum.

"Honestly Ash," I said. He *was* mean sometimes.

"Don't be such a spoilsport Ash. Bringing science into it," said mum. "Anyway look there's news Shaani."

"An invasion is imminent," said Ash, yawned and left the room.

"Oh?" I said. "Fun?"

"So sit and listen. The Dev - Sharmas are coming. The Sangeeth went so well. Mainly of course because of yours truly doing the henna and leading the dancing. Now they've decided to come here en masse for a sort of Asian Ladies Go Mad in London Shopping day."

"Haven't they wasted enough money buying up stuff in India? Pushy's wedding isn't till December!" I said.

"What are you talking about? That's only five months away, they're cutting it fine by Indian standards!" said mum. "So five ladies are descending tomorrow. Your cousins Rinki, Renu, and Pushpa obviously. Anuradha and Mausi Anuradha. But then what also happened was, during the day Nilesh phoned me to apologise for the Havan fiasco yesterday and."

"And mum was totally 'oh I didn't even notice' about it" shouted Ash from the hallway.

"Well of course I was," mum clapped her hands with glee. "But they know that we know that they…well you get the picture. And so I said, why don't Sharmilla and Giselle come along to *our* family ladies thing! And they love the idea. You know, the Dhaliwals don't really know where Southall is. And they've never even heard of Green Street or Queensbury! So you know, I'm sort of introducing them to.."

"The Indian ghettos!" said Ash walking into the kitchen with a bottle of beer, flicking it open, letting the lid fall on the floor. "Actually they're really booshettos. Bourgeois ghettos now. All those Asians have a lot of purchasing power if very little taste."

"Whatever!" said mum. "Pick it up young man!"

"Don't say that mum. It just sounds sad."

"It does sound sad mum," I agreed and high fived Ash. "Pick it up though."

Ash picked up the lid and put it in the bin, pushing his hair back with the back of his hand.

"Alright, all right. But my point is, the house is going to be full tomorrow and Shaani will you please kindly offer to be chauffeur? Because we are going to need two cars. Anuradha or Pushpa will drive their vehicle and you will drive us. And we'll spend a lovely day going up and down Southall High Street watching the Dev-Sharmas spending lots of money. Won't it be fun?"

"Good luck to me looking for parking," I said.

"Oh don't be so silly Shaani. Everyone knows Asians rule Southall. You can park where you like!" said Mum waving her hands.

"Like the Jews in Golders Green," said Ash.

"Like the Greeks in Green Lanes," I said.

"Like the Russians in Mayfair," said Ash.

"Like the Arabs in Edgware Road."

"Like the Afro Caribbean's in Brixton," I said.

"Failed! Brixton is more white than black now," said Ash and raised both his fists in victory

"Where do the English go to break the rules?" said mum. "Poor English, where's their ghetto?"

"Southall is not the Wild West it was in your day mum." I said. "It's all meters now. And every car park is full to the brim"

"Here's a Question for you, said Ash: How can you tell an Indian is a Brahmin? Answer: They tell you."

The three of us started to laugh uncontrollably.

"That is so true, so true! Five minutes in, and they work it in the conversation! But Ash, don't tell that joke to the Dev-Sharmas, they won't get it, and they'll take offence. They don't understand self abasement."

Ash started laughing. "Self deprecation mum."

"Alright clever boots. Now listen carefully, I've planned it like a military campaign."

That night we all went to bed early because it was to be a long day tomorrow. In the middle of the night I woke up suddenly from a nightmare. I was swimming. In front of me was a mound covered up with slimy leaves, turning into something, I couldn't see what, but it had nails and hair. I couldn't keep up with it, even though I was swimming hard and this leaf covered mound was bobbing like a cork. I turned to the left and I saw Mrs. Dhaliwal next to me. She was swimming too, but she swam easily, long limbed and perfect makeup while I had all my clothes on and I was pushing through treacle…

I woke up. The euphoria of the day had drained away. The rain was slamming against the house. Any minute now the windows would shatter. I got up and closed my window. Everything outside, our front garden, the street, Lovers Lane was a blur, as though someone had smudged it all into charcoal. Such anxiety overtook me that I crept into mum's room and closed her window. I looked at her and she didn't stir because she had taken her NightSleeps. I covered her with the duvet she had pushed to the ground. Then I went into Ash's room and closed his window and started to mop up his desk, which was covered with water. He was snoring, lying in an odd position. I didn't want to disturb him. The bottle of whiskey on the shelf was half full. I took the wet towel outside and threw it in the bath without turning on the light.

I stretched out my calves and hamstrings. My ears tingled. Someone's thinking of me. How can the dead think? But their nails and hair keep growing even when their brains are dead. Max had lain on the ground in a strange position and I'd thought I should tidy him up, make him comfortable. I came out of the bathroom and slumped down in the landing, with my back against the wall outside my room in the dead reception zone. The cold wall against my back was good. It's comfortable here, I thought.

My back against the wall.

Chapter 25

Morning was happy pandemonium. Mum was up at 5am and shaking me awake by 6. Ash was allowed to sleep till 7 by which time she and I were both dressed and ready. She drove to Finchley Central and got all the snacks from Mahavirs and I helped her lay them out in bowls and platters for the breakfast or *nashta* as Indians called it, a collection of tasty snacks not breads and cereals, just in time for the relatives arriving. Princey would come later and get the lunch ready for us when we returned. As usual everything revolved around food. The rain from last night was still glinting on the leaves but the sun was hot overhead.

"Shaanimeister!" shrieked Pushy as she led the procession into our house and immediately our home was full of women chattering excitedly in Hinglish, strong perfumes, bright colourful saris (not too much bling because it was Shopping day, but not too ordinary - cotton or nylon - because it was a Day in London) and gesticulating hands and delighted shrieks and shouts. And all before 9am in the morning. Everyone began to gorge on the snacks from Mahavir, taking a bite, then looking at the snack, shaking their heads and biting more and then discussing the merits and demerits of the taste and provenance. "Chick pea flour, grated carrots, grated mooli, fennel seeds, mustard seeds, curry leaves…red chillies, no, green chillies….it's a sort of pancake…it's a sort of savoury swiss roll." By 9.30 we had all got into our respective cars and were heading towards the North Circ.

We were in a convoy and mum had the Tom Tom on and we laughed because I was on the phone to Pushy who's mum Anuradha was driving behind us, and she had her own Tom Tom on which we could hear Shah Rukh Kahn, and mum said 'I must get that voice he's my absolute favourite actor, I'd go anywhere Shah Rukh told me to go' and we all tittered in our car and also in their car. In this happy way we finally reached Southall and then we had to wait around to meet with Giselle and Mrs. Dhaliwal and this gave mum plenty of time to accidently-on-purpose drop that Giselle was the great granddaughter of Tata-Khanna dynasty on the paternal side and that daddy Dhaliwal was a self made billionaire in his own right.

"No, no, too early to call and don't say anything in front of Ashi he goes mad if he thinks we're speculating. They're 'just friends' according to him," she said and all the ladies lolled their heads at the unsaid said.

We met up with Giselle and Mrs. Dhaliwal outside the Chinese Pagoda cinema that in fact had three screens and showed Bollywood films. It was noted they looked wonderful in their embroidered Punjabi suits, casual but so elegant. Mother and daughter were wide eyed and happy to meet us and together, a tribe of Asian women blending in with the other Asian women on Southall High Street, we moved towards the various Aladdin Cave type arcades selling every bit of paraphernalia needed for weddings and kitchens and occasions and well being.

"Southall is so quaint!" cried Mrs Dhaliwal. "So rustic! It's time travel, it's the India my forefathers grew up in!"

It rained a couple of times but the sun kept fighting to come out and we were all together and laughing and talking and all the time. Mum and Anuradha and Mausi Anuradha, me and Pushy, Rinki and Giselle and the rest all walking side by side, chattering and asking advice. The Dev-Sharmas bought an indecent amount of stuff.

"Did you get a chance to have your boy over," whispered Pushy as we walked past Palika Bazaar, and Mrs. Dhaliwal said "Oh look, they use the same names as the ones in Delhi, that's so cute." Pushy was in her natural Brummie accent today, a concession to her mum's pleas to not speak Black, especially in 'high company,' which I think was supposed to be us Devs of Ashley Gardens with our professor and teenage genius.

"No. It didn't really work out."

"Never mind, next time hey?" she said and punched me in the arm. "Anytime. You know you can rely on me."

Fortunately there would be no need for another time. And whatever she said, mum wouldn't just go to Birmingham at the drop of a hat. It had all been very lucky, in a way, the sequence of events.

"When will your dad come home?" asked Pushy and I said soon, very soon.

Ash and Giselle wandered off, as usual. It was as though everyone knew they would be next after Pushy and her MFI (Man from India), and even though Ash was only 15 and

Giselle was only 15, everyone sort of knew they would get engaged soon before Ash went to Oxford or Princeton. It was a subject that would keep them all busy talking and speculating because it would be a very different proposition to Pushy's wedding. It would be *mega.* The wedding couldn't take place till they were both over 18 obviously but to get engaged at 16? In this day and age? It was different! But maybe not as different as it would be in white society, because marriage in Indian families was less romance more increase. The family is what mattered and it was this benevolent beast that increased and multiplied when two small insignificant people married, because it was family that made society and it was society that made culture and this was what a civilisation was. No wonder Indians found single and gay people suspicious and threatening.

'Will they won't they' took up a lot of talking time amongst the Dev Sharmas; the speculation was way beyond the Ross and Rachel equation. Ashish and Giselle were the perfect couple in every way; they were beautiful, she was rich and he was clever—this is the way Indians liked their equations in marriage, and they would yield enough column inches in the Asian press to almost call themselves a brand. Would they do it though? Marriage was a big step and if they got engaged that would seal the deal. There would be no second thoughts and long engagements and jilted at the Temple scenario. It would be for life. The increase of Family was insatiable, unstoppable.

I thought they probably would. In their own ways, both of them had already achieved so much in their short lives – Ash was to go to university two years early, Giselle had landed the L'Oreal contract in LA, so 16 *looked* different the way they wore it. By the time they were in their early twenties they would have had one good career each. Still, an engagement at 16 would shock some people and at the same time people would be impressed by the commitment. At any rate everyone would want an invite to the engagement party of the decade as the bride-to-be family would pay. The merger of Dev with Dhaliwal-Tata-Khanna would be a big deal in every sense of the word. Our status would go up. Our value would rise. There would be more respectability, more acceptance, more of everything.

And yet, this prospect of high status didn't touch me, perhaps because I couldn't imagine it. The Tata-Khanna-Dhailwas would always be the outsiders, *them*. We were the Devs. What mattered that day more than ever was cohesion within our ranks. On the way home I thought one day, very soon, dad would return having won or lost the land and we would all be together again. I felt very sure that exactly this would happen and we would be a tight little unit attached to a trailer. Us in London the core Devs, them in Brum the Dev Sharmas, us the sedate intellectuals and they the raucous earthy element, together in our own intact world within all these other worlds. Free from fracture, malice and fear and blackmail.

By the time we got back home everyone was exhausted. Princey had done a brilliant job and the house was really shining from top to bottom. It was 1.45pm and the late lunch was laid out as a buffet.

"Shaani..." whispered Princey.

"Hi Princey!" I cried and mum introduced her to everyone.

"This is my lieutenant. Without her my house would fall apart. She's a very important part of our family and the one person who keeps me afloat," said mum smiling at Princey who blushed.

Princey was beautifully turned out as usual. She did a sort of embarrassed bow and retreated into the kitchen saying, "Shaani, please give me a hand for a minute. Quickly now."

Mum said, "Yes Shaani, go and help Princey please."

"Yes, in a minute," I said and went into the front room with the throng.

For the first time in my life I really felt connected to this family. I wanted to be part of it, absorb it, feel it. Not just pretend. It was as though a missing piece of the puzzle had fallen in the right place and now I saw the whole picture. I stood in the middle of what seemed like a whirlwind of laughter and chatter, swirling around me. Everyone here was related to me. Yes, I thought, and one day I'll marry a man who is like us and we will increase and the train will move forward with full force as it has always done, gathering more speed, momentum, certainty, memories. I stood in the middle of the room amongst my relatives and felt the power of seduction and the deep desire to submit to the majority.

It was almost 2pm. Giselle and Mrs. Dhaliwal said they were going home but they had loved meeting the Dev-Sharmas and they already felt part of the Dev family because Anuradha invited them to Pushy's wedding. The Dhaliwals had never been to a brown chav wedding and it would be their first. Mum was chuffed to bits. You know, I'm going to reclaim the word Chav, she said. Mitch Rosenthal always says very proudly that he's a redneck, because his father and his uncles worked hard in the fields and got red on the back of the neck from the sun and that's what it originally meant before the word got corrupted! We all tittered. The Dhaliwals might have gold pouring out of their orifices but *we* the chavarati were real, *asli maaal*, we were authentic with our different shapes and sizes and oddities.

As soon as we said goodbye to the Dhaliwals, Mr and Mrs Singh turned up. They put on the video of their nieces wedding and everyone settled around to watch. I was carrying some plates from the front room into the kitchen when Princey grabbed my arm.

"You've done so well today Princey. Everything was fantastic. I can clean up the kitchen. You can go home now if you want, I'm sure mum won't.."

"That man is here Shaani," she whispered.

"What man?" I whispered.

"Mortea'zar"

Shit

"Where is he?"

"He knocked on the door and I put him in the garage."

My throat went dry.

"I told him it was a Wedding party and there were too many people and…he was asking for your mum. And I said everyone was out but he wouldn't go away and so I told him to sit in the garage and I would bring him food. He could smell the food, and it was nice and he was hungry and so he agreed."

"You mean he's been here all this time! He's sitting in the garage? We've been back for half an hour at least! What if he comes in, oh God what if he charges in?" I said.

"No, he won't come."

"Hello Singh uncle!" I said as turban brain went past us to go upstairs to the loo.

"You must build a toilet downstairs. I will bring some plans and quotes," he said climbing the stairs. "I have a fellow who can do it cheap. He is from my uncle's village and he lives in Southall. No papers, no English, but strong fellow."

Mr. Singh had a disease called TMUI. He gave Too Much Useless Information when none would do. I went into the kitchen with Princey.

"He wants to speak to your mum! But I think it's better you speak to him. Yes?"

"Yes, but how do you know he won't come in?"

"He is sleeping. Very deeply," she said and smiled.

From the kitchen I could see the small narrow cupboard in the hall where we kept long things like the golf umbrella and the window pole. And Naani's walking stick, which we had bought with us from Chesham. It wasn't there. It hadn't been there since that dark and terrible day when I had been

264

to the Brook. I had noticed its absence the very next day and I'd asked her about it and Princey had simply said 'I took it. I gave it to a lady in my street. She needs it.' I hadn't said anything to her, just nodded. Princey looked at me now and I knew suddenly that I could trust her. She had been suspicious all along, she knew something was wrong the first day Mortea'zar had come to the house. Maybe she knew about mum and Max too.

"I took him a plate of Tandoori Chicken and the Mughlai Karahi Gosth and Naan. I ground up a handful of mummy's pills and I mixed them in with my home-made pickle," she nodded. "He will be snoring for some good few hours."

"You *roofied* him?" I gasped. "What made you *think* of it?"

Princey pushed out her bottom lip defiantly.

"I would regularly do it in my useless husband's tea. After he came home from dancing with girls he used to throw me about. I took it for some years but after my babies were born I thought No sir! There was no other way to knock him out. I am small and he is big. But he is the son of an owl and I am a fox!" she raised a finger to denote her superiority. To Indians a fox wasn't sexy, it was wily and the owls progeny were fools. "I would grind in my mortar and pestle. He thought he was deeply sleeping only. Pills are good. They scrub out memory. So it was easy for me, with this fat gangster goonda."

"Well done Princey!" I was breathless at her audacity, her ingenuity. "But I'll have to go and see him."

"He was quite happy to wait. I think he was hungry too. He said he will wait only. And I said as soon as everyone came home I'd send your mum to speak to him in the garage and he said ok. Was it ok?"

"Yes. Yes you did the right thing. I'm going to go and see him. I've got to haven't I?"

She nodded. I put my hand on Princey's shoulder. She took the plates from me.

I felt my blood boiling. Fucking Sahayle! He said he was going to sort it. He said trust me. He said I'll get you your jewellery back. I'll keep Mortea'zar off your back. He hadn't done any of it. And now Mortea'zar was in the fucking garage. And the house was full of people. I can't see him. I can't see him.

But I have to.

But I've got to hang on just a little longer. Everyone has to go away, or go to sleep. Someone's going to see me leaving the house and going to the garage. I stood in the hallway feeling helpless and furious. Everyone was in the front room fixed on the video. It would be at least two hours long, but they might not watch it all. Come on, come on you've just got to go out there. Take the risk.

Chapter 26

Mr. Singh came down the stairs.

"Going out?" he said.

"No uncle, I'm just opening the door for ventilation."

He went into the front room. If only I could somehow close the door…but that would look funny. Princey was in the kitchen stacking the dishwasher. She turned around and saw me standing like a lemon in the hallway, halfway between the front door and the lounge door. Immobile. She turned round and carried on stacking the dishwasher methodically. She had done her part, now I had to do mine.

Sahayle! So much for dealing with it. He's done nothing! I was glad for my anger, it stopped me being afraid.

I opened the front door.

The lounge door swung open behind me and a blast of cheers and shrieks spilled out. Mum caught my elbow and closed the door.

"Hey you, my lovely girl, come in, come in and be with us, won't you?"

"Yes mum."

All my saccharine fantasies of seduction and Family evaporated; I just could not wait for them all to get out. All the goodbyes took over 10 minutes and finally, finally everyone was out of the house. It was 4.15pm. I knew mum would want to go upstairs for a kip and it was as if Princey read my mind and said go and sleep, I'll clear up. Mum immediately agreed. As soon as she had gone upstairs I went to open the front door and Ash was standing there.

"Timed it so well," he said. "Any food left?"

"Ash where've you been?"

"Just out with the Dhaliwals," he said and went into the kitchen. 4.18pm

"Can you do me a favour Professor of Physics?" said Princey. "Can you please go to Indian shop in Finchley Central and get me spices? Here is a list."

"Now? What for? There's all this food…"

"I need them for tomorrow. I have to make the fresh subzis. You don't want stale food."

He sighed and frowned.

"Can't she go?"

"I've got plans for her," said Princey and winked.

"*She* went and got the meat last week," I said.

Ash laughed. "Alright. But I'll be a while because I'll have to walk. I can't drive because the driving laws in this country are ridiculous and age-ist."

It was almost 4.20pm. Princey gave Ash a list and he went to the kitty box.

"Oh," he said.

"I took it to get mum's birthday present. From both of us, obviously."

Ash nodded and gave me the thumbs up, without asking what it was.

"Laters," he said and the front door closed.

"Now?" I said to Princey and she nodded.

I'd kept him waiting for over two hours. He's been sitting in the garage like a ticking bomb. I walked down the path and back up to the garage instead of crossing over the hedge as usual. As I pushed open the see saw door the creaking corrugated iron set my teeth on edge. I bent down and got inside and closed the door behind me. The light was on, a single naked light bulb rigged up in the corner of the ceiling. At first I didn't see him and I thought he's woken up, he's gone!

But I knew he hadn't.

He was there, sitting on the sofa at the far end, in that same cheap suit, his stomach bulging in the shirt. I could smell him. The plate of food Princey had bought for him was on the floor, two chicken leg bones gnawed to almost clean, empty bowl of Mughlai Karahi Gosth, half a Naan, a bottle of Johnny Walker Black Label and a crystal glass on the table next to him. How dare he help himself to dad's whiskey meant for special guests? Why wasn't he sleeping? Why the hell was he still awake?

"You again!" he said blithely as though I'd walked in on his sitting room. The garage stank of the spices and his sweat.

"Mr. Mortea'zar..." I started to say.

He dismissed me again with those fat fingers, his puffy face unconcerned. "I don't want you, tell your mother to get out here now. I've been waiting for too long. She owes me money. What does she think I am, a chump?" He was groggy and a little slurry but he's supposed to be unconscious. Maybe he was too fat to be affected by the pills. Something told me that anyone who hated rich and educated people must be a little intimidated by them. Use the Gleaming White Dental Practise voice. It's all you've got. Extreme politeness.

"But we're having a wedding party Mr. Mortea'zar. You understand don't you? Whatever it is you want, surely it can wait a bit."

He bought his fist down on the table.

"It can't wait. They've gone! I heard them. I've been sitting here like a fool. Tell your mother the price has gone up to £8,000 and I want it now!"

I stared at him.

He drank down the glass of whiskey and then smacked his lips. His eye fell on his plate and his fingers moved the Naan. There was the mound of pickle. He scooped it up and ate the whole lot, munching greedily. Then he wiped his hands on a towel and threw the towel to the ground. Princey's pickle was to die for, spiked with tamarind, limes, green mangoes, astefotida, black salt and sugar cane. And clearly

271

the NightSleeps didn't taste bad, as he kept smacking his lips.

"But.... I don't understand what you mean, Mr. Mo--"

"Don't understand, don't understand! Will you stop talking and get your mother? I don't want to deal with you. But I will."

"But I gave Mr. Sahayle all I had. I honestly."

He leaned forward and made as if to get up but then sat back in the sofa. His fat hand went to his head and he pressed his temple and said something to himself. It sounded like the Urdu word for sisterfucker, a word I was forbidden to use.

Then: "It's you. All the time it's been you?"

His eyelids began to droop. That stuff worked fast! His speech began to slur.

I couldn't speak. Sahayle had told him he was dealing with mum. My brain was racing. I felt sick at the thought of this thug seeing those pictures, having them in his fat sweaty hands. I felt like going across and slapping him across the face. I didn't move.

"So it's been you all along," he said slowly trying to keep his eyes open, looking at the ground and then back at me.

"Yes."

"You've been stringing my boy along but now you get me the money. Now!"

"No, I won't!" I said. "I can't. I can't get any more. Don't you understand?"

"What do I care about the money? I've got plenty."

"Then what is it? Mr. Mortea'zar what do you want?"

He was staring at me now and shaking his head violently, keeping sleep out.

"She's no good. Your mother is a whore and your father is a simpleton who can't see what's in front of his nose. What use are his books to him? You're all fucked," he said mumbling as though to himself. A stream of abusive words came out of his mouth like gobs of venom. I didn't know what they meant, only that they were obscene. He had drunk most of the bottle. He started to scrabble inside his suit jacket and took out his phone, waving it about carelessly.

"I'll put them out on the Internet with one tap, the world will see..."

"For what? What good will it do you?"

"Look at Max, he got involved with her and look what happened to him! Max wasn't a bad guy, he was just taken in."

"He was a nasty piece of work!"

"But he didn't deserve to end up head down in a river did he?"

"It's nothing to do with me. It's nothing to do with me."

"Why I could swat you down with my hand like a fly and they'd find you in your own garage."

"Try it," I said, "Just try it."

He started laughing.

"Go *away*."

"No."

He poured himself another drink but he was swaying badly, he could hardly stay awake.

Mortea'zar leaned forward and pointed at me, the other hand holding the bottle.

"If her pictures were splashed over the Internet he'd kill her! Your dear daddy. Your perfect Brahmin. How the mighty will fall. She'll be found chopped up in her own suitcase. Hahaha I wouldn't have to do nothing."

He just wants to do us harm. He hates us, I thought dully.

"I haven't got the money, honestly I haven't."

"Sure you have. Ask your future in-laws they've got shed loads of it."

"I can't. That's ridiculous!"

He heaved himself up and I stepped back—"You!"

The garage door swung open and Sahayle was there, in his immaculate white shirt and chinos and camel coat. He closed the door and stood in front of Mortea'zar.

"What is going on? I can hear you both from outside. As can the world."

I stood to one side as Mortea'zar approached Sahayle, but Sahayle stood his ground.

"What are you doing here Baaba? Why did you come?" he said softly.

"You're a fool. You've been a fool about this. Nassir told me and Bilu told me."

"No they didn't. That's rubbish"

"Yes, it's not rubbish. It was Nassir, he saw you"

"He did not because I know for a fact that Nassir was in Edmonton yesterday. And Bilu was on a job in Leeds. So this is not right Baaba. For you to be here. It's not your business."

"Oh stop talking boy. Do you think you can go around in the world eating pig pies and no one will notice?"

"There were no pig pies!"

Chapter 27

I stood apart from them. I felt limp, like a rag doll, standing aside, letting them talk. I had no business being there. I just wanted to melt away. I had no energy. I wished I could just curl up and fade away. They just kept talking, these two strange men in our garage. One large, lumbering suddenly full of gesticulating hands, his voice like a whine and the other still, calm, arguing but not shouting.

"I see the picture now clear. This is what you've been reduced to."

"I can't see the reason you had to come Baaba. There's no reason for you to harangue her."

"Harangue her? Listen to you. It's a good thing I've alerted Nassir and Bilu."

"What have they got to do with it? Why do you get so angry?'

"Why do I? - " Now a glint came into Mortea'zar's eyes and I could feel it in the air, something changed, something crackled. Adrenaline, anger was surging in him giving him life. I felt my stomach contract.

"To have to hear of you passing around a begging bowl. Getting six hundred here, a grand there, twenty pounds from this and that. And they laughed when they told me. Your boy Mortea'zar, your boy has become a puppy. Can you know what such humiliation is? You may as well have stabbed me in the heart. Look what she's reduced you to."

"Now stop it Baaba. There's no reason."

"Yes there is every reason. You think I want that money you begged? For *her*? You disrespect me boy!"

"It's in your head, all in your head. Come now Baaba let me--"

Sahayle moved toward him and in grotesque slow motion Mortea'zar came for him, and Sahayle put out his hand to stop him but Mortea'zar stepped back as if he was running backward and lost his footing.

I screamed and then put my hand to my mouth and Sahayle was there, on his knees next to the vast body on the ground. He had his hand on Mortea'zar's face and Mortea'zar was furious, lashing out, throwing a punch, which Sahayle caught like a man catching a baby's fist.

"No Baaba. Stop now."

"You fool! Nassir and Bilu will come and finish."

"No, you can't mean it. What have you done, what have you done?"

"Get off me, help me get up!" said Mortea'zar but Sahayle put his hands on his shoulders and started shaking him.

I heard the garage door shuddering.

"You will not do it. This girl has done nothing wrong."

"Won't I?" said Mortea'zar and then a sound came from him, like a whistle or air from a balloon. Sahayle had his hands on his neck.

"No!" I said, "No Victor, don't!"

Mortea'zar went limp and everything went still and Sahayle's lifted his hands, staring at them. His legs had stopped kicking.

"Oh God, oh God Victor?"

"He's not dead. He's passed out," he said with a frown.

"Princey." I couldn't get the words out. "Princey. She…she. Sleeping pills."

"How many? How many? I need to know. I need to know how much time I have."

"I don't know, I don't know…I—do you want me to ask her. I can't Vic, I can't."

"Calm down now," he said "Just calm down. And go back into your home."

I couldn't stop shaking. My hands and my body wouldn't stop. That terrible night when I had found Max came back to me. It was like I was there again, watching myself. That terrible moment when I saw his face.

"I c-c-c-an't..!" I said and Sahayle picked up the glass and gave it to me to sip. I took one sip and spat it out. "His glass!"

Sahayle got up and got the bottle of Johnnie Walker Black Label and held it for me. "Drink a bit, it'll calm you down."

I drank from it. It was like fire inside but it soothed me, calmed me. Sahayle didn't take a drop. Mortea'zar was on his back, snoring. Loud creaking snores.

"Don't worry about this. Just get yourself together and go back inside. They'll miss you and then there'll be trouble."

"Then there'll be trouble? What are we going to do?"

"I have to act fast now, just let me think."

"What—what's …" I couldn't get the words out.

"Just go, just go back inside. Leave me with this. You have people to see."

"Yes, Mrs. Dhaliwal is coming to talk to me," I said in a daze. "But what will you do?"

"I'll manage, don't worry. Go back you."

"But how? How?"

"Just let me alone. I'll manage it. Somehow. I'll wait till dark and I'll call a friend to get me and we will shift him…."

"You can't stay here till dark!"

"I'll have to. But please, don't get upset now. Just go back. I'll manage this. You see, this changes everything. When he wakes up…Well I'll be as good as dead."

"You could drive him," I said putting my hand on his arm. "Put him in the boot and drive him away, drop him somewhere."

"No I could not."

Sahayle was looking at Mortea'zar without any emotion. He was just lying there, his huge stomach with the bulging buttons. He had slunk to the floor and was sound asleep. I couldn't look.

"What do you mean? Of course you could. I'll get the car. You can take our car!" I said.

"No. No you see I can't."

"What are you talking about? You can't wait here till dark and get a friend to come here? Then what? He'd wake up by then anyway."

"Look, just go home. And if they come, the police, you'll stick to this story all right? You'll say Mortea'zar came to see you, to find me. And you told him to go to the garage and wait. Because you were busy with your party. And then I came along and you told me to go to the garage too. And that's all you know. If they ask you, you'll say those two started having a fight, and that's all, you saw nothing."

"But it won't work—"

"Never mind, just say it for me. Just repeat what I've told you. Please darling."

"Ok, he came, then you came and I sent you off and you probably had an argument in the garage. Yes but what are you going to do Vic, where will you take him?"

"I'll manage"

"No, you won't! You're an idiot. Your plan isn't going to work, don't you see? You've got to drive him away now, before he wakes up. Get him away from here, out of our garage! I'll get the car for you."

"He will kill me with his bare hands. It's over for me now. It's God's judgement on me."

"What? Don't be such a wimp! Get yourself together."

"I can't. I'm not in myself," said Sahayle standing still, his head bowed a little.

"Vic. Get yourself together. I'm going to bring the car to the garage and then-"

"No, I don't want to pull you further into this," he said

"You're not thinking straight. We just have to get him away, and if you don't help me I'll do it by myself," I said. "I've done it before."

"I will help you," he said forlorn as a cat in the rain, his hair all wet stuck to his head. He kept looking at Mortea'zar lying on the floor.

"I'll get the car, and you'll get him up and together we'll get him in the back seat. He got drunk. That's the story. You're. You're just going to sober him up. That's the truth, near enough. And we'll drive...I'll drive you. I don't know further than that. We'll decide once we're driving. Ok, ok Victor?"

He nodded.

I pushed the door up a bit, blazing sunlight bashed my face and I came out and straightened up. Don't run, just walk, and if Mr. Singh pops up, just ignore him. I got to the car and drove around the corner then backed up till the car was in front of the garage door. I pushed open the door and saw Sahayle holding Mortea'zar up, one arm around his shoulders, the other hanging loose. Sahayle had propped him up against the wall. Mortea'zar's head was swaying from side to side and he was making groaning noises.

"Quick. Let's put him in the back seat."

Sahayle nodded but he couldn't move, he was like someone frozen in time. All the blood in his face had drained.

"Can't you do it?" I said helplessly and he just looked at me like a dazed kitten, weak next to this lumbering moaning bear.

"Alright, I'll get someone who can," I said and strode back to the house and went inside. Princey was waiting for me. She looked wary but alert and perfectly composed.

"Mum's out for the count," she said pointing upstairs.

"Princey," I said. "I need your help now. Mr. Mortea'zar has had too much to drink and his friend Mr. Sahayle wants to take him home. To sober up. I'm going to drive them."

She looked at me and nodded, wiping her hands on a cloth. Then she put on her apron and followed me out silently, leaving the front door on the latch.

"Shit, this is not happening," I thought but Princey didn't say a word and the expression on her face was unreadable.

I opened the garage door and Sahayle was stood like a statue looking at us, Mortea'zar groaning ever louder next to him, scratching his head. Princey moved fast. She took something out of her apron pocket and shoved her hand inside Mortea'zar's mouth. Then she held his head back and poured the whiskey in.

"Jesus!" said Sahayle.

"He will be asleep again," she said calmly and wiped her hand on her apron. "For a good time."

"Princey, I'm donating some of the junk to Mr. Sahayle's charity. I've put it all in a bag. Mr. Sahayle's friend isn't feeling very well and I'm going to drive them to the warehouse."

She nodded and quickly I helped Sahayle get Mortea'zar in the back seat. We pulled and pushed him until he was sitting propped up against the window. I shoved a bag of books next to him to prop him up. I closed the door.

"Thanks Princey, I'll be back later," I said and she looked at Sahayle for a moment and went back inside the house.

Just as the front door slammed, I saw Ash at the top of the street swinging a Tesco plastic bag. He had seen us. He raised his hand.

"Get in quick," I said.

I put my foot down. We went roaring past Ash and then we went out of sight.

Chapter 28

"Jesus," said Sahayle. "You just drove past him."

I took the road towards Hendon at a steady pace.

"How long before he wakes up?" I said. "Which way now?"

"I have no idea. I don't know this area. Keep driving."

I was completely dehydrated. I picked up the big bottle of Evian and took a big gulp. I took the road that became Brent Street and then turned right into the A1 towards Brent Cross and we were suddenly in a formation of cars, like a funeral procession. I kept in my lane, making sure to keep within the limit, even though plenty of cars were driving over it. In my rear view I could see Mortea'zar slumped against the window. What if he died? How many pills had she crushed up the second time? The alcohol would have made it worse. The whiskey, dad's revered Black Label would become evidence, exhibit A. Was it already evidence? Was it wrong what Princey had done? She had done it for me. Victor had got into a fight because of me. What if he'd killed him? What if...

I took a deep breath to stem the flow of anxiety. Shit, everything is being recorded on the CCTV and the speed cameras I thought dully. But if I keep to the limit. I took a quick look at Sahayle and he was sitting with his hands between his knees, his head bowed. We've got to talk about it, I thought. We've got to *discuss* it. But he's in shock. I've got to leave him alone. He'll be all right in a minute. He just needs to come back to himself. I concentrated on the road and my speed.

Then he said, "You saved me back there. I'd lost my mind. I would have gone to pieces if not for you."

You might have killed him, I thought and I knew he was thinking the same thing.

Thank God he was still alive. I wanted to turn around and shake him awake, slap him around the face and say go away, go away, and watch him walk away out of our lives the way he had walked away when mum sent him off. Max's staring eyes suddenly flashed in my brain. But his eyes had been closed. You can't rely on your memory. The way he was lying there, like a crab. I'll never get rid of that picture.

"There," Sahayle said, "Take a left there, it looks all right."

I turned and drove under trees that bent over and met like clasped hands above the road, dappling the sunlight on our faces through the windscreen. Mortea'zar moved forward like a dodgem car butting up against our seats, too big to fall to the floor. I thought I heard him grunt.

"He's going to wake up, Vic he's going to wake up," I said and right away I knew that would be the worst thing in the world. When he woke up, Mortea'zar would kill Victor. My brain went into overdrive. If he were dead, Victor would be a killer. If he were alive Victor would be dead.

"There, up ahead is a good spot. Stop the car there."

I stopped the car.

He said 'drink this.'

I turned to look at the bottle of Evian in his hand, his long tapered fingers that had been around the neck of Mortea'zar. His other hand lay in his lap, upturned, the slim tapered fingers.

I haven't touched it since you put it to your lips, he said anxiously.

A lorry went past.

"Shit, he's seen us." I said turning to look at Mortea'zar. He was snoring like a bear, his cheek pushed up against the glass. Any moment he could wake up, bloodshot eyes staring at me. And then all hell would break loose.

"It doesn't matter. We're just in a car talking."

"No but the lorry driver he'll be a witness, don't you understand?"

"There's nothing to witness."

"We've got to talk about it. We've got to have--"

"I can't just now. My mind is a blank. But I'll be all right, let me relax a little and then I'll be all right. I need to think ahead a little bit.

I nodded and waited. You could hear a pin drop. Come on Victor, come on I pleaded silently, holding my breath.

"Let's get out of the car," he said finally.

"Get out? Where to? What about him?"

"Just away from the car, just a little way."

So I got out of the car and he took my hand and we walked a little further up the road until it turned the corner and there was a little green hill there and we sat down at the foot of it looking at the cars driving past below.

"But someone will see my car. And he'll wake up. And the---"

"Don't worry so much. Be here with me. It'll be all right. Drink a little more water, it'll calm you."

I drank some more from the bottle but my throat was parched, so I gulped it down. We were sitting on the mound of grass, no one about, the sun on our heads. There's a roofied killer in my car. And I'm sitting here with a blackmailer. It's absurd. I closed my eyes, feeling something ebbing out of my body.

"Listen now. Look at me. We've got to have a story," he said. "And we have to stick to it other wise we'll both be sunk. Forget what I said before. This is the story to keep to ok? Mortea'zar came to your house and you sent him to wait for me in the garage and you were busy. And then I came along and took the bric a brac for my charity. He was drunk and we had been quarrelling but I begged you for a lift with the bric a brac. And because you felt sorry for me, you said you'd drive me to the warehouse. He and I both got into the car and you drove. You can't remember where exactly because I was giving you directions, but somewhere near a church, be vague. And so you drove me to this place and then my friend came to help me with Mortea'zar, and then you drove back.

"That's ridiculous, that's not a plan. It doesn't even make sense. It's just cobbled together. We'll never get away with it."

"Yes, we will if you keep your head."

"But how do you know? Have you—have you ever been arrested?"

"Six times," he said.

"What?"

"Yes. Six times. They never had enough evidence to keep me. I've never been convicted. I don't even have a record."

"Six times?" I said.

"Just listen and do what I tell you to. There's not much time left now. You'll go away to that shopping mall now and keep to that story. What will you do?"

"I'll..go away and say that you and Mortea'zar came and you took the bric a brac and I drove you to the warehouse."

"Exactly that. You'll go away for four hours. And in that time, I'll get a friend to come and help me. And later you'll pick up your car from the car park and go home."

"What if your friend isn't home?"

"He's always home. He will help me with it. And I'll get your car cleaned. I mean cleaned. What I want you to do now is walk up towards that mall—Brent Cross, yes that's it. Go right past the car and go in there and walk about, do some shopping. You'll have to go now. I'm sorry. But we haven't any time anymore. We won't see each other again. I'll have to disappear you understand? I shall be on my way. My friend will help me."

He got up and I got up but my legs were jelly.

"I can't – I can't do any of it. I can't"

"Yes you can. Look how you drove right past your brother earlier. You were fearless. And in four hours your car will be in the car park. Remember I won't be calling or texting you. You'll have to trust me and go and look in the car park there. It'll be there in four hours. My friend will leave it there. And you'll get in and drive home. You can do that can't you?"

"It'll never work. There's CCTV everywhere, why even as we're talking we might be being filmed. We'll never get away with it."

"We will if you keep your nerve. Just walk and go away from me now."

He was back in himself.

"How come you came out to the house today?"

"Princey phoned me. I told the roofer to give her my number. I told him to tell her that if I was ever needed she could call me."

I was startled. What a strange thing to do.

"But you don't even know her," I said. "I know she gave you a candle but that was just the once, a year ago."

"Yes I know her. She showed me a small kindness. She reminded me of someone I had known once. A Christian lady at the orphanage who was always fretting for me. She was a dead ringer for her. And just for that, I felt I could trust her. And she seemed to know it too. She saw me and it was as though she knew something about me. I don't mean she liked me. But she didn't dislike me. And then she saw me at your house, that day. She knew of me but she didn't give me away."

"I'm glad she called you," I said miserably. "Are you? I mean are you all right? I'm sorry I...She roofied him, *I didn't ask her to.*"

"Ah, she knows of Morte'zea. She has a vendetta against him. It was her husband Sonny that Tazer's poodle slayed. He was a small time criminal and in prison for a long time. Five years ago they offered him early parole if he talked. He sang. That was the end of him. The police still didn't have enough to arrest Baaba, but Tazer's poodle cut Sonny from ear to ear on the direct instruction of the boss. She has known of Mortea'zar for many years but what could she do to him? She is illegal and she is poor and she is a woman. Here she saw her chance, perhaps to balance the scales of justice. But she did not kill him, it was not in her."

"Vic, I didn't know any of this. I thought Princey's husband was in India, he was dancing with girls..."

"Very many of these ladies let it be known their husbands are living back in the old country, when in fact they are imprisoned in the UK, or just working illegally. It is a common ruse. It is safer. They would not be hired if their employers knew they had a husband inside."

"Are you all right Vic? What will you do?" I said suddenly.

"He was going to set Nassir and Bilu on to your family and I couldn't allow it. They give Rottweilers a bad name."

"Are they—gangsters?" I whispered. It seemed idiotic to say that but I couldn't help it.

"No," he said.

"What are they?"

"You don't need to know. Just please, go now. Do as I say."

"Are you all right? You'll have to go abroad now. As soon as possible."

"Yes, I will."

"You won't go will you, you're just saying that. I can see it in your face. Are you—do you feel?"

"We don't have to talk about it. Maybe you could try to forget it?"

I snorted. "I'll never forget it as long as I live. How could I?"

"He is a *sanki*, you know. That's what some call him. An obsessive. He never lets anything go. He feels disrespected everywhere and it makes him angry and violent. Fifty years ago there was a woman in a shop in Birmingham who refused to serve him when he was a kid because she didn't like foreigners, and he still wanted to find her and get even with her, all these years later. He feels the world is laughing at him. Always, always."

I nodded. Mortea'zar might not have been dead but this was Victor's personal eulogy to him, and I was the only witness.

"Mortea'zar wanted to go to school but his father thrashed him at the first and forced his face into the freshly cut sheep's stomach when he was only 9 years old. In those days no one checked and Baaba was taken out of school and put to work as his fathers assistant in the butcher shop. His father made sure to give him the worst jobs, to toughen him up or maybe he hated him. Baaba thought he should have had a better deal in life but he was afraid of his father and worked for him until he was a grown man. Well, there it is. The world is as it is. I shall never see that old fool again and if I do it'll be my funeral."

"You—like him," I said

"I love him."

Sahayle went quiet then, looking at his hands, eyes half closed.

"Without him I would have perished. It's true, he found me and he took care of me. I didn't fit anywhere, church temple or mosque and neither did he. But he really cared for me. He has done a lot for me. He made me learn English correctly at evening class. He paid for those lessons. He said your accent counted for everything, most of all respect. And I have betrayed him as he said I would."

"You're not going to drive it, are you? You're in shock."

"Yes, I'll meet my friend somewhere in his car and we will drop Baaba somewhere, best you don't know, but it will not take him long to re surface and regroup and by then I must be away. I've got all the money for him, he will have it, and he will not bother you. It's me he will come after."

"Let me see your face," I said and he turned to me and laughed.

"What's so funny?"

"It's the kind of thing a wife would say."

"Sorry," I said. "I didn't mean."

"You don't have to worry about me. I've been taking care of myself for a long time."

"Ok," I said.

"Will you please go now? They'll be waiting for you. Mrs. Dhaliwal is coming."

I stared at him. How could he remember that?

"Alright. Will you get a word to me somehow, once you're out of the country? You could call Princey. Let me know you're ok."

He reached into his inside pocket and drew out a pack of two pills. "Take these. You might need them. They'll just get you to sleep."

"These are the same as my mum's!"

"One at a time won't harm you. From the look of him, I suspect Princey gave him ten or twelve and the alcohol intensified the process. Liquid cosh they call them."

"You don't take them do you?"

He nodded

"But why? They're so strong."

"I don't like to lie awake at night. A couple won't do you harm."

"Alright," I said and put them in my jean pocket.

"Go," he said

I walked up the hill and I didn't look back. I had to spend four hours in Brent Cross. I looked at my phone. Ash had called twice. I went to my memory and deleted Victor's calls. The police are clever but it was his own people that Victor had to worry about now, it was his own that would finish him once Mortea'zar came to consciousness. Where would they dump him to sober up? In a field somewhere? In a reservoir like the Welsh Harp?

He might still die. He might still overdose.

I wish he was dead, I thought miserably. He had ordered the murder of Princey's husband and who knows how many. And he had killed with his own bare hands. But if he died, another Mortea'zar and another would rise up. There would always be evil in the world. Why don't I believe in God, I thought suddenly. If I did, I'd be down on my knees praying. But what sort of God would save me? I disposed of a dead body. I helped a blackmailer dispose of another. *He* does. He believes, I thought. He's been a criminal all his life and yet he said it was God's judgement on him.

Brent Cross was unusually crowded and I was glad. I forced myself to not think. I had been to Brent Cross just a day ago with mum and Ash and now it felt like I was in an entirely different place. I tried to bring to mind the Asian Ladies Day out to Southall and all the warm sentimental feelings I had experienced but I couldn't recall any of it. All of it seemed like something that had happened elsewhere, to someone else. I sat down on the bench exhausted, spent. I looked at my phone. A text from Ash.

"Call me asap. Don't come home before contacting me. Trouble."

Chapter 29

The closer we got to our roundabout, our road, our house the more wretched I felt. I had no idea what my face looked like. The taxi driver had frowned when I'd got in. Maybe I smelled, I know I didn't look right. I needed a mirror. I took out my phone and tried to turn on the selfie camera but it wouldn't work. I need to correct myself before I get home. As soon as I got out of the cab, Ash came running down the path.

"We've been calling and calling –where the hell have you been?'

"What Ash?"

"Shaani, you've been gone for over 6 hours! You just drove off with that guy and who was that in the back? Mum's convinced you've been kidnapped or worse."

"So what, leave me alone."

Ash caught hold of my elbow

"What the hell were you doing with him Shaani?"

"I just gave them a load of books and bric a brac for the charity they work for. Can we go inside and have this conversation?"

"But who asked you to drive them?"

"Well no one. I just thought I should."

"Listen," he pulled at my sleeve. "Mrs. D came to see you. She waited for an hour! We didn't know what to say to her. Finally mum went out with her and then her driver dropped mum back and you *still* weren't here. And the--"

"Oh so what? Who cares?"

Ash gripped my arm. He put his phone to his ear. "Yes, yes. She's here. Ok, yes. Hurry up."

"Get off me. I've got to take a shower. I feel sick."

"Mum's on her way. ...I don't know where she's *been*. She was frantic Shaani, never seen her like that. It's one thing when she gets flustered and silly, that's just funny but when you weren't here she just went haring off. She's on her way back, she keeps saying she must see you, talk to you, she was really scared that you've been."

"I don't want to. You talk to her."

I wrenched myself away and tried to enter the house but Ash put his arm out and barred my way.

I sighed. "Alright I'll wait."

As I walked into the hallway I saw Princey framed in the kitchen door, standing at the counter chopping vegetables, as neat and compact as ever. She didn't even turn around. So she had stayed here all this time. Unusual. She rarely came to us in the evenings and whenever she did we never let her go home on the bus, we put her up. But maybe Princey didn't feel like being alone tonight. She may have roofied Mortea'zar for her own reasons but she had also done it to protect me and by extension the Devs. We had an unspoken secret between us now.

I went into the lounge and sat down. And then Princey was there, with a cup of hot very sweet tea.

"Tell her Princey. They phoned up for you Shaani, the police."

"He said to pass on the message that they will come and see Miss Shaani Dev tomorrow afternoon."

"They want to question you. I wonder if you should have a solicitor? They can make you say things."

"I haven't done anything, what do I need with a ---"

"Drink the entire," Princey said and I obeyed. "It's all right Ash, Shaani is fine and mum will be home in a minute. Just be calm everyone."

I rubbed my face and took a deep breath. The sugar whooshed energy around my body and zinged me up. I was in myself again. I was sitting in the lounge. The light was dappling in through the window and Ash was standing over me, helpless. And Princey had a towel in her hand. And then the front door opened and mum came running in.

"Where have you been? Where have you been?" she shouted.

Her hair was mussed up and her pupils were dilated and her handbag was tangled in her elbow and her jacket. She looked comical.

"Where've *you* been?" I said staring at her.

"Looking for you! I thought you'd just gone to the Leisure Centre. Ash said you drove off at top speed. Princey didn't know where you *were*---Ash said you went off with that man, Sahayle. I thought he'd abducted you. I thought you'd been kidnapped. I didn't know what to---"

I started laughing.

"It's not funny!" she sat down on the sofa with a thump.

Princey looked at me and went back to the kitchen. She returned with hot black coffee for mum.

"Mum?" said Ash with disgust. "You're *drunk*. I just can't believe this family. You're meant to have been looking for Shaani--"

"Oh do be quiet Ash. Thanks Princey. Shaani, are you ok darling? I couldn't find you anywhere and I couldn't ask Mr. Singh to drive me around, he would have made it into something, and I couldn't ask any of those low lives at Dollis Cars, so I. And I couldn't ring Sharmilla and say come back, help me find my daughter. I just had no one to ask. I went to the Leisure Centre but they didn't know anything and then, I panicked. I just panicked. I went into The Mill at the top of the road by the roundabout. I had a drink. I needed it. I didn't know where you *were*."

You've had quite a few, I thought. And your hair!

"For Gods sake mum. Get it together," said Ash. "Stop laughing Shaani. Are you off your head? This is serious. Did you hear what I said? They phoned up! They're coming to question you tomorrow. The --"

And then Princey was there, her hand on his arm.

"That's all right Ashish. Dolly sister, that's all right. Drink the coffee it will do you good. And then sleep. And I'll tuck you up."

"But I want Shaani---"

"She'll come up and see you in bed after she has had something to eat. She is very fine, she is safe. Ashi you stay here."

Ash came and sat down next to me while Princey took mum upstairs. He looked at me with such a mournful face that I felt like laughing. He's brilliant but he cant cope with anything that isn't perfect. It makes him uneasy. Mitch had said that.

"What the hell's going on with her?" he said eventually.

"She just got freaked out. And you know mum, she can't handle stress too well," I said. "I take it she doesn't know about the phone call from the police? She'll be having kittens."

Ash said, "I thought you were dead!" and looked at his buzzing phone.

"Is that Giselle?"

"Never mind her."

"Aren't you meant to be going to her birthday party? On Brighton Beach?"

"I can't, not when---"

"Ash, go! I'm here and Princey's here and mum's just a bit. Tired and emotional. I'll go up and talk to her. Honestly, I'm sorry I worried you. You're not supposed to worry anyway. What's the matter with you? You're the Indian boy baby!"

Ash smiled lopsided.

"Listen brainbox, I'm fine. I just forgot the time, the car broke down, and I started wandering about the shops. No big deal. What I need is a shower and sleep. And basically Ash, we all know you are more hindrance than help around here so get lost!"

"Where's the bloody car?"

"I left it in Brent Cross car park! I couldn't start it!"

"Why didn't you ring the AA?"

"The cover's lapsed. Mum didn't think it was worth--"

"Oh for Gods sake, what is going on in this family? These are essentials!"

"Relax Ash. Look it's just gone 9pm. Tell Giselle's driver to come pick you up. When you come back tomorrow everything will be back to normal."

"Really?"

I knew he was desperate to leave.

"It's her 16th. She'll never forgive you. Bring us back cake. And listen don't say anything to that lot. They don't need to know the police are coming to our house. And you don't need to be here either. I'll keep you informed."

"Are you sure? I'll get my jacket and stuff from my room."

I was glad to be alone. I didn't bother to turn on the lamp. The evening light lay soft across the room. The day not yet done. I could hear Princey moving about in mum's room and mum's small groans. I felt nothing. I couldn't be bothered to worry about mum. She was drunk. It was dull. Tomorrow the police would come.

He's been arrested six times, I thought scornfully. And you couldn't convict him, none of you could. He knows how to look after himself.

I heard footsteps bounding downstairs.

"Text me," said Ash pushing his hair back with the back of his hand, a winning smile on his face.

"I will. And by the way?"

He stopped and looked at me earnestly, his hair up in tufts. The little man of the house.

"I'll outlive you every time little brother."

He left closing the door softly and I heard the Daimler drive off.

Ash is safely away, mum is in Princey's capable hands, now I can *think*. I can't not belong to this family, I thought suddenly. It's the glue to everything that matters. If you don't belong to a family, you don't have an anchor. However much people say it isn't true, it is true. Without family you drift, you become air. But *he's* not like that. He's a real person. He's done things and he's street smarts and he's.

He's tangible. He isn't air. He'd know how to answer the police. He'd be much better than me.

Anyway, he's gone. He's on his way to Mexico. He's on a train to the airport. He's gone.

I walked over to the window and was shocked to see how it looked out there in the world; everything bathed in a clear lemon light; the coarse grass looked yellow, the leaves on the young trees were trembling.

He's gone now. He's on the train. He's on his way to Mexico. But in my mind, I could only see him in that layby where we had sat on the little mound of green when he had come back to himself. His hair perfectly combed, the way he held himself so proud and elegant.

There were footsteps overhead; a door closed. I went into the kitchen and sat down and waited.

Everything was still and snug. Princey had put on the lights underneath the cabinets, which made the worktops glow. I looked at the perfect same size cubes of potato and florets of cauliflower in their own bowls steeping in water so they wouldn't discolour. The knife and the chopping board. The small jars of cumin seed, coriander, turmeric and chillie powder neatly stacked. The fresh bunch of coriander standing in a glass of water, because it came 'alive' when you did that instead of leaving it in polythene in the fridge. The back door with a homey gingham curtain on the top part.

Princey came. A cold rush of breeze enveloped the space around us.

"Princey, we haven't got long. Do you. What did the policeman say exactly? What did he want?" I said lowering my voice.

"I just took the message like he asked me to"

But what do you *think?* What do they suspect? What shall I say tomorrow? There's so much about your life I don't know. It's terrible that I don't know the losses you've endured. You're so brave Princey. I love you. I thank you for what you've done for me. Please stay with us always. Don't ever go away from us, how would we cope?

I stood in the kitchen looking at her but I couldn't say any of those things.

Anyway, he's gone. He's on a train to the airport now.

"Shall I make you a plate of roti and subzi?" said Princey.

"No don't bother now Princey," I said. "You'll stay won't you? Please. I don't want to be alone tonight."

She nodded. I wasn't alone. Mum was home but she was useless. Princey knew I needed her there. In the middle of the night I might go off my head or something. I'll take those pills and go straight to sleep. What was the story he said we had to keep to? I can't remember. Anyway, it was stupid. He's gone now. That's good, he's long gone, they won't catch him.

"I'm sorry for your loss Princey," I said.

It had happened five years ago but I'd never said it. I'd never known it.

"He was not a good man. But he was mine," she said. "Mortea'zar got him killed for spite."

The setting sun made a gold dazzle on the front door but the brilliance didn't reach Princey; she stayed in the shadows.

When she stayed the night she slept on the sofa bed in the study downstairs and I asked if she wanted me to set it up but she said no, she'd do it. She wouldn't look at me. I went upstairs and thought I must write to dad tonight, I must! I got out my writing paper set and sat down at the desk but I couldn't think of anything to say. So I took out an old letter I'd written and rejected because it was too boring, full of the weather and I just copied it out word for word and put the new date on it.

Chapter 30

I took out the pills Sahayle had given me and swallowed one with a glass of water. I don't even know how strong they are or what's in them, I thought. I don't know what it will do to me. Only I knew it wouldn't do me harm. Not from his hand. I wasn't afraid. I got undressed in a hurry and took a shower. What if I didn't make it to the bed and fall asleep in the shower and woke up and it was still running? How long would it last? What if they can't wake me up tomorrow? Just eight more and I'd be unconscious, ten more and I'd be dead.

Mum took them all the time but we'd never discussed the subject. I felt weird about drugging myself to sleep—it was one of those things I suppose I disapproved of. I've never said it to mum because she's sensitive about it. I'll get up early and go for a swim tomorrow. I don't want her to come in and start trying to talk to me, I couldn't bear it. I've got to have a clear head tomorrow.

They're going to ask you about Max. Is it just routine questioning when they come to your house? What if Hodgkins takes me down the station and there's a tape and another officer present? Is that an official police interview? Is that when they caution you before they arrest you? And if I start babbling or speaking gibberish because the pill's made me go loopy? How do I know how it will affect me? I've got to talk to Ash tomorrow. I've got to tell him something. Nothing is as important as getting through this night. Just becoming unconscious.

But what is there to stay awake for? It's all out of my hands. He's on his way to the airport. No, he's on the plane now. He must be on a plane now. How many hours behind is Mexico, maybe he has to change in Miami? I snuggled down into bed, waiting. What's the matter with that pill, I thought? When's it going to start? I'll give it another ten minutes and then I'll take the other one.

I closed my eyes, and a face formed like in a kaleidoscope. A long mournful face. Oh yes. Mr. Kyriacos, our maths teacher in year 10. Pythagoras, real person not just a triangle? Really! I heard he died. Mr Kyriacos. I didn't know he was married, we all thought he was gay. Why did we lock him in the language lab?

"Mr. Kyriacos?" I asked apologetically but no one answered.

I rolled the pillow in half and dug my head into it. What was it they used to call those rulers? I stretched my legs, yes it was very relaxing trying to remember. School days. Did I miss them or was I glad they were over? Uni would be different. Did I really want to go? I wasn't really worried I thought if the pill worked or not, as long as I could just lie here and feel floaty.

Princey's voice was buzzing in my ear.

"I'm sleeping. Go away!"

"Wake uppppp shake up"

"Princey, go away!"

"You've got to hurry up now," said Princey and put a cold sponge on my head. The water dripped into my neck and I sat up.

"Come on, quick," she said.

"But I'm still asleep Princey. I'm not awake yet," I said tearfully.

"Quick put on your coat and be very quiet."

As she helped me on with my coat I thought it's like my head is a pumpkin or something, it's just sitting there.

"Whassatime?"

"Almost four o clock" said Princey.

"It's going to be light soon," I said and started crying. "I didn't get enough sleep. I've got to have more---"

"I know dear, but you've got to come now, quick as you can."

I followed her down the stairs and we went into the kitchen. The moonlight was streaming in through the window.

"It's raining," I said.

"Not much,' she said and we went out of the back door.

I saw a man moving along the wire fence to the golf course and disappear into Lovers Lane.

"Now," she said. "Go across the road and walk into the Lane. I'll stay here."

"Now?" I said, tears running down my face. I tried to wipe them off.

I looked left and right, nothing was stirring. I didn't look back. I walked across to the entrance of Lovers Lane. Now I was wide awake. This was no dream. As I walked into the entrance, the path seemed to glisten, its little pools of water and mud glinting under the light. I walked a little further until I saw him standing further down. He was wearing the Burberry and he had a hat on, one of those bakerboy hats or caps with a bag slung over his shoulder. He was smoking a cigarette and I could see the smoke and the outline of his face.

"Thanks for coming out to see me," he said politely and it was so formal, like a job interview or something.

He's supposed to be in Mexico. And yet, here we were in this dark silent clearing, with the trees meeting overhead, and it was like a tunnel. I knew it went on forever into darkness. But I was awake now.

"I wouldn't have come, only the thing is I had something of yours and I didn't know how else to get it back to you."

"Are you all right?"

"Oh I'm all right."

He took out an envelope from his inside pocket. "It's in there. The SIM card. There aren't any duplicates, or transparencies. You can be sure of it. You can destroy it any way you please. You have no need to worry about them now."

"You've got to get away Vic," I said.

"Take it won't you? Take it," he said. "And I have the jewels for you too. I told you I'd get them for you didn't I? They're in this box." He took out a flat blue velvet box from his rucksack. "They weren't as fancy as I thought they'd be."

"Vic…"

The huge wave was coming, threatening to plunge me and the street and the trees out from under my feet, lifting me up and smashing me against the rocks.

"You've got to get going."

"There's no big hurry," he said and sighed. He took a long drag off the cigarette and threw it away.

"Yes there is. Of course there is. There's a policeman."

"Oh yes, I saw him earlier. He's just community patrol, neighbourhood watch scheme. I kept out of his way."

"Listen, you've got to go through this lane, it's dark and it leads all the way to Hendon. You can run along it, no one will catch you."

"Don't worry, he won't bother me."

"Of course he will. That's why he's here! They have Neighbourhood Watch, local Bobbies on the beat here. Because of burglars."

He smiled nicely. "Don't worry, he's not after me."

"The police left a message for me. They want to question me tomorrow."

He was looking at me now, alert and thoughtful.

"Vic."

"That's what Mortea'zar meant. It's what the poor man meant when he tried to tell me."

I couldn't understand the words he was speaking, only the tone.

"You'll tell them everything. You won't be able to help it," he said. "The police frighten people. It's how they do their work."

"But it'll be about Max, not. Not anything else. That's all they're interested in. That's all they're looking for, a lead to Max. Nothing else. I mean there's nothing that can hurt you in it at all. I would never say anything about the."

"You'll always think of protecting your family first. You're a good girl. You're bound to them like no other thing. And you'll go to the ends of the earth to make sure they're safe. It's how you're made."

"I'll never say anything about you. I never will."

"I believe you," he said.

"Why don't you believe me Vic? I honestly won't say a thing. You don't know me."

"I know you've got guts! The way you ran across the road and grabbed that child. Jesus. The way you helped me when I'd lost my mind! You were incredible. I've never seen anything like it. Quick as a flash you came to my rescue. Really, I've never seen such a girl. And the way you dismissed your brother! Hah, and we were away, in the car, nothing doing. You've been fine to me."

"No I haven't."

"Well, it's more than I've ever known," he smiled.

"No, you've got to get away."

"Yes, I'll go. The air is so very fresh here isn't it? Don't they call it Lovers Lane?"

He took my hand and held it lightly. He didn't look at me at all, but averted his eyes like a shy little boy.

"Lets walk away from the light," I said.

I wanted to go deep into the darkness where they wouldn't see us or hear us. And we walked a little further in. The light was gleaming on the leaves.

"Did you get rid of him?" I whispered into his ear.

"Yes, but he'll be conscious now. Raging somewhere," he said. "My friend helped me. And the car was fine?"

"Where did you leave him?" I said.

"Better you don't know. There's nothing to tie you to Mortea'zar. Don't worry about a thing."

"You've got to get to Mexico."

"I won't make it," he said. "They'll start looking for me. After they question you."

"What? Don't be mad. They can't hold you! They've got nothing on you!"

315

"But still they'll catch me."

"But even if they catch you."

He took out another cigarette and put it in his mouth.

"Don't do that! They'll see a light."

He smiled like he was high. He was still holding my hand and I pulled it away.

"_Not listening to me!"

"Listen. The birds have started to sing."

"You've got something in your mind. Give it up Vic."

"You see every time I tried to sleep I'd see Baaba's face. I'd keep seeing it wouldn't I? What kind of life would I make for myself? Knowing I'd betrayed him. Knowing that one day he would find me and kill me?"

"Get yourself together. Come on!"

For a very clear second in my head, I thought of course I must go with him. Right now. We'll go on our way wherever life takes us, whatever comes we'll drive on through like we did before. There seemed nothing else that made sense.

I took his hand.

"You'll let me know you're all right?"

"I'd buy you a drink in a bar," he said. "If you were ever in Mexico."

"I've only ever drunk shandy."

"And that, too fast."

"You can't believe what Mortea'zar believes. My family isn't like that. I'm not like that. He hates people. You're not like that Vic. You're good."

"Don't worry. I never believed him."

Something welled up inside me. Now, now I have to say just the right thing, I have to choose the right word to make sure he goes and with full confidence, to safety.

And before I could think, he turned his head and said "Goodbye Shaani."

A pale sun was in the sky, and the day had begun and the birds were singing. Soon, they would be going to catch their early morning trains. I went to the kitchen door and knocked. Princey let me in.

"You're cold," she said. "I'll make you a cup of tea."

"No, I'm going to bed now." I said and started walking up the stairs.

A sound outside, like a pop.

He'll be gone, he'll be away, melting in with the commuters.

And in the midst of the blanket of birdsong I thought I heard someone running on the thick heavy wet earth in Lovers Lane. But that's impossible, it's too far away. The heating had switched on and even though it was summer, there was always a chill in the morning and I thought, it's warm and I'll sleep now. I'll be very still and go to sleep. I don't know what to do except sleep. I'll take the other pill if

I need it. It was on my dressing table next to a half empty glass of water.

Chapter 31

It was 4pm. I'd been asleep for 3.5 hours. I was still asleep and it was the *afternoon*. Mum woke me up. She was all dressed up but she hadn't gone to work. She told me to get ready because the police were coming at 4.30pm, she had spoken to them. When I went downstairs the sofa bed was all made up. I sat down and waited until I heard them come in.

"Hello Shaani," said DS Hodgkins. "I'm DS Hodgkins as you know. This is DC Nelson."

"We've spoken to your mum and now we just need to talk to you. Is that all right?" said DC Nelson.

"Hello Mrs. Dev. Please take a seat. We've come to ask Shaani some questions following your statement."

"What statement?"

Mum came and gave me a hug and then sat down.

"I went to the station earlier and made a statement."

"Whaaaaat?"

"Can we please proceed?" said Hodgkins.

"I just told them that I knew—about Max. How I met him and—"

"We're not bothered about that Shaani. We're glad your mum has admitted the relationship. However, she is not a suspect."

His phone rang, and he took it out and listened. He put the phone back in his pocket and thought for a second. Then he looked at DC Nelson and said "Code G" and DC Nelsons's eyebrows lifted.

I looked at mum sitting on the sofa, composed. I thought she would have been all in pieces as she had been last night. Had he said *she* is not a suspect, meaning I was? Or she is *not* a suspect, meaning no worries.

"So where did you go with Victor Sahayle?" said Hodgkins lifting a hand to indicate mum should be quiet. She fell quiet. "And who was with you?"

"It was his friend, I don't know him. I was driving them to this warehouse where they store the Charity stuff, and the car broke down. So what?"

"Shaani! Don't be rude and just answer the questions," said mum.

"Alright lets move it on," said DS Hodgkins with an impatient sigh. "Is this yours?"

He handed me a clear folder with a card attached to it.

"It's got my name on it, so yes" I said.

"So this *is* your Gym card?"

"So?"

"It was found by the side of the Dollis Brook. Care to explain?"

"I have no idea. I must have dropped it there. We go there sometimes. I mean it's a place. In Barnet, it's quite well known you know, like the viaduct."

"Indeed. Did you go there on the 16th or 17th of July?"

"How do I know? I know I went there last year when we went to some allotment fair nearby. It's a nice spot."

"Yes, but did you go there more recently?'

I see what you're trying to say now.

"No I didn't."

"Are you sure?"

"It's my gym card, I lost it there, sometime. I don't see why it's relevant."

"Not sometime. You lost it there on the 16th or 17th."

Mum looking confused went to say something but Hodgkins silenced her.

"No I don't think so, because I only went there last year, so. Or it might have been last month even."

"The body of Pietr Maximillian Kalnikoff was found 10 miles away in Woodside reservoir on the 28th and forensics put the death at 11 days. We have a witness that says they saw two people at the Dollis Brook on the 17th throwing something in. And your card was found in that vicinity."

"Maybe it got lost and ended up there.'

Lost and blown away by the wind to the spot where Max was pushed into the Brook?

"Do you know what Retinal Identification is?"

"Yes, they use it in passports"

"And gym cards now. Your card has a Retinal ID. But they didn't bring that in at Barnet Leisure Centre till the 15th and cards were issued on the 16th."

The i-ting, wicked innit? Troy had meant the 'eye thing,' not some iPhone app. Now I saw what Hodgkins was saying. I couldn't have lost my card before that day. The card before that day had been an old variety.

"Can you suggest how your gym card could have got to the Dollis Brook during that time?"

"I don't know. I can't remember using the card, they just let you in if they know you."

"So much for security," said DC Hodgkins.

"I'm often in the area, for shopping and whatnot further up the hill. To get the car. Well, washed or whatever. It might have dropped after that day.."

"You've had the car cleaned recently?"

"We always get it cleaned on the 1st of the month. But I had it done a bit earlier. Or later. Whatever. But it was still a Monday."

"What? Why?"

I shrugged.

"You always get it cleaned at the same place?"

"At the Slo Fast Car Wash. It's probably about a mile from the Brook. Because they're Slovakian. But they're fast."

"Ok, so your Retinal Identification gym card. Let's just go back to that."

"I might well have dropped it at the Car Wash and anyone could have picked it up. Or it might have blown away."

Blown away over a mile and just to the point where Max's body may have been dumped in the water?

"Ok," agreed Hodgkins politely and waited, but I didn't say anything. He obviously didn't believe a word. They've already checked the day I got it cleaned and they know it was the 17th.

"So on the 17th, it was a dark and stormy day," Hodgkins paused and smiled. "If you happened to be in the vicinity, did you happen to see two people by the Brook?"

"Doing what?" I said.

Hodgkins shrugged. "I don't know. Throwing the body of Maximilian Kalnikoff in the water?"

He was playing with me. Don't rise to the bait. Be polite. It's the police.

"I just got the car washed then went to the gym and then I came home. Oh I went for a coffee in Costa while they were doing the car. I had a latte no sugar. But why are you asking me about it? I thought you'd arrested someone ages ago. It was in the local paper. And you said so."

"We did, but we had to let him go. His name was Wojcik, a character known to us, but we didn't have enough evidence to hold him. Also, between you and me." Hodgkins leaned forward and looked me in the eyes. "I don't think he did it. Do you?"

I don't like his tone. I don't like what he's saying.

"I don't know."

"Just a few more questions, ok Shaani?" said DC Nelson. "You sure you wouldn't like a glass of water? We understand this must be difficult for you."

Is that meant to calm me down? The police these days have to be seen to be respectful and courteous, fair and impartial. Why's she being so patronising then? That's not in her Police Charter. Is it because we're Asian and they don't want to be accused of racism? Maybe she's just being nice. What's mum told them? A voice in my head told me to play it cool, very cool. They are trained, they are watching you constantly for signs.

"Right," DS Hodgkins cleared his throat.

"So we have a witness that puts two people at the Dollis Brook, struggling with a large item which they then threw in the water. On the 17th."

Mrs. Dhaliwal is your witness, I thought appalled. But he knew she was short sighted. He knew she didn't see two people. Why was he telling me this rubbish? He'd told *her* it wasn't reliable evidence. It's a game. He wants to find out something.

"We understand there is a little conflict of interest, and I've asked your brother to stay out of it. For now. But. This is serious Shaani. I need you to answer me. Or I'm going to have to ask you to come into the station for questioning."

I started to say something but my stomach lurched and I leaned forward and puked. They had no chance to step back, and their trousers got the brunt of it.

"OMG, sorry, sorry," I said but it was definitely better out than in.

"Can I…" said DS Hodgkins and Mum left the room to get a towel. She came back and gave it to DC Nelson who started mopping up her own trousers and DS Hodgkins trousers. The pile of vomit on the carpet lay unattended. Bits of the Mahavir snacks were riddled in it, carrots and chillies and something cream and bubbly. Looking at it made me feel sick.

"I think I'm going to throw up again. I drank some whiskey earlier. That's why I couldn't drive my car."

"Don't listen to her. My daughter doesn't drink. She never drinks. She's a very good girl!" cried mum.

"Please calm down Mrs. Dev, I know this is difficult for you."

"Where is your car? We want to take a look at it."

"I left it in Brent Cross car park. It's closed now. I."

"What were you doing there?"

"I was driving Mr Sahayle to the Charity warehouse---"

"What Charity?"

"Prostate Cancer."

"And what did you donate?"

"Books, books. We've got too many."

"And what did you put them in?"

"A sleeping bag I think."

"Why not cardboard boxes?"

"Well, it was just a way to get rid of the sleeping bags."

"Oh you had several to give away did you?'

"Yes."

"And you put the books inside the bag."

"Well, or stacked them up with the bag in between, I don't really remember. There was other stuff too. Bric a Brac and whatnot. The car was full actually. Lamps and other things."

"Prostate Cancer?'

"That's it."

"They don't take books or Bric a brac"

"Oh, well they must have made an exception. Mr Sahayle said it was ok."

"Mr. Sahayle,' said DS Hodgkins patiently, "Does not work for a charity. I assume you know that?"

"Yes. I just assumed he was collecting, volunteering. I didn't think that was his actual job. He's a teacher. Isn't he?"

"How do you know him?' said DS Hodgkins ignoring my question. The air smelled of vomit. Were we supposed to pay for their dry cleaning bill? "I don't really. He came to the house. He said he used to be my dad's student. And he wanted to take a look at the Middlesex Uni campus and had been hoping my dad would show him around, but my dad's away. And so I showed him the campus. I thought he was a teacher, or a supply teacher, lecturer whatever. And we got talking and he said he was – did we have any junk to get rid of. I—what? What?'

"He isn't a teacher, he's a criminal," said DS Hodgkins and sighed. "He's been arrested several times. For various kind of fraud. Counterfeit goods mainly. Passing and receiving."

"But that's not really criminal, is it?"

"Passing and receiving counterfeit goods? Yes it is criminal. Don't you know that?"

"Well, of course, Of course I know that. Sorry. Can I please go and wash up."

"Alright but put your clothes into a bag. DC Nelson will go with you. We won't stay longer, it's late and we all need to wash up. But take a shower and come back down. I haven't finished yet. I will need to take you down to the station tonight."

"But can't I come tomorrow morning instead? It's late now, and. It's late."

"I'm afraid that makes no difference."

I went upstairs with DC Nelson and she searched me.

"Sorry," she said.

Then she stood outside the door of the bathroom, which she told me to leave open. What did she think I was going to do, jump out of my window? I put everything in the bag and got into the shower. I stank. I had to wash it off. It's just about Max, I reminded myself. It's only about him. Maybe if I tell them everything at the station it'll be ok. They're just looking for Max. They don't know anything about Mortea'zar, they don't even know who he is. Mum had gone to the police station to tell them about her involvement with Max because she saw the state I was in. She wanted to protect me, but maybe she'd made things worse. She didn't know the whole story.

The shower was powerful and I bent down and let it massage my back, looking at the suds at my feet. Bloody Mrs. Dhaliwal, she was such a liar. She was so desperate for the limelight. She must have called him and insisted. Surely he knew she was liar. But what if she stuck to her story? What could anyone do to disprove her? I felt furious with her. She was blind as a bat without her glasses. Maybe part of it was the guilt but I didn't feel guilty. What had I done that was so bad? What she was doing, bearing false witness, was much worse, much worse. Wasn't it?

When I came downstairs I handed the bag over to the DS Nelson. Mum had a bowl of cornflakes for me but they told her no I couldn't have it.

"Was it you and your mum who were at Dollis Brook that day?" said Hodgkins.

"What?" mum and I said at the same time.

"We know your mother was in a relationship of sorts with the deceased. She told us. We know you went to see him at Pumping Iron and told him to keep away from her. And we know that on the night of the 16th, there was a meeting planned between them. Or so she says."

"What? Hang on, what are you on about?'

"You went to see him at Pumping Iron, right?"

"I did."

"And you told him to keep away from her?"

"Of course I did, but it didn't do any good."

"How's that?'

"Mum was angry with me. She said she'd sort it."

"Right. Well she told us that she did indeed decide to end it. And on the 16th, she says she went to meet him to say goodbye in person. But she's lying. She says she met him in The Mill their usual rendezvous –well no one remembers her, or him on that night. I think she's trying to cover for you. Which naturally leads me to wonder if you had anything to do with Max's disappearance. Perhaps you were at Dollis Brook not with your mother, but with Mr. Sahayle? Answer the question or else I'm going to have to take you in right now. In fact I will be getting forensics on your car as soon as we can get someone over there. Might not be for a few hours."

"If the car parks closed," I said wide eyed. "Can you still get them to open it?"

"Never mind that. Did you perhaps take the body in your car and together dump it in the Brook?"

"No."

"And was Mr. Sahayle here yesterday not to collect stuff for charity, but in fact to get rid of evidence that pointed to his involvement in the homicide of Maximillian Kalnikoff? Maybe Mr. Kalnikoff had come to the house to see your mum and you and Mr. Sahayle knocked him out, took him to the Brook? In a sleeping bag. And maybe Mr. Sahayle had come to dispose of any evidence that had been left behind…"

Disposing evidence a full 20 days after the event? Hardly likely. And what evidence would he have come to dispose? Even to me that sounded like a crazy conclusion for the police to come to. No, Hodgkins was trying to trap me into saying something else.

"No, definitely not."

"I'd like to speak to Mr. Sahayle."

"I'm not stopping you!"

He'll be able to handle himself. He's been arrested six times. Anyway, he'll be out of the country now.

"Got his number?'

"No."

"You sure about that?"

"Well, he called me a couple of times, about the junk in the garage, so that might be on here."

I took out my phone to look, knowing full well it was number unavailable, which I had deleted anyway. Mind you if he took my phone they could easily access the data.

"He probably had a burner. Does anyone else in your family have access to him?'

"No."

"What about …Mrs. Deshpande?"

 "I don't think so."

"She says she did call him a couple of times because he asked her to call him"

"Oh," I said. "I didn't know that."

"She called him on a number that doesn't seem to be available."

"Right."

 "How much do you know about Mrs. Deshpande? Her status and whatnot."

Whatever happened, I could not get her into trouble.

"Look…Princey works for us. She's really nice. She's just a simple lady. I mean, couldn't you just let it go this one time?"

Hodgkins smiled. "You're asking the police to do a special favour?"

"No sergeant," said mum curtly. "No one is asking any special favour. My daughter is being emotional and using inappropriate language. Please extend her some latitude in this matter. She's a very young nineteen."

Hodgkins looked at his phone and put it away.

"Have you already interviewed her?" I said quietly.

"Yes. But we'll need to interview her formally. At the station. She may have information on an associate of Mr. Sahayle who we are very interested in."

"Oh—will she need a lawyer? We can arrange--"

"My daughter is very attached to her. We all are," said mum. "Be quiet Shaani. Please!"

"You know she's illegal?' said DS Hodgkins looking pointedly at me.

Mum was looking at the floor. She looked up and said, "No Sergeant, she is not illegal. I checked her papers when I hired her, and they were all in order. I wouldn't hire someone illegal. It's against the law. I can vouch for her."

"Surely you're aware that many papers are forged these days Mrs. Dev. Her papers are not in order."

"I don't know anything about that. I can show you the photocopies I made of the references and visa she gave me. I took them in good faith," said mum. "We have to make the same routine checks in my work place, Gleaming White Dental Practice, in Golders Green. I'm very aware of the checks that all employers must make. I'm the receptionist there. But you know that. We don't hire illegal labour. It's unethical."

"I'm afraid we don't have the luxury of dealing in ethics. I deal with evidence. Systems and procedures."

It was a mad cat and mouse game they were playing. He knew Princey had been paid cash in hand and he knew that we knew she wasn't exactly totally 100% legal and that we had turned a blind eye to it. Everyone did. He knew it and mum knew it but they were talking in technical terms, covering themselves. About our beloved Princey.

"Her visa expired a while ago," he said. "As did her husbands."

"Maybe she's outstayed her visa but a lot of." I said and mum grabbed my arm.

"Shaani!"

OMG she's right, stop talking. This is not a conversation, it's the police questioning you. Don't volunteer information. What's the matter with you Shaani, you've got verbal diarrhoea all of a sudden.

"You don't seem to understand the fine line between what is legal and what is illegal," said DS Hodgkins looking at me and ignoring mum.

At the Havan he had been so ...different. Had I really thought he was a friend? He'd asked me about things to help him with his daughter. But he hadn't not really. He'd been setting a trap for me. And now, he looked positively hostile. I'd vomited on his feet and he knew I was lying. Or did he?

"I do, of course I do, honestly. I just thought…a lot of people do that."

"Just because a lot of people do it, doesn't make it less illegal now does it?'

"No.no.."

"Not paying tax is illegal. You know that? Right? Paying cash to someone not on the books is illegal. Living in a country without the proper documentation is illegal. Driving a cab without the proper papers or insurance is illegal. And dangerous. Buying Indian mangoes that are not passed by the EU are contraband. Shall I go on?'

"Are you going to inform on her?" I said looking straight at DS Hodgkins. "Because if you are, then we have to get her a good lawyer."

"Shaani, stop talking right now," said mum sternly. I'd never seen her so self assured.

"Well, immigration isn't my remit."

"So you'll overlook it?'

"I might. If she helps us."

His phone buzzed and he went outside the room to take it.

"My daughter's just being emotional," said mum. "She doesn't know the law. If you're illegal, you're illegal. She knows that. She isn't asking the sergeant to do anything. You understand don't you?"

DC Nelson smiled at mum and nodded. She was a nice looking young woman, I felt bad that I'd soiled her trousers.

"I know how difficult this is for…"

Hodgkins came back in the room.

"Right ladies. The interview is at an abrupt end. We won't be requiring any more information. We'll be leaving now."

"What?" I said. "What's happened."

"We've got a confession," he said.

Chapter 32

After the police left I was in no mood to sit and have a post mortem with mum. I didn't feel like sitting down with her at all. She had "confessed" her affair with Max to the police and she felt better about herself, and now they had someone in custody for the murder she wanted to be able to discuss it, gossip about it, but I didn't. There was too much going on in my head. I needed to be alone with my thoughts to separate them. I went upstairs and locked my door and got into bed. All I could see was Victors face in the darkness of Lovers Lane.

Was it him? Had they caught him after all? Had he given himself up? What had he confessed to? Or was it someone else altogether?

I lay wide awake looking at the ceiling. A long legged spider was making its way across and I pulled my duvet to my chin. I hate spiders! I held my breath as it finally, laboriously crossed the entire ceiling, it's long legs revolting me, it's jerky journey filling me with disgust. I couldn't take my eyes away from it, until it had disappeared in a crevice somewhere. I breathed out through my mouth a long slow breath the kind they tell you in Tai Kwan Do. Empty your stomach and allow the chi to be free.

All at once I felt like crying. The evidence Hodgkins had on me was real. My gym card at the Brook. Regardless of the false witness statement of Mrs. Dhaliwal, it put me there and whether they knew already that it was not the scene of the crime—and they surely did---they definitely knew from simple forensics that the body had been dumped somewhere along the Brook in order to reach the gap at Woodside park. He had evidence against me. It hadn't hit me hard when he was questioning me, but it hit me now like a hammer to the head.

He could have taken me for questioning at the police station with a tape, and I'd have to have had a solicitor. He could have arrested me. Mum had been on the ball, she kept trying to make me stop talking. It had not struck me so hard before, this awful realisation. The police were clever and they would extract the truth within minutes. I had come so close, so very close to I didn't even want to think to what. Imprisonment? I was old enough to be put in prison. Would they do that to someone for moving a body? Would I have had to go to court and plead my case? I had no case. It was just my word. Who was to say I hadn't knocked him out and was laying the blame on my brother who was too young to be imprisoned? I was the one who had gone to Pumping Iron, I was the one who knew of the affair.

And Ash would have been called in, and he would have that injured, dazed little chick look on his face. Yes he had chased a burglar down the road, but he had no idea of what had transpired, no idea. The whole thing would have come out. No Oxford and no Princeton, but also no marrying into the Tata-Khanna-Dhaliwal dynasty. And further, utter disgrace. How it would have affected us was beyond my imagination. We'd be finished.

Hodgkins had enough to bring me in to the station. He was going to do it. And just at that moment, a man had been arrested and he had confessed and set us all free.

Who else could it really be but Vic?

Goodbye Shaani.

Had he done it for me? This sacrifice? Had he known, or understood that I was implicated in some way with the Max disappearance and death? But who did that? Why, he didn't even know me. He didn't owe me anything. He had every right to hate me, because it was my fault that he had had to become a fugitive, estranged from the man who had bought him up. Mortea'zar was the only family he had. His Baaba. Vic should hate me and yet I thought maybe he had loved me. We were from different worlds. How could he have loved me? When did he have time to discover he loved me? Yet he had gone to some trouble for me. Almost from the beginning he had been sympathetic to me.

I remembered how we had walked together that day when he had come for the money at 11am and he had said it wasn't for him, and I had scoffed. That was the day the red ball had bounced onto the road and I had shot across towards the toddler. Those Chinese women! The mother who had collapsed at my feet. I'd never seen such a display. Vic had looked at me in a strange way. Why? Hadn't I done what anyone else would have? He said he'd never seen anything like it. And in the pub, he had told me personal things, but I couldn't remember what they were at the present moment, all I could remember thinking was "He's not going to harm me, ever." And in the pop up shop, why had I put on all those crazy clothes? I had felt so happy, elated. Was that how it felt to be in love? He had bought the jewellery back for me and it had delayed his departure considerably.

I kept tossing and turning. Sleep would not come. I mean, you can't have loved me Vic, you didn't even know me, that's not how it happens, love is something that takes time, it isn't instant coffee. But Vic let me look at you. Let me see your face darling. No, no you must run now, go quickly, you must get to Mexico. Oh leave me alone Princey, I'm still asleep, I'm dreaming, leave me to dream. Oh yes, it's not you, you don't want the money. I hate you, I hate you. Is that your real name? Are you Ukrainian or Indian or what? He can't even pronounce his name, it's Sohail and he says Sahayle. He's never had a proper job in his life, what sort of a man is he? People always do, yes you'd know wouldn't you? Blackmailer, Criminal, wretched half breed orphan without a real family, without a place in society.

And yet despite these jagged voices I drifted into a sound and sweet and gentle sleep. I was free. It was over. I could live the rest of my life.

A week later mum declared she was going to have a little Tea Party for our *desi* neighbours.

"Why?" I said.

"Well we've been here four years and we know this one, and that one to say hello to, but the Singhs are the only ones who've ever come to the house. It's time to consolidate. It's time to stake our claim and establish ourselves in the community of our neighbourhood."

"But, dad's not here," I said

"So what? Aren't we a unit by ourselves? Anyway, this is the 21st century Shaani. It's not as if we're going through some secret divorce. Vinod is in India for the highest of reasons and Indians more than anyone will understand that. He's there for us! Our piece of India. What's more important than your identity? It's the same as family? We should be proud of your dad. Yes, we've been hiding ourselves under the bushels for too long. Yes, we're going to be part of this community. It stuck me when I was wildly searching for you; I had no one to ask! It was between Sharmilla and Mr. Singh and the drivers at Dollis Cars. That's not right. We should be a community. And we will be."

I left the house and walked to the Leisure Centre. I had been walking there ever since the police questioning. I didn't feel like using the car which we had got from Brent Cross car park the next day. It was cleaner than it had ever been but neither mum nor Ash had commented on that. Mum had just said, I'll drive, and just like that I'd realised I didn't want to drive that car, not now. For now, I'd walk to the pool. It was good for me.

A 'thank god it's all over' Tea Party is what it was. Mum didn't know the half of it, but she too could breathe at last. Perhaps in some way this tea party was also about another kind of consolidation. She wanted to keep her base here, put down roots with the neighbours who were more like her, who would be her confidants and well wishers, before we entered the hemisphere of the Tata-Khanna-Dhaliwal Dynasty. The likes of Mrs. Dhaliwal and her kind would never be the people mum could depend on, even though she would have an elevated social status as the groom's mother. She needed her solid constituency close.

While I did my lengths I thought of how I could possibly verify whom the man was that had confessed? I couldn't just call 101! There would be a trial at some point. How could I find out about it? We hadn't heard from DS Hodgkins or DC Nelson. I don't know why I had thought we would. After all, it wasn't their job to tell us what had happened in an investigation. There had been nothing in the paper or the news.

How could I find out who it was? Why did I even *want* to? If it was Vic, then it was Vic. And if it were someone else, what good would knowing do? Whoever it was and whatever reason he had I knew it was the wrong man. I knew he hadn't killed Max, but if he had confessed to it we were free to live, so why disturb a hornets nest?

As I ploughed through the water I remembered the dream I had dreamt of Jacek Wojcik being accused of a crime he had not committed and how I knew he was innocent and it had seemed a whole other league of wrong to bear false witness. They've got the wrong man, it isn't case closed, I'd thought. And yet, when I got out of the water and stood under the shower I knew I felt differently. I was ashamed because I was relieved. It was over and I could breathe. I could breathe. It was a beautiful lie and I preferred it to the ugly truth.

The next few days were spent in a flurry of activity. Mum had drawn up a list of invites, seven people and with us it would be ten. She planned for a Sunday afternoon and with the help of Mr. and Mrs. Singh she called everyone and was delighted that everyone could come! Most of these names were a blur to me, but they were Indians who lived close by in surrounding streets, and mum had met them variously at the post office, or in Tesco, or she simply knew of them through another Indian. Indians were champions are finding connections one way or the other and we joked that some bright IT spark could probably use algorithms to find a family connection between every one of the billion and counting population of India, never mind in the Diaspora.

Mum wanted to cook everything from scratch, which is what this kind of Indian guest would expect. There would be no chef bought in, or even takeaways bought in, no *sir,* everything would be cooked in her kitchen and she set about it with gusto. Princey wasn't answering the phone and so we assumed she was sick or her credit had run out as had happened before because Princey was not used to this 'western' way of keeping us informed. If she was sick, she was sick, she didn't prioritise informing us, in the same way as if she was late, she was late, it didn't merit explanation, it was just the way things were.

Mum went to Brent Cross for her Botox injections and I waited on the bench next to Lola Cakes, eating a red velvet one. It tasted of sawdust. Thank you darling for no judgments, she said. I shrugged. It was her choice. What did it have to do with me? She was in the Botox place for over 40 minutes and I saw her having a coffee in there. I looked in the passbook quickly while we were in the car and I saw she had withdrawn 2k. I didn't bother to question her about it. She didn't even look that different but according to her, she had had the deluxe melt away the wrinkles option and it was some special doctor that did it. Hence the expense, she explained scrupulously.

Then she drove us to Ealing Road and we did all the vegetable shopping and later in the day she began to draw up lists of menus, surrounding herself with cookbooks and her own recipes. She was utterly absorbed and she put the shenai music on and sank into the books, determined I suppose to create the perfect menu. How quickly and seamlessly we had slipped into ordinary living! We hadn't discussed the events of the last few weeks at all, and nor would we. I felt sure of that.

I had cut up the sim card into little pieces and I had replaced the jewellery. Max was dead and someone, possibly Vic, had confessed to his murder. Ash was unofficially engaged to Giselle and dad had phoned to say he was coming home in a few weeks. The land now belonged to us, although as he pointed out, it would stay as a piece of land surrounded by barbed wire for some time yet, until we as a family decided what to build on it. If anything at all. In a few months I would be at university and a new life. Change was in the air and we were onwards and upwards.

And there was another bonus! A tiny miracle. Mitch's cancer had reversed. His number had gone from 129 to -3 and no one knew why. Ash told us in his usual low key casual way but we knew Mitch being well meant the world to him, and we decided our little Tea Party would be a celebration of this triumph. One good thing it seemed had led to another and there was no stopping the Devs.

Things can only get better, sang mum as she pored over recipes and raised her hands and eyes to the heavens when Princey's phone still didn't yield a reply. But hadn't Princey been to *other* houses, said mum because she thought she had heard on the grapevine that Princey had been to other houses, but for some reason she wasn't coming to us. I'll find out at the Tea Party, she said.

I didn't say anything. I wasn't surprised. In some way I had expected it. Princey had to look to her interest and she wouldn't want to connect herself with us any more. It was sad, so sad, but understandable. She had to think of herself and her family first. So many good things had happened and maybe to offset this balance of nature, a few bad things had to happen too and you had to live with that. In a few months I'd be gone to uni anyway, so I wouldn't even see her, so what was the difference?

"Hey yaaa eye?" shouted Troy. "I been in the back doing office work for the last few, so I aint seen you. So boring."

"Is it part of the job?" I said.

"You know? Because they want us to do the paperwork for the courses as well. No more pay obviously. We're like modern day slaves eye. Like there isn't even air con in the back, eye. Sweating man."

"Eye," I said nodding apologetically holding my plastic bag of wet clothes.

"Good swims?"

"Always," I said.

"You know dem mekkin inquirees coupla week ago?"

"Um---"

"Yeah. This guy they look for? The Pumping Iron guy? You know e was murdered? Shot five time I heard. With a Kalashnikov. Or maybe that was his name, anyway. His brains was splattered all over the road yuh know! It was drive by I bet you. Gangland execution and tings. That's what I heard anyway. It's Kill Hill innit? They caught him though. The killer."

"Oh—"

"No but listen, get this right? They got the accused behind bars right? They hextract the full confession. I bet they beated it out of him. Then they said man went and killed himself. Suicide to raaaas! Not even two days in custody. What do you think of that?"

"I don't believe it."

"Feds innit. Two days later? Man found dead in the cell? Man not a Hinglish man? You do the maffsyeah?"

"Not an Englishman?"

"Inside job innit. Po-po. What they do, innit."

"The police did it? What even after he confessed? Why?"

Troy scratched his chin. He looked like the confused emoji. The Botox wouldn't let him frown.

"It's a mystery. Aye."

I left the building and started walking home. It was boiling hot but super windy. The wind was from Sibera and it cut to your bone. This was August! And then this happened. It actually happened dad. If you read it somewhere you would never believe it, but I promise you dad it happened. It was like a sign. No, it wasn't like a sign, it *was* a sign. I think.

A little tornado of litter started circling my ankles. Rubbish, leaves, sweet wrappers, twigs, a sheet of newspaper, tiny stones, little pebbles, it was gross and disgusting. The newspaper got stuck flat to my calf while the rest blew away. I peeled it off and was about to chuck it when I noticed it was the front page of The Hendon Times.

The headline was **"Met Police to weed out Corruption"**

Ever since the national directive of the Metropolitan Police eight months ago, a serious investigation has been put in place. One of the real life Line of Duty detectives from Internal Affairs who "police the police" DI Maycock said, "It is our mission to drain the police force of all undesirable elements. There are unfortunately policemen at the highest levels who have been working in collusion with criminals, giving out classified information, meting out vigilante style 'justice' on behalf of gang warlords and this is not a situation that the Met is prepared to tolerate. Given the secrecy and fear at all levels of…"

I threw the paper away. My legs felt shaky and I walked even faster. It's a judgement on me, he had said and I'd told him there's no such thing, that's just superstition. And it was. I don't know about the creepy coincidence of the newspaper wrapping itself around my leg but I know that Vic did not give himself up because he was scared of judgement. He was a criminal, he knew what he'd done, and even if he felt remorse, even if he lost his mind for a bit with grief, even if he had developed a soft corner for me, he didn't confess because of *guilt or self sacrifice*. He had a plan. I know he did. He knew there was no evidence to link him to Max's death, none. He had a plan worked out.

But he had forgotten one thing. *'Tazers poodle.'* He had already slayed Princey's husband Sonny for Mortea'zar. Tazers poodle was the inside man high up in the Met.

What if Tazers poodle had executed Vic?

Chapter 33

I can't remember much in the days leading up to the tea party. None of it stayed in my head. I went through the motions. I did what I was asked to do. I wore the right clothes. I helped mum put out the dishes in the hostess trolley. Guests arrived. I went into automatic "Namaste aunty, Namaste uncle," although they were all strangers to me and afterwards when the lounge was full of chattering Indians stuffing their faces with samosa and cachoris, they all looked the same. Fat ladies with bulging spare tyres shown off in their saris, wiry henpecked husbands nodding like dogs, they all seemed the same to me, off an assembly line in a factory where they produced Bland Asians.

They didn't talk, they complained. About the catalytic converters getting robbed in front of your nose off of your BMW, the Soods who owned the dry cleaners and ruined your clothes; the Sri Lankans who were the new owners of the Spar and had hiked the prices up; the recent spate of burglaries which had skyrocketed ever since the neighbourhood had become expanded with social housing for *lazy white people* because Asians had always worked hard and never demanded anything from the government, taken the insults blah blah blah; the best house alarm systems that were a racket for printing money because nobody paid attention to them and that local locksmith must be a billionaire by now, and as for the Barnet Council who kept spending the taxes on traffic lights no one wanted, dear Gods let them all come back to earth reincarnated as dung beetles.

One topic of conversation was Princey.

"No, I haven't seen that witch," said one fat lady.

"Maid problem is worser in Barnet than Bombay," said a thin lady.

"They always leave, it's in their culture," said another. "You can't depend on them."

I was passing the snacks around and I suddenly thought Princey's gone back. Princey's gone back to Malad without saying goodbye. The compliments for mum's food came thick and fast and the snacks disappeared from the plates. I bit into a samosa but I couldn't taste it. It was like cardboard. That's strange, I thought. I can't taste anything. I remembered when we had gone to the Hospice for the last time and Naani was asleep for the last time. She didn't say goodbye, I'd thought.

"Shaani? *Shaani,* aunty is asking you a question. Where is this girl these days, in daydreams that's where," said mum.

"Sorry aunty," I said. "Well I just wasn't sure if I really wanted to go to university and then I didn't want to be in debt and—"

Ash walked in late as usual and every head turned towards him.

"Come come," cried Mr. Singh who had made himself official replacement head of household. "Now then Ashish, please tell us all about Physics!"

"Yes please tell us. Tell us everything."

"You are a genius, so you will know how to explain to us silly aunties na?"

"Oh but Physics is not just one thing," said mum proudly. "He can't just tell you. It's like asking what is India?"

"Well that's easy," said a fat lady. "Corruption top to bottom, terrible toilets, lovely food."

Ash grinned and sat down among the adoring throng and took an aaloo cutlet and bit into it.

"Quantum Physics is the study of…"

"No no no," said one uncle wagging his index finger. "We cannot understand quantum shwantum."

"Ok, so Einstein's theory of…"

"No, no,no, Einstein the Movie, I saw it on Netflick. Could not understand," said the same uncle, turning his hand into a lotus. "Tell us something we can understand."

Ash giggled.

"There is something to do with apples, I am sure of it," said the same uncle, wagging his finger and lolling his head to Mr. Singh. "Or is it pears?

"Maybe it was a mango," said Mr. Singh hopefully.

"Yes, that's right uncle. An apple fell on a mans head and he discovered gravity. His name was Isaac Newton."

"Ohhhhh Suck Neutron, that's right, and then?"

Ash looked across at me and winked.

"Yes, Suck Neutron established three laws of motion. One, a body will remain at rest unless acted upon by force. Two, a body will accelerate if a force is applied to it. Three, for every action, there is an equal and opposite reaction."

Everyone nodded wisely, none the wiser, and began a fresh list of complaints about the neighbourhood.

I stared at Ash.

"Hey sis, what's up?" he said walking over to me and stood by my chair.

Something told me to run, get away from there.

"Ash…" I started to say and then I saw the spider. It was the same one, entering from the hallway, it's long awkward spindly legs crawling now across the room. This spider had traversed the entire house. Everyone was talking at the top of their voices and no one saw it except me. It was coming towards me, slowly, deliberately. I put my hands over my mouth to stop from screaming.

And then Ash walked over to it and put his foot down with one single stamp.

"Nooo! Ash! Ash!" I cried.

He bent down and scooped it up into his cupped hand. He turned his head towards me and slowly his face formed into a winning smile.

"Don't look so shocked Shaani. I didn't kill him, I just gave him a scare," he said and walked out of the room with the dead spider in his hand.

Something like an earthquake went off in my head.

I got up and followed him out into the hallway and out of the house.

"Shaani! Aunty asked you---" mum was saying, but I wasn't listening. I wasn't going to ever listen again.

I closed the front door behind me. Ash was crouching down, flicking the spider into the ground.

"Ash."

He sighed and stood up, almost towering above me.

"Ash," I said, my bottom lip trembling.

"For Gods sake Shaani, sort yourself out."

He had that expression on his face, the dazed chick, the injured confusion. The expression I had always labelled as a kind of innocence. The look of the very clever who have no subterfuge, or guile, or irrationality.

But it wasn't that at all. It was a mask.

"What you just said back there.."

He folded his arms.

"The penny's dropped. At last."

"You knew he was dead when you left him there that night."

"Of course I knew," he said with irritation. "What am I a moron?"

"You knew you'd killed him. But you didn't mean to…it was an accident…"

He sighed again and rolled his eyes.

"Your trouble is, you keep analysing everything and jumping to all the wrong conclusions. You want the world to be as you see it. Not as it is."

"How could you Ash?"

"Oh how *could you Ash, oh oh*," he mimicked. "For Gods sake Shaani, he was a nobody. Who cares? He wasn't a Mitch Rosenthal, a great mind. Or an Ashish Dev for that matter. What productive or important thing did a person like that ever do in his life?"

"Are you serious?"

"Come on are *you* serious? All lives matter? Come *on*!"

I couldn't speak.

"But..but… he was a poisern! He was a youman! Life is sacred!" said Ash in the voice of Bugs Bunny.

"It's a joke to you? A body will remain at rest unless acted upon by force."

Ash started giggling. "Of course it's a *joke*. A pretty good one, don't you think?"

I shook my head. "No, no Ash. I….For *you* I…To protect you, I…"

"Yeah yeah yeah, Shaani sister to the rescue again. Well done. Gold badge. Now we're getting to the real subject at hand. It's all about you isn't it? Your pain. Your outrage. Your feelings."

"You knew I'd moved him?"

"Well, duh it didn't take an Einstein to work it out. That was your choice. A rather idiotic one if you don't mind me saying, but of course it was exactly what you would do. Shaani knows best. Shaani the super saviour sister. Anyway, the entire thing's over now, it's boring. What's the problem?"

I stared at my brother in disbelief.

"It's been you all along. You put that spoon in the sink so it would splash up and ruin mum's blouse."

Ash giggled.

"And it was you who hid her phone."

He giggled again.

"You didn't like it when she said it was bad luck. You wanted us to know it was deliberate. Clever."

He made the same gesture that Mitch makes, slicing his open palm across as if to usher in good times. But Ash is not

Mitch, he never will be. And he isn't you dad and he isn't me. Or is he? Are Ash and I different sides of the same coin?

"Why Ash, why?"

"Hmm, let me think. Fun?" he said making jazz hands. "But you don't like that answer do you?"

"How could you? *How could you?*"

Ash shook his head and smiled.

"Listen to yourself. You're so full of it. You're a narcissist Shaani. You want to control everything. You think you're street smart and wise and you're the only one who knows best because you're good. You think you're above everyone and normal rules don't apply to you. A normal person doesn't dispose of a dead body, for whatever reason. A normal person doesn't go and sell the family jewels, yes I know you tried to do that, I knew that junk was in your bag. We're not so different you and I."

"You and I? No Ash. Whatever we were is finished. You're not my brother. I can't look at you."

"You're running out of family members to look at Shaani. You can't look at mum because oh she's let you down by oh shock horror, having sex! You can't look at me because oh…I killed a spider, an insect. Who's left? Oh yeah daddy. Our great and wise old man. With his wonderfully lofty ideals. Our very own Gandhiji. Our very own statue on a plinth. Why don't we put him up in Trafalgar Square?"

"How can you be so hateful? Doesn't anything matter to you at all?"

"Sure it does. But the way you go on, it's so. Boring. It's all so boring. You think if I say something about dad I've disrespected him and I should be banished to hell? Who cares? You can say anything, you can do anything. None of it matters."

"Yes it matters. He's your father and he's a good man. He doesn't deserve your disdain. Max wasn't an insect. He didn't deserve to die."

"And why are you so up on your high horse? It was ok for you to move the body when you thought it was an accident, but now you're simply *outraged* because it was deliberate? What's the difference? It's just your vanity."

"My vanity? But you killed him. And you don't even care."

Ash laughed and pushed his hair back with the back of his hand. He looked at me earnestly.

"What is it that bothers you most? Is it that I stuck the walking stick under his chin precisely to cut off his windpipe, or is it that I don't care? Would you prefer me if I sat with my head in my hands, full of remorse? What difference would it make to the outcome?"

"It makes all the difference Ash. Don't you know that? Don't you know that?"

He yawned.

"I'll be out for dinner. Save me the leftovers." He started walking and then stopped before stepping into the silent street and turned to look at me.

"You should have let me drown Shaani."

There was no expression on his face. It was a blank screen.

Chapter 34

For the first time in my life I did not get up at the crack of dawn. I was still in bed at mid day when I heard the postman. I couldn't get out of bed at all. I lay there looking at the ceiling sans spider. What am I supposed to do now? Tell the police the whole story and go to jail? And then will a psychiatrist come to assess Ash because he's too young for prison? If I do nothing, then what? What if he does it again? Or was it just a one off? Has he done it before? Why did he say I should have let him drown?

I started to write to you dad, the whole sorry saga. So many thoughts had raced through my mind all night and they didn't stop, they just got slower like tired runners in the marathon. With each fresh one, I seemed to lose who I was. My spirit, my faith, my beliefs. I could see them collapsing like the walls of a house under a wrecking ball. Ash my genius brother, who I had saved and loved and protected and known. Ash who I thought would always have my back and me his. I didn't know him at all.

Was he a boy who enjoyed wicked acts for their own pleasure? Was he actually mentally ill? Was he a hater, a fascist, a kind of Nazi who thought all lives really didn't matter? Even in his twisted state, had he been clear sighted about me? The sister he had known all his life? Shaani knows best. Was I controlling? What kind of a normal person disposes of a dead body? Why hadn't I trusted mum and shared the information? Had it been my vanity all along that had escalated the situation from bad to worse?

A man was dead because of it all.

And another man was dead by his own hand.

And yet I didn't want to say anything to the police. Ash would one day do something great for the world and we the Devs would belong to the Fuck You side of the family. The alternative was devastation. If I went to the police, I would be arrested, Ash was too young, but the marriage would be off, dad would know about Max, and our family would be no more. Perhaps Mortea'zar had been right all along about us. We lived in a swamp of lies. We preferred the beautiful lies to the ugly truth. Mortea'zar the evil man was still out there on the loose and Ash the brilliant boy was still out there on the loose. Both of them were part of my life.

I lay in bed for five days straight. Mum thought I had the flu. I could hear them downstairs. I couldn't make out what they were saying but I knew Ash was sitting at the breakfast bar and mum was cooking. There was an absence of Princey in the kitchen and in my life. The chink of glass, the knock of stainless steel saucepans, the supermarket music from the radio were still there but. O my beloved Princey had gone and I knew not where. Back to Malad under her own volition before they deported her? Or just deliberately far away from us? Still in London, doing for other people, living in the invisible cities of workers who live under the parapet, forever afraid. How would I ever know? She was like the dead and they don't talk.

And yet in my bed during those five days, the dead spoke to me, they engulfed my thoughts. Naani sitting on the couch telling me her 'best friend' all about her 'boyfriend' who was so sophisticated because he drank foreign whiskey made in a country far from Uganda. Princey squeezing the sponge over my head, wake up shake up but I'm still sleeping don't you understand? A man called Max who had shown a kindness to my mother and who had paid for it, asking me if I wanted a drink.

And other dead people who I had never met, they kept talking to me. A beautiful lady in a covered rickshaw asked me if I would look after her son who was across the black water and every day her heart broke a little because no airmail letter came. A doctor with white whiskers who couldn't write to save his life asked me to tell that pharmacist it was high time he stopped giving out the NightSleeps to vulnerable women who could not sleep, high time. A geeky teacher that a gang of us in school locked in the language lab one day for no reason other than entertainment, and he was too embarrassed to report us.

There were so many dad.

A young girl, Slovenian I think she was, and she had her arms cut off but she kept asking me if I'd just arrange her properly, tidy her up, it would be a great service. A man lying in a ditch, dead drunk telling me to make sure his wallet was out of reach, hide it, quick, it has my days work in it, I need to give it to my family but you see I bought a bottle of vodka. A turncoat, a snitch and a bad man who had fallen down in the showers told me he never danced with

363

that many girls, he never did, not that many and could I please be sure to tell someone this fact.

The loudest voice, the voice I couldn't get rid of was another man in a cell. He was making a noose with the sheets.

"But aren't you going to throw that out of the window and escape?" I said.

"No, it's for my neck."

"No Vic, don't. Please don't."

"It's a judgement on me."

"That's silly."

"Don't worry, I'll fix everything."

"You've got to go, you must go. You'll be on a plane now, maybe you'll have to change flights?"

"I know you're a good girl. Goodbye—"

"No Vic, don't you dare! Don't you dare!"

"Goodbye---"

"No! I won't let you. I won't let you. Look how strong I am? I won't let you. Vic, I wont let you."

These conversations go on for hours dad, there's no respite. The dead are stinking up the rooms in my brain. But they are not ugly. They are beautiful to me dad. They teach me things I didn't know. They bring me peace. There is nothing I like better than to sit among them at a table where delicious food is served. They all come and sit, one by one and they argue and tell each other stories, and they eat, my god they eat! They slurp and chew and mumble and burp and shriek and laugh and swallow and smile. I'm glad I invited you, I say, I didn't think you'd come. It would have been rude not to come, they say.

I turn the pages of the catalogue the university sent me. I'm expected to go to something called "pre Fresh" which is an induction day for all those who took a year off. Will it be like school after the holidays when they asked you to write an essay on what I did on my holidays? I look at the photographs of the buildings I will inhabit in three months. It's a shiny place in a green town. Everything happens on campus. I'll join all the societies. Try it out, see if it's me, meet people, we don't have to be friends for life.

I'll change from the introspective girl I used to be. I'll have three BFF's and we'll go around together and swop stories about makeup and boyfriends because normal girls are always in a group of four. I won't be a loner anymore. I'll dive into student life. I'll get around by the little buses there. I won't drive. I know mum's going to offer to buy me a car but I feel scared that I'll forget how to drive when I'm in the middle of the road. You can't forget, mum says, it's in your muscle memory. She's wrong. You can forget everything you know.

I'm banking on it.

I think about Victor Sahayle's face. I can't get rid of him. I hardly knew him. And yet my heart aches to see him again, just the once. My heart is like the ocean. It is uncontrollable. And I think about what Mitch said about projecting. Or did

I say that? Isn't it possible to bring things into existence? Doesn't the law of attraction tell you if you want something enough the universe will provide it?

But the Professors of Physics are angry because Physics says no such thing, the mumbojumbocrankies have twisted an idea and tried to authenticate a spurious claim about the law of attraction. It is opposites that attract, not the same that attracts. But what about the possibilities of the little miracles Mitch? 129 to -3? How come? I'm glad you're not at the dead table by the way. I want to call you soon but I don't know what to say to you except I'm so glad you're still with us. But I'm not really here.

I'm somewhere in between the living and the dead.

Sometimes when I'm having trouble getting to sleep which is every night and every day, I have this idea that he's alive and kicking somewhere, that he made it out of the UK and on a plane and got to somewhere in the world where he was free. Mexico or anywhere. It's possible. Almost anything is. He's resourceful, I know that. Victor Sahayle was a survivor. He'd never waste time on being unhappy.

You didn't put that noose around your neck Vic, you couldn't. I don't want your sacrifice, don't you see? I want you to be free and happy. I know that you're alive and you're just going in that direction, towards the good. Princey's gone, did I tell you Vic? I loved her you know? I don't think I ever told her though. Do you think she knew? You didn't tell me that you loved me but I knew.

On the sixth day I heard a nightingale behind my door.

Go to sleep, my little angel go to sleep.

My precious little baby, go to sleep.

You don't know how you lit up my life

And now all I want to do is look at you

Go to sleep, my little angel, go to sleep

Ah Dolly. I love your voice. I haven't heard that since I was this high. Tears started running down my face. I've never let her in because I've never trusted her. But she's never stopped trying to get in with me. It upsets her that I don't ask her opinion, and it crushes her that I don't trust her judgement, and she has awfully low self esteem and she's a very silly Dolly most of the time, but she ...

The door opened and mum walked in. I was so shocked I didn't have time to wipe the tears away.

"Get out, get out," I screamed, wiping my face furiously with the sheet, but mum just sat there like a Buddha. She just sat there. I turned my back to her and buried myself in the bed but she wouldn't leave. Finally I turned around and she was looking at me, her perfectly made up doe eyes all soft and puppy like.

"Have you got a key to Ashi's room too?" I asked eventually.

"Of course I have. I'm always nosing about in there. And I check his Twitter feed even though he's blocked me. I got Gosia at work to show me how to do it. How else do parents know what's going on with their kids? I didn't find anything out though. He just writes riddles and sentences I don't understand."

I stared at her.

"Total violation of privacy," I said.

"I don't care. I've sent him---He's spending some time at the Dhaliwals. He's been there for the last week. He's coming back today. It's just been you and me here sweetheart. Did you know?"

"No, he's been here, downstairs, with you." I said.

"No sweetheart," she said gently.

"But I heard him. I heard you both."

"Do you know what you've been doing this week?"

"Sleeping."

She sighed. "Not much of that. You've been pacing, mumbling, a bit of screaming."

"What?"

"Humming. Lots of humming."

I stared at her. I felt shaky. She was lying. But I didn't remember the days only the nights and the dead people.

"Have you been in here watching me?" I shouted.

"No, I didn't come in. I listened at the door. I was right outside all the time. All I could do was sing to you. Do you know how useless I feel? All I could do was sing. But six days is too long. It's an eternity to be without my daughter. I had to unlock the door and see your beautiful face. "

"What's wrong with me mum?" I said and started crying.

"I don't know sweetheart. But whatever it is, you've been all by yourself in it. Please talk to me. You've been all alone. That can dismantle you. Feeling all alone. I know how that is Shaani."

"You don't know."

"Ok sweetheart, forget me. At this moment I'm focussed on you. I know you've gone through something huge, I don't know exactly what it is but I suspect," she pointed at the shoe box. "The answers are in there. I wouldn't mind reading those letters."

"How do you know they're letters?" I said in irritation.

"Don't you know you hum when you're writing?"

"No I don't!"

"Yes you do. And I know you've been writing airmails because I saw the bundle on the shelf, and the bundle is a lot less now."

"I'm going to put a new lock on my door. You have no business coming in here it's unethical and disrespectful."

"Only in English houses. We operate under Indian law here."

I let out a huge sigh cum grunt. I was too exhausted to be angry.

"Anyway, I don't need to come into your room. I know everything about you. I've been studying you since you were born. Actually I was talking to you even before you were born. Did I ever tell you that? And I'd do your voice so we could have a conversation. You see, I--"

"You *made* me, yeah I know." I rolled my eyes.

"I didn't say I made you. You made yourself. I mean, you're not finished yet Shaani, you're still making yourself. Don't think you're finished sweetheart, there is a long road ahead. I didn't make you....But the basic material came from me I suppose..."

A shadow passed over her face and suddenly I knew.

"You've always known about Ash," I said quietly. "Or suspected. That there was something not right in him. That's why you've sent him away."

Mum put on her Gleaming White Dental Practice smile.

"Well, lets not talk about it now Shaani. We'll talk about it later. For now he's at the Dhaliwals but I can't stop him coming home. Dad will be home next week. So, it's just us for a few more days. I want you to stay in bed and get well. I can't have you getting sick. Do you understand? I can't --"

The words got stuck in her throat and she coughed a dainty cough to cover it up.

"I'm fine mum," I said looking at her face.

"I won't come into your room again, I'll cook your favourite and leave it on the hob and you can go and eat it when I'm at work."

"You didn't have any botox last week did you? You sent Princey away. You knew her papers were false. You bought her plane ticket. You gave her money."

"Make sure you eat something. And drink a lot of water."

"You did the right thing mum," I said with a lump in my throat.

"I did what I had to do," said mum looking at the floor. "Wasn't she lovely Shaani? We'll never forget her will we?"

"I'm sorry I can't talk to you mum. I…know I should be able to."

"You know what Shaani, from the age of 13 to when I met your dad at 18, I was fighting. I never asked for anyone's help, because I was stronger than the rest."

"What, you?" I said.

She was puny and if she broke a nail she'd be crying all week.

"I was a bulldog, I never stopped. I had my teeth bared and my fists up 24/7. In the playground, at teachers, doctors, social workers, nosy neighbours, you name it I would take them all on. I was the school bully. Girls were scared of me in the playground. Some boys too. I had to be tough because if I got soft for one second, if I got flabby, that would be it, I'd be buried. Getting married and having kids was the privilege of my life. I got to be soft."

"I didn't know that about you mum. I mean, I knew bits but---"

"Well you didn't need to know it baby girl, it's my—excuse my French—it's *my* shit."

I burst out laughing.

"What," she said eagerly.

"Mum honestly!"

"What?" she said smiling from ear to ear.

"One, you're so...*genteel* or you try to be. Who says, 'excuse my French' before they say shit, it's so...retro sitcom mum! And two, it's pathetic how you light up like a Christmas tree when you make me laugh, you're like an eager little puppy panting away!"

"Well you're a tough crowd Shaani," she said. "See, we're talking. The trick is to get to when you don't have to talk. You just know."

I nodded. I looked at her. We are family, I thought. Me and you and Princey and naani and her mum, we're all from the same place. We do what needs to be done.

Mum put her hand on mine.

We both smiled and it was a precious thing, the sort of thing you would put inside a cloth bag and swaddle up in a drawer. Something to keep safe. It would be the last time we made a joke. From now on we would be careful, very careful with each other. A branch tapped against the window almost politely. The wind was whistling through the trees and I imagined it coursing through Lovers Lane whilst a dark unfathomable beast moved noiselessly on the wet earth, ever forward.

I looked at the shoe box full of airmails and some personal poems and thoughts and diary entries, and I started thinking they might not be for you after all dad. The more I looked at the shoebox, the more this idea took hold. You weren't ever going to see them dad, they were destined for Dolly. They had always been for Dolly. They were to be the secret bridge between me and mum. Once the storm had passed.

"I'm going to work," she said getting up. "I'll be back by 4pm. Ash will be back at 5pm."

"Alright mum," I said looking at her.

O mother o' mine, I thought.

Downstairs the front door slammed shut. Outside the storm was brewing. The branch kept slamming against the window. I got out of bed and did my stretches. No one keeps Shaani Dev down, no one, I said out loud. I was unnerved. I opened the window and caught hold of the swaying branch, twisted it off, and let it fall to the ground. I couldn't hear it land because it was swept up by the wind. I closed the window and took a deep breath.

The unexamined life might not be worth living but I'd done enough examination; it was time for action. If you don't act now Shaani, you'll turn in on yourself. You'll implode. You'll take on all the guilt and responsibility. And what good will that do? What would be the outcome of such self sacrifice?

I made a list.

Feel sad, mad, bad, glad all day long and then the next day too?

Sink into depression and start taking blue pills?

Stop eating and sink to a size zero?

Cut yourself with a broken bottle so you can feel something?

Throw yourself off a tall building

Feel sorry for yourself 24/7?

No!

Fuck that, I don't like those options! I'm not doing any of that. I know exactly where I'm going and why.

I walked down to the roundabout with its cluster of shops.

Chapter 35

By 3.45pm the man had done it and I paid him. It was extra for same day. I stood behind the front door waiting till mum came home.

"Hello mum," I said opening the door.

"Sweetheart," she said and smiled but it was strained.

She went upstairs to get changed. I went into the kitchen and wiped down the counter. The clock overhead burped. 4.20pm. I straightened the homely gingham curtain above the back door. Then I got out the three bowls designated by Princey for the chopped vegetables. All the vegetables had to be cut to the same size to allow perfect cooking. I opened the kitchen drawer and saw dad's airmail there. I bypassed it and took out the knife and laid it on the counter. I switched on the lights underneath the cupboards. Princey's courage was everywhere in the kitchen; her sense of order and her little feminine touches. She had sewn the gingham curtain by hand at home and bought it in.

Mum came in wearing her lounge clothes, palazzo pants and long cardi. She was carrying an Indian magazine called Time Pass. It was full of household hints, film gossip, quizzes, games, factoids, astrology, cartoons.

It was 4.38pm

She sat down at the breakfast bar and opened the magazine.

"Look Shaani," she said. "Come and see this."

I exhaled and came over to look, my mind elsewhere.

"Look," she said and started reading it out. 'Definitions Of Your Name. Nishani is a Hindi word and not at all commonly used for a name. In English it has many meanings.' I've never seen your name mentioned before, have you?"

"No," I said. "I thought it was unique."

I bent down to look as mum traced her finger across the page as she did when I was little to help me read.

निशानी {nishani}

Nishani (noun) = souvenir

Usage: This gift was a souvenir of my birthday

Nishani = Keepsake, Remembrance

Nishani = Momento,

Usage: The vase is a momento of our time in Italy

Nishani = Trail.

Usage: There was a trail of blood.

Nishani = Token

Usage: Ram gave Hari a book on birds as a token of appreciation for his help.

We frowned at the slightly tilted descriptions and the strange little worlds the usage sentences conjured up with a little version of me hanging on to the track like a monkey, in the middle for the Hindi characters hanging off the same track. We looked at the magazine blankly and mum said without conviction, "That's quite interesting isn't it?"

The huge wave was coming.

For a tiny moment I let my mind drift into another space. I imagined waking up on a beautiful morning and bounding down stairs and finding all the junk mail on the floor. I pick it all up and something flies out and lands at my foot. I stop and bend down, the other junk forgotten. It's a postcard with two palm trees and the word Mexico written in fat letters like a hammock between them. Inside the letters are pictures of sun kissed beaches, sombreros, Tequila bars, jazz musicians and cacti. I turn it over and there's something written in loopy handwriting. I squint, I can't make it out. The postcard slips from my fingers and I go to pick it up and then I stop. It's only a souvenir.

Don't touch it, I tell myself. Don't go near it.

Ash was putting his key in the door. I went out of the kitchen and stood in the hallway. I heard him try to put the key in the lock, stop then try again. It wouldn't fit. For a moment there was a deadly silence, and then he pressed the doorbell. I waited. I knew he could see my form through the mottled glass.

"Shaani!" he said.

I didn't say anything.

"Shaani, let me in. My key's not working."

I walked up to the door and put my face against it.

"I've changed the lock."

"What? Why?"

"You know why Ash."

"For Gods sake, stop messing about. Pull yourself together Shaani, let me in. It's raging out here."

"Ash," I said quietly. "Listen to me."

"Mum!" Ash yelled over me. "Mum!"

It was a blood curdling scream, like the scream of a small abandoned baby.

I waited. The hallway stayed empty.

"Mum!" he bellowed, angry now. Demanding.

I kept my nerve. I knew mum was sitting in the kitchen, head bent over the magazine, trying with all her might to keep her nerve too. She had done what she had to do; I was doing what she could not bring herself to.

"Ash," I said. "You won't be coming back in the house. Go and stay with the Dhaliwals."

"You're ridiculous. You can't get away with this. What are you going to tell everyone?"

"I'm not. You're going to tell everyone that you want to stay with the Dhaliwals. You've moved out. You're a genius. You need space and fun and different people to be with. We're too boring."

"Let me in you stupid bitch!" he barked and I stepped back as if I had been slapped across the face. Something like my heart seemed to shrivel dry. It was possible for love to evaporate in a moment with a word or a gesture. Something as strong as love was also air.

"You won't enter this house again," I said.

"You're crazy. Let me in. You stupid stupid girl. You're making a fool of yourself don't you know that? There's no proof you idiot."

"That's the thing Ash. There is proof."

I looked back at the hallway. Still empty. I knew mum was listening to every word. Now Shaani, you have to say exactly the right thing.

"Rubbish," he said and banged his fist on the door.

"You were seen," I said keeping my voice low. "There was a witness."

"Who?"

"Mum," I said. "She saw you."

I waited. I thought he would kick the door, or shout, or bang his fist but there was an eerie silence in which all I could hear was the wind whistling through the trees and a low moaning. It was Ash. A strange plaintive noise that could have been the sound of an animal caught in a trap. I waited. I heard his footsteps running along the outside on the wet grass. Something about the emptiness frightened me. I swallowed and took my key and hung it up on the little hook. The old key lay in the bin by the door. I pushed open the door of the kitchen.

And then Ash was banging on the kitchen window, his form blurred by the mottled glass. His small fist looming large then blurred, back and forth, back and forth.

"Mum!" he screeched. "Mum!"

Dolly was perched on the stool by the breakfast bar. She got up and walked across to the cupboard, took out a glass and walked to the sink.

The handle of the kitchen door turned again and again but it was locked. Princey had been adamant about the double lock.

Mum turned the tap on and filled up her glass to drown out the noise. Then she carried the glass of water back to the breakfast bar.

"Let me in!" bellowed Ash from behind the door. "Mum! Let me in, let me in, let me in!"

The storm was raging. Soon it would be over.

I put the duplicate key on the kitchen table and mum put her hand over it. I put my hand gently on top of hers. Our eyes met. Hers were glittering with unshed tears. I remembered how I had stopped her going out in the rain to meet Max, how she had looked at me, full of fear and the scars of her unhappy childhood. Now she was more fragile than ever. I knew I would never again use my physical strength against her. I would always treat her gently. It was my duty. She had lost a limb. She had lost her son.

"Let's chop vegetables for tonight's meal," she said.

"Yes I'll get them mum," I said. "I'll get them."

I opened the fridge and saw my lifeless hand reach in.

It'll never be over, I thought.

Bite-Sized Books Ltd

Why not sign up to our mailing list here:

Why not browse our BOOKSHOP?

Find out more about Bite-Sized Books here: